Praise for Christina
No Place Like Here

"A contemporary spin on the classic *Hansel and Gretel*, Christina June's *No Place Like Here* is the story of a girl struggling to find her footing amidst unthinkable family hardship. Main character Ashlyn sparkles, the retreat center setting is fresh and fun, and June's prose is, as always, lovely and affecting. A delightful story that's sure to charm fans of young adult literature."

—KATY UPPERMAN, author of *The Impossibility of Us* and *Kissing Max Holden*

"*No Place Like Here* is a *Hansel and Gretel* retelling that focuses on an important but often-neglected relationship in young adult novels—the one between a teenage girl and her father. Christina June tackles in a direct way the common struggle that many YA readers can sympathize with: the realization that your parents are not always right, and how do you forge your own path that's right for you? Ashlyn is a brave and relatable character. Through the course of the novel, she slowly comes out of the shell of who she thinks she *should* be to become who she knows she *can* be. It is a hard-won personal journey, and by the end of the book readers will be cheering Ashlyn on as she makes decisions from this newly cultivated place inside her. The retreat camp setting is fitting both for the modern-day fairy tale theme and for the romantic ideology of Thoreau, in which one goes to the woods to find herself. Fans of June's other books will enjoy references to characters they have already come to know and love from *It Started with Goodbye* and *Everywhere You Want to Be*, and new fans will welcome the chance to take a break from their lives and retreat into the woods."

—FLO @ BOOK NERDS ACROSS AMERICA

No Place Like Here

Also by Christina June

It Started with Goodbye
Everywhere You Want to Be

No Place Like Here

Christina June

N K®

BLINK

No Place Like Here
Copyright © 2019 by Christina June

Requests for information should be addressed to:
Blink, *3900 Sparks Dr. SE, Grand Rapids, Michigan 49546*

Library of Congress Cataloging-in-Publication Data

ISBN 978-0-310-76692-6 (softcover)

ISBN 978-0-310-76698-8 (ebook)

ISBN 978-0-310-76859-3 (audio download)

Interior design: Denise Froehlich

Printed in the United States of America

19 20 21 22 23 /LSC/ 10 9 8 7 6 5 4 3 2 1

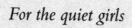

For the quiet girls

"Owning our story can be hard but not nearly as difficult as spending our lives running from it."

Dr. Brené Brown

Chapter 1

There is never a good way to find out your father is going to prison. Some are worse than others, though. For example, learning that your father has committed tax evasion via a social media post is on the top five worst ways list.

I might have missed it, if I hadn't logged on to see if my best friend, Tatum, had posted any new messages for me. We'd spent the last school year apart—me at boarding school in the Shenandoah Valley and her at home, just south of Washington, DC—and we had been making plans for not only my big return home, but for the upcoming school year. Not that I'd actually asked my parents if I could come back for senior year yet. But I would. Soon.

And there, below a photo of Tatum and her boyfriend, was the news article from the *Washington Post* about my father. And the cherry on top? Cassie Pringle, the girl down the hall, hadn't even posted it. Her mother had. With the message, "Cass, doesn't this guy's daughter go to your school?" Thanks, Mrs. Pringle.

The headline was the worst: "Millionaire Real Estate Developer Evades IRS." It made my father seem like some creepy super villain who was ducking into shadowy alleys to avoid getting caught by the police. But, in a way, it wasn't that far off. Instead of an alleyway and the police, my dad hid from the federal government behind a shiny exterior and seemingly pristine business.

I inhaled and exhaled in short, panicky little bursts as I skimmed the first few paragraphs.

Prominent. Community leader. Disappointing. Seven years without paying. Dead to rights. Plea hearing. Guilty. Sentenced. Jail time. No comment.

I swallowed the lump in the back of my throat and shut my laptop harder than I meant to. There was no way. Right? My dad going to jail? I scoffed aloud. No chance. It was a misprint. Had to be. There was no way my parents would keep something like Dad committing white collar crime a secret from me. Was there?

I felt around in my backpack for my phone. *I'll just call home and clear it up. Easy.*

I dialed my mother but got her voicemail.

"You've reached Celine Zanotti. I can't answer my phone right now, but please leave me a message and I'll get back to you as soon as I'm able. Have a fabulous day."

Fabulous was my mother's favorite word. She thought my elitist private boarding school was fabulous. She thought her closet full of shoes was fabulous. She thought our vacations to Miami Beach each summer were fabulous.

Is Dad's alleged impending doom fabulous?

"Hi, Mom. I just read an article saying Dad is going to jail and thought that was something you would tell me before it hit the national news. So, please call me and let me know what's going on. Please."

Two pleases. I'd done it without realizing, but once it hit me, I knew I was scared.

"Call Dad," I said into the phone. It practically slipped from my sweaty palm. It rang once. Twice. Three times. I was about to slam the phone down on my bed when my dad answered.

"Hello?" Dad's voice was gruff. Short. Like he didn't have time for this.

"Hi, Dad." My voice quavered. "It's me."

"Ashlyn, hi. How are you? Getting ready for exams, I hope." Did I hear him take a deep breath? Was it fear or relief? Regardless, here he was, still managing to tell me what he thought I should be doing. Classic.

I gritted my teeth. "Of course. You know me." And the kicker was, he didn't. But that was neither here nor there.

Dad cleared his throat. "Well, I'm guessing you're calling because you've heard about my little setback."

Little setback? Is that what going to federal prison is? I almost said. "So, it's true? I wish you had told me yourself."

There was a moment of silence before he spoke again. "Sweetheart, your mother and I have been trying to determine the best way to tell you. My lawyers and I were able to make a deal with the prosecuting attorney, which thankfully avoided a big trial and the media circus that comes with it. However, it seems we took too long to fill you in. I'm sorry if you were shocked by what you read."

Sweetheart. It left a sour taste on my tongue. He only used terms of endearment when he was trying to convince me of something. And he was *sorry* that I was shocked? What a non-apology. Like it was somehow my fault that I'd been surprised by the news he had failed to mention to me.

I pursed my lips. "I'm sorry I was shocked by the fact that you didn't tell me before the internet did." As soon as I said it, my stomach dropped like I was on a roller coaster. Clapping back at him never went over well.

My father exhaled into the receiver. "Unhelpful, Ashlyn. This is a very difficult time for me right now. It is certainly not the time to be disrespectful. You were not raised to act this way."

My chest tightened the way it always did when he criticized me. I wanted to tell my dad it was a very difficult time for all of us right now. Because of him. I wanted to tell him I was angry something catastrophic was happening to our family. Because of him. I wanted to tell him I felt embarrassed and ashamed. Because of him. I wanted to tell him that despite my anger, I was scared. Because of him, and *for him* as well. But I said none of those things.

"Yes, sir." It never failed. If I said, "Yes, sir," he nodded his head and we moved on. But how did we just move on from this?

"Now, here's what's going to happen. Are you listening?"

"Yes, sir."

"One, I will turn myself in to the Williams Correctional Facility in two weeks' time. I will be there for fourteen months and one day, possibly less. Sometimes a sentence will be reduced when an inmate demonstrates good behavior." He called himself an inmate. I wanted to throw up. "Two, your mother is not herself right now." *Who is she*, I wanted to ask, but kept quiet. "She will be checking herself into the Hart Canyon Rehabilitation Center this summer."

A shriek got stuck in my throat and came out like the whine of a wounded animal. "Is Mom on drugs?"

"No, Ashlyn, your mother is not on drugs," he said, like I should know better. What did he expect? I just found out my father was a criminal. Anything seemed possible now. "She is exhausted."

Exhausted was sometimes code for depressed; I knew what that was from my Introduction to Psychology course this year. But a rehab center?

"So, you're both leaving me," I said flatly, while my stomach bottomed out.

He sighed loudly again, annoyed. "Your mother and I are handling our business so this family can move forward." He sounded so matter-of-fact. No nonsense. As if this was just another business transaction and not the total destruction of our family.

I shouldn't have been surprised. A year ago, I'd had a little run-in with the law myself, but no real harm was done. Unfortunately, my father's solution to me making one mistake was sending me away to boarding school, where they would be better able to "teach me to make the right choices." All our conversations over the last eleven months were related to my grades. The two times I'd been home in the past year—Christmas and Thanksgiving breaks—had been a preview to what death must be like since our house was as silent as a tomb, and nearly as empty.

But this? This was something else entirely. Both my parents were abandoning me. My mind emptied itself of the annoyance and filled instead with fear. What was going to happen to them? To me? I imagined everything from having to beg Tatum's family to let me live in their spare room to living on the street to going into foster care.

Lost in my spinning thoughts, I didn't realize my father was still talking, taking advantage of my silence to advance his plans for my life. "Instead of spending the summer at school, you will go live with Uncle Ed and Aunt Greta. I want to make sure you're supported during this transition."

My mouth dropped open. I was glad we weren't video chatting. Better that he didn't see my red cheeks and the steam coming out of my ears. "In Pennsylvania? The middle of nowhere? That's so unfair. Why can't I just stay here? There will be plenty of girls here to support me." It was a page right out of his book as a seasoned business executive: use the other party's words to make your own argument.

My father blew out a breath that crackled in my ear. "This is so typical of you. Do not talk to me about what is unfair, Ashlyn. We all need to make sacrifices right now. This is not a negotiation."

My chest seized again. "Fine." The only person who

seemed to be making any sacrifices in this arrangement was me, but that was, unfortunately, normal.

He went on. "I've arranged for you to have a summer job. You and your cousin, Hannah, will be working at a wilderness retreat center. The kind of place companies bring employees to do team building. Hannah worked there last year. She loves it. Because Greta and Ed know the owner, Greta was able to pull some strings and get you in as well. You'll be doing something productive with your time. It'll be a nice leadership role to put on your résumé when you apply to college in the fall."

"That's very nice of them," I said quietly so I didn't start shouting. If I were to shout at him, I'd probably say, "You're ditching me at the edge of the forest?" very loudly. Not that I ever shouted at my dad, but if there was ever a time to start, this was it.

My aunt and uncle were nice people. Aunt Greta was a social worker and Uncle Ed was a high school biology teacher. They sent thoughtful birthday cards and a family newsletter in their holiday card. I knew Hannah had been president of the environmental science club at her school and her older brother Dylan was studying abroad this summer in France so he could "improve his fluency while also getting in a bit of history." They had all the outer trappings of a perfect family. However, my faith in the accuracy of outside appearances had become significantly skewed over the years. My dad liked people to think we were perfect because he had a job that paid a boatload of money, we had a huge house, he drove an expensive car, and had shiny shoes and could afford to send me to the "best school in Virginia," which was the line he came up with to avoid telling people I got arrested. Clearly, we were far from perfect if you looked past the surface.

"So, it's all decided."

"All decided," I echoed with zero enthusiasm. I knew better than to complain further. The sureness in his voice and the fact that he wasn't trying to convince me that spending my summer in the middle of the woods was a good idea just proved how much he was still in charge. Even when he was about to be locked up.

"You'll have fun, Ashlyn. This place looks like a stand-up operation. You'll love it. Hannah wouldn't go back for a second year if it wasn't great."

Hannah and I are not the same kind of girl, I didn't say. But for my father to know that, he would've had to have read the annual holiday newsletter and I would've bet my college fund that he hadn't taken the time to read it further than to confirm that his brother and his family were alive and kicking. He would also have had to pay attention to me beyond making sure my report card was flawless, my clothes were acceptable, and my posture was straight.

"A town car will be coming to pick you up at the end of the week," my dad rolled on. He, apparently, had been restricted from travelling any farther than a short radius from our house. Mom, he told me, wasn't up for the drive. I said nothing to protest and wrote it all down in my planner.

When we hung up, I stayed perched on the edge of my bed, staring at the seam in the bedspread. *What just happened?* My entire plan for the summer, the next school year, and potentially forever, just went up in a puff of smoke. My life was suddenly completely unrecognizable. And I'd said nothing to protest. I couldn't move. I couldn't breathe. I opened my nightstand drawer, took out my purple pocket-sized quote journal, and selected a matching purple marker from my pencil cup.

I twisted my body to get a good angle and wrote on the inside of the drawer:

> SILENCE IS A SOURCE OF GREAT STRENGTH.
> *Lao Tzu*

A tiny knot of tension in my chest unraveled and I was able to inhale deeply. Maybe whoever lived in this room next year would see those words. Maybe it would be a source of strength for them in the midst of their own crisis. I didn't feel strong, but if this quote had survived thousands of years, there had to be some shred of truth to it. Or so I hoped.

A timid knock at the door snapped me out of my daze. When I opened it, Cassie Pringle stood there with a look that was one part sympathy, one part curiosity.

"Hi, Ashlyn," she said, the corners of her mouth turned down. "I just wanted to see if you were . . . okay. I saw, um, about your dad."

"Bad news travels at the speed of light around here, I guess," I said, trying to keep my voice steady.

On a scale from one to ten, my year at Blue Valley Academy earned a five. I'd managed to get good grades and do well in activities, but I hadn't really made friends.

Plenty of acquaintances, but not friends. I wasn't surprised. The other girls were mostly from small towns nearby, while I was the "city snob," as I'd overheard one girl saying in the hallway. No one had been rude to my face, and some had been pleasant—Cassie was on the nicer side, for sure—but I wasn't invited on weekend trips home and no one decorated my door on my birthday. I couldn't really blame them. Trying to break into any clique during junior year, when everyone else had known each other since birth, was nearly impossible.

"So, it's true?"

"It seems that way." My face was blank. I didn't know Cassie well enough to trust her with the fear and confusion that was hiding behind my emotionless mask.

Cassie sighed and cocked her head to the side. "Can I . . . do anything for you?"

You can just go, please. I shook my head. "No. But thank you. I just want to make it through finals. And then I want to go home."

Cassie nodded. "I understand. Let me know, okay?" She smiled sadly at me and retreated to her own room.

I shut the door, lay on my bed, and squeezed my eyes shut. Forget surviving exams, I just wanted to go home. But what did that even mean now? No one would be there anyway. I shook my head, fighting the urge to cry. I'd had this grand idea that I'd have an amazing year here, prove to my parents that I was making good choices, and they'd turn in the paperwork to transfer me back to Henderson High, where I'd spend my senior year with Tatum. But now? It felt like home didn't even exist.

Chapter 2

When the town car dropped me at the edge of the driveway, I nearly teared up at the sight of my house. *Not that I'll be staying long.* I rolled my suitcase into the garage and bumped it up the three steps into the house. When I came home for winter break, at least my mother had greeted me at the door in her Christmas sweater. But now? Nothing. I turned my ear toward the foyer. Silence.

"Hello?" I called, pulling the giant bag in behind me. "Mom? Dad?" I rounded the corner into the kitchen and watched an imaginary tumbleweed roll by. *Where is everyone?* My cheeks heated. *Don't they even care a little bit that I'm back?* I dropped my bag in the middle of the kitchen, slipped off my sandals, and padded up the stairs to my parents' bedroom. The double doors were wide open, and my mother was sitting on the edge of the bed, a pair of socks in her hand, an open but empty suitcase at her feet.

"Hello? I'm home," I said softly.

She looked up at me, as if I was a ghost. "Ashlyn?"

"Hi, Mom." I sat down on the bed next to her. I'd

never seen my mother wear pajamas past eight in the morning. It was three in the afternoon. I studied her—this woman who I knew was my mom yet seemed to be only a shell now. Light brown roots peeked from her normally pristine honey blonde highlights. I leaned in, expecting to smell her familiar perfume, but wrinkled my nose instead. When was the last time she'd taken a shower?

"When did you get home, honey?" Her voice was distant, as if there was a pane of glass between us. Like in a prison. Would that be how I'd soon talk to my father?

"Just now. Didn't you hear me calling?"

My mom turned to look at me for the first time, her face without affect. "No. I guess not."

This was normally the part where she'd wrap me in a hug and I'd be smothered by her signature scent—a smell I didn't know how badly I missed until right then. But she just sat there for a moment before turning her attention back to the socks.

"Are you packing for rehab?" I almost couldn't get the word out.

"Yes. They said to bring things that make you comfortable. I don't . . . I can't . . . ." Mom's voice disappeared completely.

"Can I help you?" I stood up and walked to her dresser.

"Maybe in a bit, sweetheart. I'm so tired right now. I think I'm going to take a nap." She shifted higher on the bed and slid her slippered feet under the comforter.

I pulled the covers up over her shoulders as she turned on her side. "Okay, Mom."

She closed her eyes and I just watched her for a moment, holding my breath. She looked frail, like if I breathed too hard, she might blow away. A moment later, my mother was snoring softly. Was this what it felt like to be a parent and watch your helpless child sleep?

Where my dad had been a lifelong opponent, Mom was more of a silent ally. Our relationship consisted of measured glances that said whole conversations with just one look, followed by shopping trips and pedicures after he'd been particularly cruel. And we rarely discussed things further. I knew she worried about me, about us, but just like I had, she'd convinced herself that staying quiet was best for everyone. Like, if we said it out loud to each other, it might get worse. So, we carried on. Now it seemed like she'd worried herself into nothingness. *Thanks, Dad.* I tiptoed out of the room.

I crept to my father's office at the end of the hallway. The door was cracked, with yellow light spilling out, illuminating my pink-painted toes.

"Yes, I'm taking care of it." His voice, loud and sharp, suddenly cut through the silence.

I paused outside and listened, knowing that I probably shouldn't.

"No. Yes, I'm sure you are." Pause. Heavy sigh. "Fine. Uh-huh. Speak to you tomorrow."

The phone slammed down on the desk, echoing through the hallway loud enough to make me flinch, causing my eye to twitch. I fingered the single pearl I always wore around my neck. My dad had given it to me on my thirteenth birthday. I'd only taken it off a handful of times. He was typically a gift card kind of present-giver. Or, more accurately, his administrative assistant was. Dad rarely picked out his own gifts. Or even remembered gift-worthy occasions for that matter. But when he handed me the blue velvet box when I turned thirteen, he was almost shy. As I opened it, he said, "Ashlyn, you're a teenager now. On your way to becoming a grown up. Pearls are classic."

I thanked him quietly, admiring the iridescent sheen on the pearl. It was lovely. And a rare reminder that somewhere beneath my father's cool, slick exterior was someone who was occasionally thoughtful.

I inhaled and pushed the door wider, revealing myself. "Dad? I'm back." I almost said *home*. Almost.

My father was bent over his desk, his eyebrows pushed so close together they became one black line over his eyes. Papers were strewn about and his briefcase lay haphazardly across the loveseat, pens ready to spill at any moment. This was more than unusual. It was just plain wrong. Dad was the kind of guy who never had even one paper clip out of place. I cringed at the irony—now his whole life was askew.

"Ashlyn." It wasn't a greeting. It was barely an acknowledgment of my presence. He looked up at me from beneath his furrowed unibrow. "How was the ride?"

Who the heck cares about the ride! Everything is a disaster! I didn't shout.

"Fine," is what came out instead.

"Good, good," he said, nodding. "I guess you'll need to do some packing for work. Do you have enough pairs of shorts? Athletic shoes? A bathing suit? You'll want a one piece." I resisted rolling my eyes at his wardrobe suggestion. "Maybe some water shoes. Your uncle sent a list. I'll email it to you now. Take the credit card tomorrow and get what you don't have."

"Okay."

He shuffled some papers into a pile. "Did you say hello to your mother?"

I nodded. "She's napping now."

"That's to be expected. She's worn out."

Is that what we're calling it now? More like clinically worn out. Why can't you say depressed?

I just nodded again. "I guess I'll go start the laundry." And with that, I turned and ended our little reunion.

"Good, good," he said, eyes already back on his laptop, hand reaching for the phone. "I just need to square some things away with my lawyers and . . ."

His voice trailed off as I reached the stairs. I retrieved my suitcase from the kitchen, bee-lined to my bedroom, and shut the door, locking it for good measure. I wrapped myself in my quilt, letting the weight of it settle around me, and turned on my favorite sad playlist. As the heaviness in my chest began to lift, I dialed my best friend, Tatum. Her grinning face appeared in the middle of my phone.

"Are you here? Are you here? Are you here?" I'd missed her puppy-like enthusiasm.

I grinned back, I couldn't help it, and panned the camera around to verify. "I. Am. Here."

"Hooray!" She pumped her fist into the air, shaking

the camera. "So, what's first on the agenda tomorrow? The pool? Trip into DC? Binging on all the TV you missed this year? I'm game for anything. Your choice."

My grin slipped away. "How about you come over while I do laundry?"

"Well, that doesn't sound very exciting. Can we pair said laundry with some TV at least?" Tatum pouted and then grinned again, eyebrows up and waggling.

"Yeah, about that." I flopped down on my bed and held the phone above my face. "There's been a change in plans. Have you seen the news lately?"

"About your dad?" I knew she'd been waiting for me to bring it up, instead of pressing me, and I loved her for that.

"Yep. Turns out I'm only here for a few days, given the house is about to be totally empty."

"Wait, what? Where's your mom going?"

I filled her in on all the gory details and her brown eyes grew wider and wider with each new bit of grisly information. By the time I got to "work" and "cousin," her jaw was at the bottom of the screen.

"But . . . but . . ."

"I know."

She slumped down on her bed. "Gosh. That sucks. All of it. I'm so sorry, Ash."

"Thanks. Me too." I pursed my lips and blinked back the tears welling up in my eyes.

"At least there wasn't a trial. That would've been a nightmare."

I imagined reporters peeking in our windows at all

hours of the day. "Thank goodness for small favors." Not that it changed the outcome of this whole mess.

"And it's nice that you'll be with family?" Five years of best friendship had given her intimate knowledge of the Zanotti family dynamics. Or lack thereof. Uncle Ed, Aunt Greta, Hannah, and Dylan—they were more like characters in a book I'd read once or twice, not close relatives. I could barely remember the last time I'd seen them in person. "Maybe this is your chance to get to know them better," Tatum added.

"That's true." My father didn't care to spend time with his own brother, for reasons that had never been clear to me. But, I guess their relationship wasn't so nonexistent that my dad wouldn't ask for a bailout when he really needed it.

"So, a retreat center, huh? That could be fun. Lots of time in the sun? Maybe there will be some cute employees to hang out with?"

I groaned. "Even if there are, that doesn't take away the bugs and the dirt and the pretentious corporate participants." I was picturing groups of men in suits, just like my father, side-eyeing the ziplines and checking their expensive Swiss watches.

"At least you have lots of experience with that type." We both snorted. "You'll be great." That was easy for Tatum to say. She wasn't the one venturing into the unknown.

"I'm glad *you* can be optimistic." I sighed loudly. "And really, this new job is the least of my worries. I was going to ask my parents if I can come home for senior year, but

now? I don't even know if *they'll* be home for senior year."
I'd had this grand vision. If I got good grades—which I
always did—and kept my nose clean—which I usually
did—all would go back to normal. If I proved myself, Dad
would forget that I'd dated a guy who was now in jail.
Sure, I'd just been along for the ride when he got busted,
both figuratively and literally, but no permanent damage
had been done and Dad covered it up, which was kind of
ironic considering my dad couldn't cover his own tracks.

My hand went to my neck and the pearl that rested at
the base of my throat. It wasn't always like this. My dad
had always been strict, but he hadn't always been a dicta-
tor. My mom hadn't always been superficial and complicit.
When I was little, before Dad got busier with work and
shorter on time and patience with me, we went to the
movies or museums together most weekends. We ate dinner around the table. We laughed. But when the money
started drifting in, we drifted apart. Now it had been so
long since the good times outweighed the bad, it was hard
to remember what the good times felt like anymore and if
they were even worth fighting for.

"Need help packing? Shopping?" Tatum asked, jolting
me back into the present again.

"Sure, that'd be great." I smiled.

"Stellar. I'll pick you up first thing in the morning
and we can hit the stores. You can pick out stuff for care
packages too."

"Care packages?"

Tatum rolled her eyes and laughed. "I'll send you little
notes and stuff to make you not homesick."

"You'd do that for me?" Tears pricked the corners of my eyes again.

"Hello! If you can't hang out with me all summer, this is the next best thing."

"Thank you," I said quietly. If summer with my best friend wasn't an option, a care package would have to do.

"You got this, Ash. You'll be brilliant. You'll see."

"I hope you're right." We smiled at each other and hung up, the promise of shopping giving me hope for tomorrow.

Chapter 3

After an epic shopping trip, thanks to Dad's credit card, and best friend time, thanks to Tatum, I somehow felt both better and worse. Better because I was equipped for my trek into the wilderness, in regard to gear anyway, and worse, because our limited time together reminded me how I was going to be far from home and far from Tatum all summer.

When I'd put away my stack of shorts, T-shirts, new backpack, reusable water bottle, and hiking boots, I came downstairs to find both of my parents seated at the kitchen table. My father had a glass of red wine in his hand; my mother sipped on club soda with lime. Family dinners generally only happened on holidays around here, so naturally I was a little confused.

"Sit down, Ashlyn," my dad said, gesturing to an empty chair.

I sat.

"Your mother and I just want to make sure you understand how this summer will go. Everything is under control. We don't want you to feel like you're unsupported."

I almost laughed out loud. *Too late for that, Dad.* "Okay," I said, quietly, instead.

Dad sipped his wine. "We'll all be leaving tomorrow morning." *Tomorrow?* I'd been home for less than forty-eight hours. I thought I'd at least be here a week. I shifted my gaze to my mother, who was staring at the lime floating in her drink, and then back to my dad, who was eerily calm for someone about to have a massive lifestyle change. "You need to have everything packed tonight. There will be a car coming for each of us and then we will go our separate ways."

It sounded like he was breaking up with me and Mom. My stomach churned and bile rose in my throat. I swallowed hard. "Who leaves first?"

"Me," my mom whispered.

Dad set his glass down on the table with a thunk. "We will all be *fine*," he said, sensing the panic rising around us, as if he could just make it all disappear with a word. "We'll do what we need to do and then everything will go back to status quo."

A flicker of hope lit in my heart. Was this the right moment to ask if I could come home at the end of the summer? Surely Mom would be better by then. I ran through my mental list of things I wanted to remind them of from the last year at Blue Valley Academy. My grades were perfect. I was captain of the Quiz Bowl team, which was unprecedented for a new student. I got a gold medal on the national French exam. I wanted to add that I hadn't dated anyone or gotten one single demerit the entire year but decided *that* might work against me. I looked from my dad to my mom and back again. It was time. I inhaled and opened my mouth to speak, but my dad was quicker.

"And, I'm sure you'll be pleased to know that senior year at Blue Valley is all arranged and paid for. Since I'll be gone and your mother's treatment is still up in the air, we can all be assured that you're well taken care of and that your future is secured. I think all three of us can feel relieved knowing things are managed, don't you agree?" He smiled at me, like a cat with canary feathers sticking out of its mouth. Smug, even. Did he know what I was going to ask? Sometimes I wondered if my father could read my mind and spent time thinking of ways to divert my plans. Like it was a game, ruining my life.

Rage bubbled up inside me like the carbonation floating to the top of my mother's glass of club soda. I wanted to scream so many things at him. I didn't need to be managed. Mom just needed some help, and she wouldn't be locked away forever. If anyone needed to be watched or supervised, it was him. I deserved better than being sent away for his mistake. But of course, I said nothing and popped the rage bubbles, leaving me feeling warm, tender, and raw.

I looked at my mother. Had she heard the screaming inside my head? Her eyes, huge and blue like mine, bore into me, full of what looked like panic. I wordlessly pleaded with her, my face begging her to ask me the question I desperately wanted to answer. She shook her head—at me? At my coming home? Did she not want me here? Mom's voice was void of all emotion. "This is for the best. Your father will be gone, and I just can't think past today right now, sweetheart. Okay?"

The lines on my mother's face were deeper than I'd ever seen them. Tears appeared in the corners of her eyes. I couldn't stand to see her hurting. I swallowed the rotten lemon taste of my anger for her sake. "Okay."

We ate a dinner I didn't even taste while my dad answered no less than five phone calls from various lawyers and advisors. I guess he had time for that since he wasn't packing anything. He disappeared into his office, his plate only a quarter eaten, while Mom and I just looked at each other again. Her shoulders sagged as she exhaled, her wispy bangs lifting slightly.

"It'll be fine, honey. It has to be," she said, in a moment of optimism. I wasn't convinced she believed it, but I imagined she'd seen and heard enough in the last year to want to believe it. And then, perhaps to convince herself further, "You're a good girl, Ashlyn. It'll be okay."

I got up from the table, shoved my plate in the sink with a clatter, and ran up the stairs as fast as I could so she wouldn't see the tears that had begun to spill, hot and stinging, down my cheeks. I shut the door, locked it, and crawled into bed.

Are you there? I texted Tatum.

She responded immediately. What's up?

I need you.

Tatum arrived in ten minutes flat, a pint of mint chocolate chip ice cream and two spoons in her hand. "Reinforcements have arrived."

I relayed the whole terrible conversation, with my

head resting on Tatum's shoulder, as she cupped the container between her hands, softening the ice cream.

She sighed when I finished, pried the lid off, and handed me the pint with a spoon stuck in. "It's not forever. None of it."

"In my head, I know that. But it feels like everything's changed, and none of it for the better. We're broken. All of us." The words brought fresh tears.

"You're not broken, Ash. And your family isn't broken. Maybe in need of a little duct tape," she said with a low chuckle, poking me in the ribs, "but not broken."

"I'm going to be the worst retreat center employee, you know. I've never had a job. I don't really know how to do anything."

Tatum shrugged, and my head bobbed with her shoulder. "You'll learn. You're smart."

"Book smart, maybe. I don't think all the random quotes and trivia I know are going to help me."

"What's the worst that can happen? You'll commune with nature, get a tan, and hang with your cousin. No big deal."

I lifted my head. "The cousin who is essentially a stranger?"

She waved my protest away with a flick of her hand, like it was no big deal that Hannah and I probably couldn't pick one another out of a line up. "Blood is thicker than water, or so they say. Hey, she's done this retreat center thing before, right? You can just ask her everything. It'll be a bonding experience." Tatum quirked an eyebrow up. "Do you know what your assignment is yet?"

"I have no idea." I hoped no one was expecting me to hook middle-aged business women and men onto the ziplines or guide them through trust falls.

"Well, I'm sure, whatever happens, it'll be fine. You're stronger than you think, you know. You got through this last year at a new school all on your own."

"True." While I hadn't made any life-long besties at Blue Valley, I hadn't made any enemies either. If I had to go back, it was a small comfort to know that Cassie Pringle and the girls on my hall would be there too. "I just wish I was going to be back here. At school. With you."

"Me too, Ash."

One of the first quotes I'd ever recorded in my notebook was from T.S. Eliot: *"Home is where one starts from."* It made home seem like a source of pride. And I *was* proud of where I'd come from. Despite the recent wealth, my parents hadn't had so much when I was born. There was a photo album collecting dust somewhere with pictures of tiny me in secondhand toddler clothes, joyfully running through the exhibits at the free Smithsonian museums. My parents held me tight under the cherry blossoms at the tidal basin, love written on their faces.

The photographs that were framed, cased in silver and glass, hanging in the formal living room, were the ones where I was posed, wearing an outfit specially bought for the occasion, my smile never reaching my eyes. They had taught me appearing perfect, doll-like, was the real source of pride. According to my dad, anyway.

Last year, during our poetry unit, we'd studied

Warsan Shire, who speculated that home was somewhere we haven't experienced yet—a place to discover. The idea of something better waiting for me in my future resonated like the clang of cymbals. When I thought about Shire's and Eliot's words together, though, I wondered if the place I was running to was the place I'd already been.

It wasn't perfect, but it was mine. My parents belonged to me and I belonged to them. I wanted what was mine to be the best, even if I didn't know how or when we would get there. And even in a twisted way, there was comfort in knowing that my dad was going to scrutinize my every move, and my mom was going to look the other way and try to make us both forget through retail therapy and spa days. It was our normal.

I wanted to go back because I was clinging to the idea that it would change one day. Every once in a while, I got a glimpse of what it could be, in the laugh lines in my mother's face or my dad's footfalls coming down the hallway. Who we used to be. I wanted to go back because what if one day I left for good and it all completely disappeared. That would break my heart. So, I kept clinging and hoping.

I slipped my cold hand into Tatum's. We sat that way, in the comfortable silence that exists between best friends, until the ice cream melted, and I could breathe again.

The next morning, I kissed my mother's cheek and told her I loved her as she slid into the car, spirited away to her treatment facility. As the car sped from the house, I imagined the conversation we might have had if she hadn't been so "exhausted."

"Do you have everything packed?" Though Mom would've already known because she would've slipped a note inside my bag or inside my quote journal, telling me she loved me.

"Packed and organized."

"You'll call me every day?" She would've made me promise.

And I would promise, of course, to call and to write and to not be embarrassed if she showed up at the retreat center just because she missed me.

Even though we couldn't have that conversation now, I hoped we could have one that was just as loving and meaningful when Mom got back. I said a silent prayer to anyone who would listen: *Please make her feel better . . . and quickly.* I went back into the house and carried my own bags downstairs. I stood there, twisting the pearl on the chain at my neck, and waited for the next departure.

My dad and his lawyer hired a security team to ride along behind them as he surrendered himself to the prison. He thought there might be media trying to "catch a glimpse of a fallen hero." *Hypocrite is a better descriptor,* but I didn't say so out loud.

I didn't say goodbye to him. He just squeezed my shoulders with a reminder and a promise he himself probably couldn't keep. "Be on your best behavior. I'll see you soon." I didn't know if he meant at our first visitation, or when he was released, but it didn't matter. I just nodded. I watched from the living room as three black SUVs whisked my father away, two local news vans and their cameras looking on from across the street. I shut the curtains with a huff.

On the blank first page of the grocery list pad hanging from the refrigerator, I scribbled,

> THERE WAS A CERTAIN SATISFACTION
> IN BITTERNESS. I COURTED IT. IT WAS
> STANDING OUTSIDE, AND I INVITED IT IN.
> *Nicole Krauss*

But it didn't matter. No one would see it. I ripped off the page, crumpled it, and threw it in the trash, hoping it wouldn't spontaneously combust.

I felt like the cliché-est of clichés, but after my dad's car had disappeared, I went straight to the bathroom and got out the scissors. Pulling up a YouTube tutorial, I started hacking away at the blonde hair that had always hung halfway down my back. In books and movies, heroines cut their hair when they need a change or they're about to start a revolution. I wasn't trying to change the world at the moment, maybe just my little slice of the world. If I had to go to be a niece, a cousin, and an employee, things I had absolutely no experience being, it might be easier to do it if I actually looked like someone else. I managed to cut a fairly decent straight line at my ears and did my best with the back. I faced the mirror and shrugged. It made me look younger; my already large eyes seemed even bigger. I thought I'd feel lighter, physically and emotionally, with all that weight gone, but I felt the same. Still angry. Still lost. I could see my dad's face in my mind, brows knitted in disappointment at my impulsivity. *You look ridiculous*, I heard his voice say.

"Get a grip," I said out loud, twisting my pearl necklace between my fingers. "It's a summer job. And one more year at Blue Valley. And then you're out of here." I gripped the sides of the sink and leaned in, nearly nose to nose with myself in the mirror. "You can get personal loans for college, so you don't need his money. You can go to school in California or Canada or on the moon. As long as it's far, far away from here. Deal? Deal."

The Ashlyn that looked back at me nodded, her newly shortened hair tickling the tops of her ears. She looked scared. A little angry, a little hurt, and more than a little scared. I swallowed. She swallowed too.

"We're going to be fine. Just fine."

I hated that I was using my father's favorite phrase, but at that moment, in an empty house, alone, with an uncertain future ahead of me, that was the only thing left to say.

Chapter 4

The ride to Pennsylvania took four hours. Or so. I wasn't really paying that close attention. I couldn't shake the anger laced with sadness that was rattling around my body that felt otherwise hollowed out. My dad had said, "we're not abandoning you," but I could hear his voice, over and over, *abandoning, abandoning, abandoning,* so many times it sounded like he was laughing at me.

I'd stuck my head in the sand more times than I could count when Dad would say something horrible or tightened the reins on our lives until it was a chokehold. It was easier that way. But, this time, the wreckage was worse than ever. Impossible to ignore. I felt bad for my mother. She had trusted him to take care of us and generally excused everything else. Until it all went up in a puff of smoke and she found herself lost in the middle of it. We both did.

When I pictured my father's calm face as he casually announced the destruction of our family last night, anger shot back through me. He didn't look sorry. No apology. No acknowledgment of the misery and embarrassment he was heaping on us.

I sucked in a sharp breath as the driver turned onto the street that I vaguely recognized as the one Uncle Ed and his family lived on. I hadn't been to their house in eight or nine years. The last time was for some kind of celebration. Maybe Dylan or Hannah's birthday or an anniversary. The only things I remembered were the crystal tumblers my Aunt Greta served the iced tea and lemonade in and my dad grumbling about there not being any wine. Those glasses looked like they were made for royalty, intricately designed with flowers and swirls. I felt special just putting my lips on them.

I sighed, and my newly short hair flew up around my face and tickled my nose. I sneezed twice as the car pulled into the driveway of the small house where I'd be making a brief pit stop before trekking into the forest. A rusting pick-up truck sat under a carport with a sagging roof, and the front lawn seemed to consist more of weeds than actual grass—a sea of yellow dandelions and white fluff. Wishes waiting to be cast. I heard my dad's phantom snort of disgust in my head and tightened my jaw as the car slowed to a stop. The driver, who hadn't said a single word the entire drive, opened his door and went straight for the trunk to get my suitcase. I remained in the backseat as he placed it on the sidewalk, until he peered in the window at me. What would he do if I didn't get out? I groaned, opened the door, and swung my feet out. At least my toes were done—my favorite shade of purple to match my fingernails. If my life was going to hell in a handbasket, I'd look cute on the journey.

Aunt Greta was coming down the walk as I slammed the car door behind me.

"Ashlyn!" She smiled warmly, showing a row of sparkling white teeth with a small gap in the front. If that'd been me, my dad would've insisted on cosmetic dental surgery. I liked it on her, though.

"Hi, Aunt Greta," I said. She wrapped her arms around me and I patted her back awkwardly, hugging her for the first time in almost a decade.

"How was your drive? Let me look at you. Goodness, girl, you are thin. What are they feeding you at that fancy school of yours? Spinach and sparkling water?"

"My best friend asked the same thing," I laughed, self-consciously looking down at my legs, bare beneath my white skirt.

"Well, I've got lunch ready for you in the kitchen. Your grandmother's special baked ziti." *My grandmother had a specialty?* Aunt Greta pursed her lips. "I would've made your favorite, but I wasn't sure what that would be. So, Hannah insisted I make *her* favorite." She chuckled and put her hand on the small of my back, taking the handle of my suitcase in the other, but not before reaching into the pocket of her shorts and handing the driver a folded wad of bills. He nodded, got back into the car, and peeled out like he couldn't get away fast enough. "Come on, let's go in and I'll show you the guest room."

Uncle Ed was at the front door when we got there. I did a double take. He looked just like my dad. A little thinner, a lot grayer, more stubble around his square jaw, but there was no mistaking the relation. We both just sort of stared at each other for a moment, and then his face broke out into a wide grin—wider than I had seen on my father's face in years and years. My uncle swept me up into a hug, my feet leaving the ground, and I had to hold onto his shoulders to steady myself.

"We're so glad you're here, Ashlyn, I can't even tell you," Uncle Ed said into my hair. "I'm so sorry for everything you're going through." Tears immediately sprang to my eyes and I quickly turned my cheek to wipe them on the soft fabric of his worn T-shirt. And then, setting me down gently, "But you're with family now. We're here to support you."

I nodded, afraid to speak and let loose the ocean of tears I was desperately trying to hold back. He stepped into the house and held the door open for me and Aunt Greta. I followed him up the narrow wooden stairs, each stomp of my feet on the steps releasing a bit of the nervous energy inside. He carried my suitcase into a small bedroom on the left side of the hallway. It was fine, but it wasn't mine. Uncle Ed set it down on the bed and wiped his hands on the seat of his jeans. He looked at me, with what looked like hope, and his face fell when he saw the grimace I knew was on my face.

"Well, I know it's not what you're used to, but it's comfortable. At least there's air conditioning, which is more than I can say for the employee cabins up at Sweetwater, but that's half the fun, right?" He chucked me gently on the arm. Was that meant to be a joke? No air conditioning sounded like a nightmare.

"Sure," I said weakly.

"Do you want a glass of water or a pop or something? Hannah's downstairs setting the table, should be ready

in a few minutes." Uncle Ed's eyes were light and hopeful. Like adding his estranged niece to his household was
absolutely no big deal. I hoped that was true. The last
thing I wanted was to be anyone's burden.

"I'll just freshen up and be right down." I clasped my
hands behind my back. Uncle Ed nodded.

"You got it." He smiled again, and his eyes crinkled in
the corners. "I know I said it already, but I'm glad you're
here, honey. We've missed you."

I heard myself say, "Me too," with a creak. I wasn't
sure I meant it but I wanted to.

"Bathroom is across the hall. You'll share with
Hannah." He nodded again and left, closing the door
softly behind him.

I sat on the corner of the bed, which was covered in
a lacy bedspread that probably used to be white but had
yellowed with age. The walls were dark blue, almost navy,
but the room was still filled with light from the large
window, framed with lace curtains. *Cheap*, my dad's voice
scorned. I stood and inspected the three-drawer dresser
at the foot of the bed. On top, conveniently for me, was
a brochure for Sweetwater Overlook Retreat Center. Did
Hannah put it there? Aunt Greta? I ran a finger down
the glossy cover, over green trees and the roof of the big,
wooden lodge. Men and women, who looked like they
belonged in suits and shiny shoes, smiled bright white
teeth at the camera as they linked arms and pointed to the
logos on their matching Sweetwater tees. They looked
happy. But how anyone could be happy in the woods with
bugs and rain and dirt was beyond me. I groaned and

silently cursed my father. If he had followed the rules set forth by the IRS like every other law-abiding citizen in the free world, I'd be sitting by the pool reading magazines with Tatum.

I read further and something caught my eye. "Sweetwater is proudly 'off the grid' so be sure to leave your cell phones and laptops at home."

No cell phone or internet? How was I supposed to talk to Tatum and stay connected to the real world? My dad talked a good game about his genius plan of ensuring I was "supported," but that seemed impossible if I couldn't talk to my best friend.

"I know you probably think you'll hate it, but the retreat is magical. People's lives change there. So just make sure you don't ruin that for the rest of us, okay?" I whirled around to find my cousin Hannah in the doorway, hand on her hip. She looked exactly the same as the picture Aunt Greta had sent in the most recent holiday card. Tanned skin—she'd benefited from our Mediterranean genes, while I was paler than a ghost—muscular thighs beneath olive green shorts, plain white tank, swimmer's shoulders, a chocolate brown pixie cut. And a spectacular sneer.

"I have no idea what you're talking about."

Hannah raised an eyebrow. "Sure."

I raised one back. "I'm not sure what you think you know about me, but I'm pretty certain you're wrong."

Hannah's navy-blue eyes widened. They were just a shade darker than my own. She held my gaze for a full minute as I felt my insides shrink. Just as I was about to look away, she shrugged. "That's fair. I mean, we haven't seen each other since, what? Elementary school."

I cleared my throat. "I think that's about right."

She shrugged again, no hint of aggression or anger on her face. She looked oddly calm and unbothered. I'd never seen anyone who could do that. "Well, maybe I *am* wrong then. I guess we'll see."

"I guess we will."

At the round table in the kitchen, Aunt Greta seated me between her and Hannah. Uncle Ed, across from me with a monster-sized helping of cheese-smothered ziti, grinned as I dug into mine, which was about a quarter of the size of his.

"Prepare for greatness, Ashlyn. My mother's recipe won contests. Your father and I used to fight over who got the corner pieces where the cheese is crispy." Uncle Ed winked at me and then chuckled at the confused look on my face.

"I don't think we've ever had this," I said quietly and slipped a small bite into my mouth. I wished it hadn't tasted like sawdust. I'm sure it would've been better had I not been here against my will. I took another, smaller bite and tried to ignore my dad's voice telling me to watch how many calories I ate.

Ed raised an eyebrow for just a second before he nodded once and said, "Well, we're certainly happy to be able to introduce you to it, then."

Lunch continued like that. Ed or Greta making perfectly good attempts at conversation, me not knowing what they were talking about or giving the shortest answers possible, and Hannah, chewing with that smirk on her face. And despite Uncle Ed and Aunt Greta's best attempts to make me feel at home, the meal only intensified the reality of how alone I was. They were this nice little unit and I was the interloper. Once I'd eaten enough to be polite, I asked to be excused, saying I needed to rearrange my bag for camp.

Aunt Greta put a hand on my wrist as I stood. "You let us know if we can do anything to help you, honey. Anything at all." I was surprised to see more than just compassion in her gaze. There was concern, fear, and anger there as well. All the things I was feeling too.

"I will. Thank you."

I slid my chair back under the table and ran up the stairs.

Chapter 5

A few days later, as I was lying on my bed staring at the popcorn ceiling, Aunt Greta knocked and pushed open the door. "Hon, your dad is on the phone. Better take it. Who knows when he'll be able to call again."

The familiar feeling settled over me whenever I heard the word dad—half-fear and half-irritation. I took the cordless from her hand. "Hello?" I said, as Aunt Greta slipped out of the room.

"Hello, Ashlyn, how are you?"

He sounded exactly the same, as if I were on my bed at school and he were at home. "Hi, Dad. I'm fine." Not scared. Not angry. Not second-guessing myself at every turn. Fine. I was a good liar. I should be. I'd had enough practice telling my dad what he wanted to hear.

"Are you all settled in?"

Define settled, I didn't say. "Yes," I said. "Aunt Greta and Uncle Ed have been very nice. They made baked ziti." I waited to see if he'd take the bait, and say something, *anything*, about the crusty cheese edges.

"Hmmm," he only mumbled. A non-answer. "And you're ready for work? You leave in a few days, correct?"

"Saturday morning." I knew what he was doing here. Instead of asking me how I felt or even asking about his brother and his family, he simply focused on the cold, emotionless logistics. He was keeping me an arm's length away. Like he always did. If I wasn't so used to it, I'd probably be more upset than I already was. I mean, if my dad and I had the kind of relationship where he offered fatherly advice and showed interest in me as a person, I bet I would've been bawling my eyes out to hear his voice, knowing I was only going to see him in a prison uniform in his cinder block cage for the next year. But it was just the same as it always was.

"Make sure you are on your best behavior. It might feel like fun—kind of like summer camp—but you are there to work."

"I will be." I gritted my teeth.

"This goes without saying but keep the flirting to a minimum. You can't let some boy distract you."

I squeezed my eyes shut. He was never going to let me live down my mistakes. I clenched my jaw so hard it ached.

Dad just kept plowing forward. "And keep in mind Uncle Ed will pick you up for our visits, so you'll need to request the time off in advance. I'm sending the visitation paperwork to Ed's house. He'll get it to you."

I realized my nails were digging so hard into my palm they were making angry red marks in my skin. I didn't say anything in response. We were talking about prison visits. What was I supposed to say?

"In case you were wondering," he said, with the certainty that only he was capable of, "I'm doing okay here." Truthfully, no matter how frustrated or angry or just done with my day that I thought I was, I *had* been curious. And scared. I felt a lot of things about my dad, but I loved him. My love for him was part of the problem. It was easier to ignore someone you weren't so emotionally connected with. "I'm still getting used to the routine, but that's to be expected."

"Good, that's really good." I exhaled into the receiver. In the background, I heard voices and scuffling.

"Time's up, Ashlyn. I'll call again soon. I have the number for Sweetwater."

"Okay. Take care, Dad."

"You too."

The phone clicked, and then there was nothing.

It took a full minute before my lungs decided to start working again. And another full minute before the bedroom door opened again.

"Are you okay, sweetheart? I couldn't help overhear." I was more stunned by the look of pure sympathy on my aunt's face than I was at the fact that she had been eavesdropping.

"I guess." Anyone's guess was as good as mine at that point.

Aunt Greta sat down on the bed next to me and put her arm around my shoulders. "I know you didn't say much to him, but it's exactly what you didn't say that came across loud and clear."

Despite her embrace, I crossed my arms over my

chest, suddenly feeling exposed. My nonresponses were carefully calculated from years of practice masking what I was really thinking from a father who didn't seem to care anyway. "What do you mean?"

She stroked what was left of my hair. "Your tone was guarded. You only answered his questions and didn't ask any of your own. He didn't engage with the ziti comment, which I'm guessing was probably pretty discouraging."

Aunt Greta did not miss a thing. I crossed my arms tighter. "You got all that?"

"Honey, I'm a social worker. My job is to read people. And right now, you are either angry, terrified, or a little of both. Which is it?"

"Both," I whispered.

"I'd probably be the same if I came home from school to find out my family was leaving me."

The tears spilled down my cheeks before I could stop them. "Why did he do it? Why did he do this to us?" *Was it something I did? If I'd made better choices, would my dad have too?* I wanted to ask it out loud, but I couldn't.

Aunt Greta sighed. "I wish I knew. I've seen a lot of people do a lot of hurtful things over the years, and the best answer I have, which isn't nearly as nuanced as the truth, is that they're selfish."

"I could've told you that." The second after it slipped out, I wanted to clap my hands over my mouth.

My aunt gave me a knowing little smile. "Well, I can't say I've spent much time with your father in the last decade, and not for lack of trying, but from the outside, it looks like selfishness is a decent assumption. If I were to keep guessing, I might also say he is a desperate man, and afraid. With a bit of pride thrown in."

I jumped up, my hands balled into tight fists again, wiping the scalding tears from my face. "What did he have to be afraid of? We had everything."

Greta's lips pursed into a horizontal line. "Maybe you should hash that one out with your uncle."

I stared at her and shook my head. "Maybe another time. I'm feeling tired all of a sudden. I think I want to lie down, if you don't mind." I wrapped my arms around myself, sat on the bed, and turned away. I'd said too much already.

"Sure, sure. You're going to be busy, busy, busy soon enough. Get your rest while you can." I glanced up as she rose and went to the door, pausing just long enough to look over her shoulder and smile sadly at me. Then she was gone.

I hated that smile. It was the same one Cassie Pringle gave me before I left school. Filled with pity, but also relief that the terrible thing that had happened to me hadn't happened to them. She was probably counting her blessings that she'd married the Zanotti brother with more sense.

When I heard my aunt's footsteps on the stairs fade away, I rolled off the bed and slid my laptop out of my backpack. I flipped the top and drummed my fingers nervously near the keys as I waited for it to wake up before typing "my dad is going to jail" into the search bar. No one in this house, and most likely no one where I was going, knew what this super-weird mix of feelings felt like, but maybe the internet would.

I found forum after forum of people—kids like me—looking for support from strangers. "My dad is going to jail for abusing my sister and I'm depressed." "My dad is going to jail for two to six years." "My dad is going to jail and he's the only man in my life who I trust. I have no idea how I'm going to cope without him." None of them were quite like my situation, and reading their words solidified my understanding of how very strange and "first world problems" my circumstances were. Even still, I felt less alone reading their stories. Even if the details were different, those kids were being abandoned too. Just like me, they were wondering how they were supposed to reshape their lives around a father-shaped hole.

I googled "tax evasion sentences" and found page after page of people who cheated their companies and the government, as my dad had done. *Selfish people*, I thought in Aunt Greta's knowing voice. I looked up Williams, the place Dad was . . . what should I call it? Locked up? Staying at? Spending time in? A lump formed in my throat and I shoved the computer off my lap.

"It's not forever. It's not forever," I whispered to myself.

"Are you talking to yourself?" Hannah called from the hallway. "I mean, if you are, I guess that's fine. It's not that odd . . ."

I stared at her, unsure if she was joking. She stared right back. Hannah's gaze was so unnerving, I had to look away. Was she making fun of me? If she was, this was going to be an even worse couple of months than I originally imagined. Finally, she broke her gaze and, thankfully, laughed. "Really, though, are you okay?"

"Sure," I said. *Not that I'd talk to you about this. Not a chance.*

"No, you're not." Hannah came in and sat down, just like her mother had. "What were you doing online?"

With all the fight taken out of me for the time being, I passed her the laptop. She scanned the screen for a few minutes and clicked two or three times.

"He's right, you know."

"Who is?"

Hannah pointed to a tab that displayed a poem written by a boy whose father had been incarcerated for five years. "He says it's not his fault. What his dad did."

"So?"

She shrugged. "Just making an observation." She clicked around some more. "Williams, huh? It's about an hour from Sweetwater. Looks brutal." I rolled my eyes as Hannah continued scanning the website. She looked up just long enough to catch me sending an eyebrow-singing glare her way. "Sorry, sorry." Hannah shut the laptop and put it on my nightstand. "Look, I know we don't know each other very well—"

"Or at all," I muttered.

"Fair. Or at all. But here's something about me. I don't wallow. Things are rough for you right now, I get it." *No, you don't,* I didn't say. "And Mom says they've been rough for a long time. And that totally sucks. I get it," she said again. I sat on my hand that wanted to clench into a fist.

"But if you sit in here and google stuff, you're only going to make it worse. Plus, we're leaving for Sweetwater soon and you won't be able to sit around and stew, you know?" I nodded once. "Some friends and I are going out tonight. Maybe a movie. Not sure yet. But you should come. It'll be good for you."

I closed my eyes. Why did everyone else think they knew what was good for me? It was exhausting. "I don't really feel up for it, but I appreciate the invitation. And thanks for the advice. I'll take it into consideration." It was what my dad said to clients, and to me, when he didn't want to do something someone was asking of him.

Unfazed, she popped up off the bed. "Suit yourself. But when we get there you're not going to be able to skip out on stuff. Especially staff campfires and dinners. The owner expects the staff to participate in all the activities."

"Great. Thanks for letting me know," I said, making no effort to mask my annoyed tone of voice. Luckily, Hannah the non-wallower moved on immediately.

"Consider yourself warned," she countered, smiled sweetly at me, and left.

Alone in my room, I picked up the laptop and opened it again. I reread the poem aloud to myself, as if it was a prayer. "You are not responsible for the mistakes of others" jumped out at me, and I repeated it. It seemed like something worth remembering, so I opened my quote journal and wrote it down in slick black ink. I may not have been responsible for my dad's mistakes, but I sure as heck could take responsibility for my own. I'd spent the last year doing everything right. Yet, here I was, in

Wherever, Pennsylvania, still trying to prove I was ready to come home.

My dad's voice, a sinister whisper, still poked and prodded at me. If I'd stood up straighter, worn a longer skirt, and gotten higher test scores, would he have reached for more? Would he still be in prison? It was totally ridiculous, but completely consuming.

Chapter 6

My sentence to work for the summer didn't feel real until the Sweetwater Overlook Retreat Center sign stared back at me as Uncle Ed pulled in to drop us off. It seemed to be taunting me, telling me I was going to fall flat on my face here, and I had to look away. We drove to the main building and parked. Hannah hopped out first and began unloading our bags, while I dragged myself from the station wagon at the pace of a snail.

My ever-observant aunt picked up on my misery. "You're going to have a wonderful time, sweetheart," she told me, her hands on my cheeks as she stared into my eyes. Was she trying to implant the idea that Sweetwater was awesome directly into my brain? If so, it wasn't working.

"I'll be fine. Don't worry about me." I was going for confident and reassuring, but it came out more dismissive than anything else.

Aunt Greta winced, but quickly recovered. "Well, if you need anything at all, we're just a phone call away, okay?" She stepped back, put both hands on her hips, and surveyed the forest of tall trees that surrounded the gravel parking lot where we stood. "This place holds such fantastic memories for me. I spent most of my summers in college and grad school here. Helping people reach their potential is so powerful. It's part of why I became a social worker. The owner, Fred Allen, is like a second father to me. He saw how much I loved it and just kept encouraging me to get more involved." She smiled at me. "Even if you don't love it as much as Hannah and I do, it'll be a good experience. Sweetwater teaches you what you're made of."

"Sugar and spice and everything nice?" I deadpanned.

Greta raised an eyebrow. "I was thinking more along the lines of strength and courage."

"Not sure that applies to me," I said, looking at my shoes. If I rewound through the movie of my life up to this point, it was pretty easy to see that I wasn't a fighter. I always knew this about myself and I always hated it, but it was so much easier to keep my mouth shut when something bothered me. I appreciated Aunt Greta's positive attitude, but if Sweetwater was trying to teach me to be strong, it might be the one and only class I ever failed.

"You might surprise yourself," she said with a wink.

Doubtful, I said, but only to myself.

Greta and Ed kissed my cheeks, hugged Hannah fiercely, and promised they'd send care packages. Hannah yelled "Cookies!" with a smile as they got back in the car. Then her smile faded when she realized we were alone, together.

"Let's go. We can't be late for orientation." My cousin

picked up her army-style duffel bag and started toward the lodge. I gathered from the brochure that this was where the retreaters slept, where conference rooms were, where the dining hall was housed, among other important places for the complete retreat experience. Looking around, I spied a few separate cabins, a gazebo, and trails that led behind the lodge to who knows where. And a lot of trees. And dirt. A fly zipped past me and I swatted at it. I grabbed my rolling suitcase and dragged it behind me, kicking up pieces of gravel that stung my bare ankles as I went.

When we got inside, I followed silently down linoleum hallways until we passed through a set of double doors and the sign that said Mess Hall. *Mess hall? Are we in the Army?* Hannah dropped her bag on the floor and ran like a track star for a group of people standing in a semicircle next to a long row of cafeteria tables. I stood off to the side and took in my surroundings. Besides the long tables, there was a smaller one set up in the front, with a clipboard and a stack of papers. I approached the table, inspecting the clipboard. It was a sign-in sheet. I scanned the names. Hannah's was typed at the very bottom—the curse of being a Z—and right under hers, mine was handwritten in a swirly blue scrawl. The last-minute addition. I quickly signed my initials next to my name, and just to be nice, wrote HZ next to Hannah's name. And, making sure no one was watching me, I scribbled,

THE BEGINNING IS ALWAYS TODAY.
Mary Wollstonecraft Shelley

across the top of the sign-in sheet.

Across the room, I watched my cousin sling an arm around an older woman with a braid hanging down her back. There were a handful of others, all ages, standing around with them. Hannah's friends looked outdoorsy. They all wore some variation of the same outfit—T-shirt or Sweetwater polo, khaki shorts with lots of pockets, running shoes or hiking boots. My gingham sleeveless top with the silver snap buttons, professionally frayed jean shorts, and cute white canvas sneakers seemed fussy and out of place now. The others seemed ready to take on grizzly bears and scale rock walls, while I looked like an extra in a movie set on a farm.

Hannah seemed to be so wrapped up in catching up with her friends that she'd forgotten about me. So instead of standing around staring like a creeper, I took a seat at one of the long wooden tables, my suitcase at my feet. I sighed. The new girl, yet again. Just like last year at Blue Valley, when I arrived right as summer school began. School was school was school, and I was good at doing school. I knew the right things to say and the routines were familiar. But here? I didn't know anyone, and even my job was still a mystery. I sat, my chin in my hand, and stared at the dark wooden beams on the ceiling, counting them forward and backward to the sounds of laughter and chatter from Hannah and her friends. *You look lazy. Sit up straighter. Impressions are everything,* my dad's voice urged. I sat up and sighed.

Five minutes later, the door swung open again. I was expecting another wilderness-ready counselor type. My eyebrows lifted into my forehead when I saw how wrong I was. Not that he wouldn't have been completely comfortable hugging a pine tree. The guy strolled in like he owned the place, one hand in the pocket of his shorts. He was tanned with rosy cheeks, as if he spent all his days windsurfing and playing volleyball on a tropical beach, and his light brown hair was sun-kissed on the ends. A carefree half-smile played on his full lips. The collar of his gray polo was turned up and his running shoes were just the right amount of worn to suggest he hit the pavement several times a week. His muscular calves confirmed it.

"Drool much, Ashlyn?" Hannah scoffed in my ear. I hadn't heard her come over. Just in time to see me staring.

I couldn't even pretend she was wrong. "Who is he?"

Hannah watched him drop a green backpack on the floor, sit down a few tables away from us, and remove a ring of keys from his back pocket. "Not a clue. Never seen him before."

Something inside of me lit up, warm and bright. He was brand new, just like me. Maybe he and I could band together, us against the dirt, forging a new path. I shook my head at myself. *Ridiculous.* He was probably a mountaineer just like the rest of them. In fact, he exuded so much confidence that I bet Sweetwater hired him to offset my lack of experience. Still, there was something about him that I couldn't look away from. Tatum liked to joke that there wasn't a boy in a polo I didn't like. Maybe she was right. And perhaps my track record with boys wasn't amazing, but there was something magnetic about the promise of flirty banter. It had always been my favorite way to take my mind off . . . other things.

"Well, if he's new, maybe he's nervous too," I said. *Should I go talk to him? We could feel out of place together . . .* As I stood, his dark brown eyes locked on me. I felt him give me the once over and my insides went molten. He was definitely my type.

"Sit down, sit down," came a voice from the front of the room. I startled and sat back down as directed. Hannah took the seat next to me and some of her friends joined us. A tall man with a shock of white hair and posture like a flag pole stood before us. His navy-blue polo sported the Sweetwater logo over his heart and his khaki shorts were lined with cargo pockets. A carabiner with about a hundred keys hung from his braided belt. The man clapped his hands and his keys jingled. "Welcome, everyone. We're so glad you're here." His voice was warm, grandfatherly, like he was ready to teach me to fish or to pull a quarter out of my ear.

A short, sturdy-looking woman with a bird's nest of curly brown hair stood next to him, rocking back and forth on the heels of her Velcro athletic sandals. She cleared her throat loudly. The man patted her shoulder and continued speaking. "My name is Fred Allen and I've had the distinct pleasure of owning Sweetwater Overlook for the last forty-two years. My wife likes to say I'm semiretired, which is her way of telling me to spend more time at home, which I intend on doing after today. I see a number of familiar faces, which is always nice, and many new ones, which is also nice. I'm sure this is going to be our best summer yet, and that's all because of your hard work. So, thank you in advance."

Fred held his hands out toward us and clapped. And because you couldn't not clap with him, I clapped too, as did everyone else. I stole a quick look over at the guy in the polo and he lifted his clapping hands in my direction and nodded, as if he were clapping for me. My face warmed and I smiled shyly, mimicking his action. Why shouldn't we clap for each other? The boy winked at me and turned back to the front.

The short woman cleared her throat again, louder this time, and rocked so hard I was afraid she'd fall over. Fred finally got the hint.

"Kids, this is Deborah Gress, our new manager." Audible gasps were heard around the room and Fred nodded, a sympathetic look on his face. "I'm sad to report that our beloved Joan Jenkins retired several weeks ago. I'm even sadder to report that Joan is undergoing treatment for cancer, but happy to share that her prognosis is good. Joan sends her best wishes to you all, says please don't worry about her, and that she's already got her grandkids running errands for her since she's not here to boss you all around." Laughter erupted from some of the others around me, including Hannah. I guessed you needed to know Joan to get the joke. "But we are lucky to have Deb here with us."

Deb stepped forward and introduced herself in a voice that reminded me of a door hinge that needed greasing. She waved her hands around as she talked, like she was swatting flies. By the time she mentioned the third hotel she had managed and "brought back from the brink of destruction," I had already zoned out. I wish I hadn't, because Deb's boasting was replaced by my dad's voice in my mind, his last phone call echoing back at me. *Be on your best behavior. Don't embarrass the family.*

The nail polish on my thumb was chipping, so I picked at it and sent tiny flecks of purple to the ground. Moments—or a half an hour—later, I had no idea, Deb barked my name. My head shot up so fast my sunglasses toppled off the back of my head and clattered to the floor.

Deb's left eyebrow was raised. "Here's your assignment, Ashlyn." She held out a half-sheet of paper. "You and I will be working closely together this summer."

I took the paper without looking at it. "Sounds good," I mumbled, and sat back down, setting my assignment face down on the table.

It wasn't until I was following Hannah to our cabin that I read what was written.

My cousin elbowed me in the rib. "What did you get?" I handed her the slip of paper. "Office assistant, and other duties as required?" she read, puzzled. "What does that even mean?" She shoved the paper back at me. "I don't like Deb. I want Joan back."

"Well, it doesn't sound like that's an option."

Hannah's jaw tightened as she sped up; I nearly had to jog to keep up with her. "Deb put me in charge of the equipment kiosk." I didn't know what that meant, but her angry tone made me think twice about asking for clarification. "This is so humiliating. I was supposed to be head lifeguard. Joan promised. I don't understand. I worked hard. I'm certified. I get along with everyone. I got a great evaluation last year. This is completely unfair." She shrugged and shook her head, as if she was trying to make peace with the job. "I will make it work, but this is *not* what was supposed to happen."

I just nodded in solidarity. Neither of us were off to a good start this summer.

Chapter 7

Hannah and I were assigned to share one of the employee cabins. "They used to be where retreaters stayed," she told me, "but once the Allens continued to build additions onto the property, including the main lodge with nicer, hotel-style rooms, the cabins became personal quarters for the staff living on site for the summer."

It was modest by any standards, but I'd been living in a standard issue dorm room for the last year, so the bunk beds, small wardrobe, and single desk didn't faze me. Hannah took the bottom bunk without asking. "I roll around a lot in my sleep." I didn't fight her for it. She flopped down on the bed, put in her headphones, and stayed that way until it was time to eat. I didn't mind the peace and quiet and did the same.

When we walked into the dining hall for the all-staff dinner, the first thing I saw was an elaborate gingerbread house on a table at the front of the room. I leaned over to Hannah and whispered, "It's six months from Christmas. Why is this here?"

"Not a clue," she said. Like moths to a flame, we both went over to inspect it.

Unlike the houses I'd made every year in elementary school, which had been a couple of graham crackers cemented together with icing from a can and a few candy canes slapped on the roof, this gingerbread house was both a culinary and architectural marvel, made from solid sheets of real gingerbread. I leaned over the roof, covered with flat candy disc shingles, and inhaled the spicy, sugary smell. It reminded me of the cookies my mom used to order from our favorite bakery at holiday time. Suddenly I was seven years old in bunny slippers, eyeing the shiny, wrapped boxes under the eight-foot Fraser fir in the living room, while my dad told me to keep my hands off the presents.

Hannah sniffed too. "Just like Mom's air freshener." She sneezed. "Smells good, but potentially hazardous to my health."

We circled the house, admiring the details. Green coconut grass in the yard. Stained-glass sugar windows. Fluffy white icing smoke coming from the perfectly built chimney. Sliced gumdrop flowers improving the curb appeal. There was even a little mailbox made out of a Tootsie Roll.

"I can almost imagine a little candy family living here, can't you?" I asked Hannah.

"More like a witch, boiling up little kids," she said with a smirk, and before I knew what she was doing, a gumdrop flower had disappeared into her mouth. My eyes widened. She smirked again and shrugged. Hannah shrugged a lot. Like she didn't care what anyone thought.

Maybe you should try shrugging more, I thought. *Mind your posture,* came my dad's reply in my head.

I was reaching out to take my own gumdrop when someone cleared her throat right behind me. "What do you two think you're doing?"

I turned slowly, while Hannah's cheeks turned bright pink. "I . . . was . . . just getting a closer look."

Deb's eyes narrowed. "Please don't touch the house. It took me a very long time to build and the oil from your fingers could damage it."

"*You* built this?" I couldn't hold back sounding impressed. Nor could I imagine this woman building something so dainty and sweet. When Deb nodded, I took the opportunity to flatter her and hopefully make her forget we were trying to eat her masterpiece. "It's fantastic. I was just telling Hannah how wonderful the craftsmanship is. Really creative. I especially love the mailbox. That's a nice touch." I knew I was being over-the-top but judging by the way Deb preened and stood up straighter, it was the right move. I elbowed Hannah as subtly as I could, hoping she'd follow my lead.

"Huh? Oh, yeah. I like the grass." *That's the best you could come up with?* I didn't ask.

"Well, thank you. Just admire it from a few inches back." Deb walked away like a proud peacock, shoulders pinned back, chin tipped up. I stifled a giggle. My father was the one who had taught me to watch people, find their weakness, and use it to your advantage. Such a great role model. A sour taste coated my tongue. *Be more like Hannah, less like Dad.*

Deb clanged a knife on a glass and gestured for everyone to sit down. "Let's take this first night on campus for some togetherness. I know my daughter, Mallory," Deb said, waving to a girl seated at my table, "and I aren't the only new members of the Sweetwater family. I hope everyone is made to feel as welcome as we do. As a thank you, direct from me to you, I've had the cooks whip up my specialty." She clapped her hands and a handful of servers brought out platters of chicken in some kind of brown sauce alongside bowls of rice. Or was it pasta? It was hard to tell, really.

"Why is she clapping at them?" Hannah whispered angrily. "They're not house elves. I feel like I need to give them a sock."

"Maybe she's just trying to be festive?" said a voice to Hannah's left, from someone I hadn't noticed. The guy looked over and reached a hand across Hannah to me. "Hi. We haven't met yet. I'm Baxter Clark."

I shook his hand, which was large and callused and scraped against my skin. "Ashlyn Zanotti. I'm Hannah's cousin from Virginia."

"Oh yeah? I didn't know Hannah had family in Virginia." Baxter raised a blonde eyebrow at Hannah, who rolled her eyes.

"Our dads are brothers. They're not close." She pushed Baxter's arm away. "But we've got all summer to bond. Right, Ash?"

I almost flinched. Did she mean it? "Right."

Baxter nodded. "That's great. Glad you're here." He smiled, showing a crooked incisor. "I work at Sweetwater year-round. Have for a few years now."

"Bax was in my year at school but graduated from high school early. He's a genius," Hannah said matter-of-factly, reaching for the chicken and scooping some on her plate. "Bax is like my second brother. We worked at the summer camp up the road together for a few years and were campers before that. He's a master of the ziplines."

"And what am I? Chopped liver?" The woman seated across from Baxter piped up, pretending to be offended. She shook her head good-naturedly and offered me her hand. The skin on her arm was deeply tanned and wrinkled, almost like a shar-pei. "I'm Ruth Newhouse. I work the ropes course with Bax." With a long silver braid down her back, I guessed she was in her sixties. She'd been the one Hannah had hugged earlier. "Been here a long time. Curious how this one," she nodded in Deb's direction, "is going to run things."

"My mother has been running hotels and resorts for years. Well, she and my dad did it together. They just got divorced, but she has loads of experience. It'll be great, I promise. Nothing to worry about," said a high voice from further down the table. Deb's daughter.

"Mallory, is it?" Ruth asked her. The girl nodded furiously, her wild brown curls rustling around her face. "I'm sorry to hear about your parents splitting up." Mallory gave her a sad smile. "And, that's good to hear. Your mother has a tough act to follow in Joan, but it sounds like she's up for the challenge." Mallory nodded again. "And what will you be doing around the place, young lady?"

Mallory perked up, her proud mannerisms like her

mother's. "I'm head lifeguard. I love the pool." Mallory beamed at Ruth, while Hannah practically growled.

I clamped a hand on Hannah's leg under the table just as she opened her mouth. "Don't," I said, so only she could hear me. She stopped and stuck a fork in her chicken, shoveling a huge bite in her mouth.

"Did someone say lifeguard?" A head swiveled from the table adjacent to ours. The guy in the gray polo. I held my breath. "I'm lifeguarding too. Does that make you my boss?" He winked at Mallory and she giggled. "I'm Marcus Toft."

"Pleased to meet you, Marcus," said Mallory, just as I said, "Hi, Marcus. Glad I'm not the only new one." She glared at me, I glared back, and Marcus nodded at both of us. So that's how it was going to be—Mallory and Marcus working together all day long in the sun while I was shut up in an office with Deb. I'd have to figure something out. And quickly. Or Mallory and her little giggle might win him over before I had a chance to get to know him.

Ruth had everyone else at our table go around and say their names and jobs as the group continued to serve themselves from the platters being passed around. I tried to pay attention to the names, but I knew I wouldn't be able to recite most of them tomorrow. I took a small scoop of rice and ladled a few chunks of chicken on my plate. It smelled strange and looked stranger. But I knew Deb would be watching and I didn't want to look ungrateful on our very first night. As I raised a bite to my lips, Hannah poked me in the ribs.

"Don't eat it."

"What?" I said, the food falling off my fork and onto the plate with a plop.

"It's rubber covered in canned gravy. Just don't do it."

"Really?" This was supposed to be Deb's specialty. Deb, who had appointed herself head of the competitive cooking activity. Deb, who had supposedly run hotels and resorts with restaurants on her properties. I didn't have any reason to not believe Hannah, but the evidence was in Deb's favor. I stabbed a piece of chicken and took a bite. Immediately I knew it was a mistake and willed myself to not spit it out into my napkin. I chewed without inhaling and swallowed as quickly as I could, washing it down with a gulp of water so big I almost choked. *That was rude. I hope no one saw what you did,* said my dad's voice.

"Told you so," Hannah said, reaching for the rice and serving herself a fresh scoop without sauce. I did the same, and we ate our plates of plain rice, while Baxter and Ruth did their best to not laugh at us.

"Ashlyn, how are you enjoying your meal?" Deb's creaky-door voice sounded over my shoulder.

For a horrible brief moment, I thought she had seen me take that bite of her "specialty" chicken and was coming in for the kill. Had I ruined this before it even started? I smiled politely at her. "It was really nice of you to do this for us, Deb. Thank you."

"You're very welcome," she smiled back, but it didn't reach her eyes. "You know, it's quite lucky we were able to find you a spot here," she continued, her sturdy voice capturing the whole mess hall's attention. People turned their heads to listen more closely, to my horror. "Your aunt's phone call came so late in the hiring season, and what with you being the youngest employee here at not even eighteen yet . . . but we made it work, didn't we?"

While Deb seemed very pleased with her ability to fit me in, I wanted to die. If crawling under the table for the rest of the summer was an option, I would've done it. In one fell swoop, Deb told everyone that I hadn't gotten this job on my own merit, that I was underage and under-qualified, and that my family had arranged the whole thing. I thought I was embarrassed when Cassie Pringle came to my door to peddle her brand of sympathy back at school, but this suddenly felt so much worse. The only other thought that went through my head—besides wanting to lock myself in Deb's gingerbread house—was whether Hannah had told anyone about my dad's "situation."

"Good things come in young packages," Marcus called from his table. I raised my eyes to his, grateful for the diversion, and he winked.

"Isn't it small packages?" Hannah said with a scowl.

"Maybe. But my version works." Marcus just smiled at her and took a swig from his glass. He turned back to me and flashed me the same confident smile. My toes curled as I grinned back, my mind started thinking of ways I could pay him back for the save.

I could feel Deb's eyes on me. Was she waiting for me to say something? How grateful I was to her for hiring me? It would be a lie. How happy I was to be there? Also, a lie. How thrilled I was to be working with her in the office? I didn't think I could get that out without laughing.

"Thanks, Deb."

It satisfied her enough that she nodded and went back to her seat at the front of the room. And in that moment, I realized something very important. Deb reminded me of my dad. She needed to feel important. *That* was her weakness. Perhaps I could use my years of experience with self-centered people to my advantage.

Thanks, Dad.

On my way back to the cabin, feeling deflated, a hand grasped my shoulder. I whirled around to find Marcus there, grinning.

"Speaking of small from earlier, '*Though she be but little, she is fierce.*'"

"Shakespeare," I said. "Impressive." I smiled, charmed that one, he had come to find me to make me feel better, and two, knew quotes. I wondered what else he was good at.

"I try." His grin brightened a few watts.

"That's one of my favorite quotes." I didn't add that it was a little bit of wish fulfillment on my part. I was definitely on the small side, but I'd never felt fierce. *Maybe one day.*

He brushed imaginary dust off his shoulder. "Lucky me. I look forward to learning more of your favorites. See you around, Ashlyn."

"See you, Marcus."

He saluted me and took off jogging, leaving me looking forward to telling him more of my favorites.

Chapter 8

*I*t turned out "other duties as required" meant cleaning up in the campus gym and filling in when an area was short-staffed, on top of working in Deb's office. In my first week as a gainfully employed near-adult, I wiped down fifteen treadmills approximately three hundred times, spilled water on half a table of retreaters during a particularly hectic lunch shift, and handed out the wrong room assignments, mixing up an all-girls high school leadership group with a bunch of insurance salespeople. Those girls were not pleased when I had to trade out their cushy rooms with queen-sized beds for cramped quarters and bunk beds. It felt like I was doing everything wrong. The dad-voice in my head criticizing constantly didn't help.

On top of it all, none of the things I'd been asked to do did anything to chase away the thoughts about my parents and about my future that kept plaguing me. Questions, really. What was my dad doing in prison? Was he safe? Was he making friends or enemies? Was he think-ing about me? How was rehab going for Mom? Was she feeling any better? Would she be the mom I once knew by the end of the summer? What was going to happen to me at the end of this summer? Where would I be? It was an endless loop, an earworm I couldn't shake. And it was causing me to stumble at my job even more than I would have otherwise.

I'd also spent so much time by myself, I felt like I was almost completely alone at Sweetwater. Sure, I interacted with retreat patrons occasionally, and I saw Hannah every evening long enough for her to catch me up on how many volleyballs she had to rescue from the lake that day before she passed out in her bed, but for the most part, everyone was kept busy. Most of the time, there weren't even a handful of us eating dinner at the same time, so I'd taken to bringing a book or my quote journal with me so I didn't look like a loser eating at a table for one. I probably saw Deb the most, though it was usually as she was rushing in from some meeting, her hair a mud-colored cloud around her head, and papers that were usually flying off her desk, drifting to the floor behind her. I, on the other hand, was much less important. The most strenuous thing Deb asked me to do was walk into town to buy her a refill of the Swedish Fish she kept hidden in her breast pocket.

By the time Friday night rolled around, I was a mess—bored from doing nothing challenging, physically or mentally, and desperate for meaningful human contact to distract me from the endless cycle of negativity and nerves. Once upon a time, I'd enjoyed things like going to football games and movies and parties. But the last year was something of a social life–desert, and I was beyond thirsty. So, when Ruth stopped by my place at dinner to tell me there was an employee bonfire happening after "last call"—when the retreaters had finished their activities and retired for the night—I lit up.

"You in, kid?" she asked.

"Sure," I said, trying to sound cool and nonchalant instead of desperately hopeful about the whole thing.

"See you at the firepit at ten. Bring a pen."

A pen? Who brings a pen to a bonfire? Sticks for marshmallows, sure. Hot dogs, perhaps. A blanket if the air got especially chilly. But a pen?

After I'd eaten and taken one more spin around the gym with my disinfectant wipes, I headed back to my cabin to grab a sweatshirt. On the way I passed Baxter, who had three logs over one shoulder like he was some kind of lumberjack mountain dweller.

"Coming to the bonfire?" he asked, adjusting the wood like they weighed nothing.

"Yep," I replied, imagining splinters jutting from his shoulders like porcupine quills.

"Good, good. I'll see you in a few then." He started walking again, careful not to knock me with the ends of the logs.

"Hey, Baxter?"

He paused and turned.

"Yeah?"

"What's the pen for? Ruth said to bring one."

Bax's faced crinkled into a smile. His crooked tooth showed, but it was a nice smile anyway. "You'll see," he said laughing, and went on his way, shaking his head.

I chose a purple pen, the one I used to write many

of my quotes down in my journal, and tugged on a Blue Valley Academy sweatshirt, the one my dad had bought me when my parents moved me into the dorm last summer. It felt like a consolation prize at the time, as if my dad was trying to say, "I know we're taking you away from all your friends and ruining your life, but here's a sweatshirt." I stuck the pen in the little front pouch of my sweatshirt and headed for the firepit.

Most nights, the firepit was used as a gathering place for whichever group reserved it, as a kind of debriefing of whatever they'd learned that day. The insurance salespeople used it the night before, and when I walked by on my way to the cabin, I heard them chatting about increased productivity as a result of team unity. The night before that, a team of math teachers were congratulating themselves on getting everyone over the giant wooden wall in the ropes course and discussing how they could use that experience in the classroom. It was the firepit of truth, where all became clear and the path forward showed itself like a beacon shining through the fog of life. Or something like that.

Hannah was already sitting by the fire when I got there. Bax had chopped the logs and was stoking the fire, with Ruth dictating how the wood should be arranged, like a backseat driver.

"You need more kindling," she advised.

"It's fine, Ruth."

"It's going to go out and then where will we be? In the dark, that's where." Her hands were on her hips.

"It's fine, Ruth."

Mallory and a girl whose name I didn't know who was on kitchen staff, strolled up and sat down. I chose a seat next to Hannah. I dusted off the seat, which was really just a big slice of log, and sat down.

"Did you really just wipe off a tree?" Hannah looked at me with disdain. "You know you're in the middle of the woods, right? There's dirt here. Pretty much everywhere."

"I'm aware."

"Just checking. And guess what else we have here?" Her sarcasm was quickly diminishing any hope I had for some much-needed, positive social time.

"What's that?"

"Washing machines. Dryers even. They're these cool machines that make the dirt on your clothes disappear. Wow. How about that?"

"How about that?" I echoed. I was trying to decide if a snarkier response was worth the effort, when someone sat down on my other side.

"Is this seat taken?" The hope suddenly rekindled and burst into flame. Marcus. I hadn't seen him much except in passing the last few days, so this was a more-than-pleasant surprise.

"It is now." I turned on the brightest smile I could muster. "How are you?"

"Can't complain. Getting paid to sit in the sun all day is pretty great. How about you?" That's right, he was life-guarding with Mallory. My smile went down a few watts.

"I'm getting the hang of things." I didn't want to talk more about work, or lifeguarding, or any other subject that might lead to Mallory. "Thanks for the save the other night."

"What save? I was just calling it like I saw it." Marcus' brown eyes sparkled with mischief.

"It was sweet of you. Thanks for the quote too. And for the record, I'm almost eighteen. Just a few more months."

"Age is a state of mind," he said, stretching his legs out in front of him. "So, what brings you to Sweetwater, Ashlyn?"

I quickly tried to think of a story that didn't invite questions I didn't want to answer. "Well, Hannah is my cousin," I said, nodding in her direction, "and our families were never very close, distance-wise." Okay, kind of a lie. But now was not the time to rehash our life story. "It seemed like a good idea to spend some time together. Hannah worked here last year. Et voila, here I am."

"That's cool."

"How about you? This is your first summer here too?"

Marcus nodded. "Yep. I just finished my first year at Columbia." Cute *and* smart.

"I love New York." My parents took me there for my tenth birthday and we had tea at the Ritz. It was perfect, until my dad told the waiter he wasn't bringing things out fast enough and threatened to leave zero tip. My smile slipped another few watts in the shadow of the memory. "My best friend's stepsister, who is also kind of my friend, is spending the summer there." My smiled dimmed even more. I shouldn't have said anything. Thinking about New York made me think about Tatum and her stepsister

Tilly and how they were going to be tourist-ing all over the city without me. Maybe even right now. Ugh.

"Oh, yeah?"

"Yeah, she's a dancer."

"That's cool."

Despite the less-than-inspiring small talk, I decided I liked Marcus. I liked his laid-back attitude and the promise of something deeper inside. That bit of mischief didn't hurt either.

"Are we all here now?" Ruth called. When I broke my gaze from Marcus, I realized there was quite a crowd around the campfire. All the lifeguards, cooks, servers, sports instructors, maintenance people, and who knows who else were seated or standing. There had to be at least thirty or forty employees and, just like Deb had so unceremoniously pointed out in the mess hall, it was painfully obvious I was the youngest one here.

Hannah gave Ruth two thumbs up, so she continued. "Welcome to the first Sweetwater Overlook employee bonfire of the summer season." Everyone started clapping. *First?* I thought. *There's going to be more of these?* "I'm Ruth Newhouse, senior most team member and self-titled Queen of the Ropes." A few laughs erupted. "For those of you who are with us for the first time, we're glad you're here. Everyone else, good to see your faces back around this fire." More clapping. "Now, I know we're feeling a loss this year. And for anyone who is wondering, I called Joan this morning and she's feeling very well. She said she hopes to visit when she's a little stronger, so we have that to look forward to. Now, I want to introduce you to Amos Turner."

A distinguished-looking man, who could've been James Earl Jones' doppelganger, stood up and smiled. I knew Amos already—he had waved to me from his classroom as I ran errands for Deb. His job was to take groups through a series of personality tests and then teach them how to use the results back in their workplace or organization. After welcoming us again, Amos asked us to all take out our pens. Finally. "This is a Sweetwater tradition," he said. "The Allen family started it years ago and we continue it tonight." He and Ruth began passing out little slips of paper.

"What are we doing?" I pressed Hannah.

"Impatient much? Relax."

I took a slip of paper when the pile came my way, passing it on to Marcus. Once everyone had a paper in hand, Ruth and Amos took the stage again.

"We're in the business of helping people reach their potential," Ruth announced. "Or, at the very least, trust themselves and their peers a little more. We build teams. We repair teams. We build families." It took every ounce of strength to keep the skeptical look off my face at the word "families." A family was the thing you were dropped into at birth without a choice. You didn't get to build it. It was built before you got there, cracks and all. I knew that better than anyone.

Amos held up his own slip of paper. "In the great Allen tradition, we will now write down our hopes and dreams for the summer. What do you wish?"

You're kidding, right? Are we back in first grade? I looked around to see if this was some kind of joke. It wasn't. Everybody else was lost in thought.

What did I wish? I wished my dad wasn't in jail. I wished my mother didn't have to deal with depression and go to rehab. I wished we were the kind of family who talked about stuff rather than letting it fester until our bad decisions bubbled up to the surface and everything was infected. I wished my dad had been the kind of father who took me camping so I wouldn't be the kind of girl who wiped off a tree stump. I wished I'd been allowed to get a part-time job like everyone else my age instead of being a fish-out-of-water here. I wished I was with Tatum, instead of Hannah, who probably wished she was with someone else too. I guess, when I really thought about it, I wished for an awful lot of things.

"Write down your wish for the summer, fold it up, and toss it into the fire," Ruth instructed. "If you want something bad enough, it just might come true." Thirty heads bowed over their laps, scribbling wishes. No one else thought this was ridiculous?

I blinked and looked down at my paper. I wrote, "I wish to survive," crumpled the paper up into a tiny ball, and threw it into the center of the fire, where the flames swallowed my wish and made it disappear.

Chapter 9

"What did you wish for?" Marcus asked me after Ruth and Amos had bid us all pleasant dreams. We all had an early day ahead, so most people drifted away from the fire and back down the trail toward their respective cabins or their cars to head home. I had lingered a little longer, not quite ready to go to bed yet. Marcus, to my delight, stayed too.

"You first." I gave him a half-smile.

"I wished for an intelligent, beautiful girl to appear before me," he said, the corners of his mouth lifting.

I wagged a finger at him. "Ah, but you fell for my trick and told me, so now it won't come true."

"It was already true before I even wished," Marcus said, leaning his face close to mine so there was no way to mistake he was talking about me.

My face flushed with pleasure. "What did you really wish for?"

Marcus squinted at me, a little of his bravado fading. "Do you really want to know?"

"I wouldn't have asked if I didn't."

He sighed, shoulders sagging. "Just to have a relaxing summer. I didn't have the best first year at school. College isn't always the great experience everyone tells you it will be."

"What happened?" I asked softly. "If you want to tell me."

Marcus inhaled. "I'll spare you the gory details, but in a nutshell, my grades weren't what I expected, which meant I didn't get the internship I wanted. My parents were not pleased. Thankfully, this job came up." He looked at me with a small smile. "So, it wasn't all bad."

I was touched he'd opened up. "I'm sorry. I know what it feels like to be disappointed."

"Yeah?"

"Yeah."

His brown eyes were warm on mine. "I shared. Now it's your turn." Marcus smiled again, this time wider, encouraging me.

Something in my heart tugged. *Maybe he understands.* "Well, speaking of parents not being pleased. Last June, I got arrested."

Marcus's mouth opened and then he clamped it shut. "Not what I was expecting you to say."

I offered a wry smile. "Not what I was expecting either. I was dating this guy, kind of the stereotypical 'bad boy,' and he decided to shoplift a ton of stuff, while we were together, and keep that plan a secret from me. It was awful. My parents were, obviously, furious, and I got my best friend mixed up in it too. So not only was everyone mad at me, my dad took it five steps further than every other parent on the planet and sent me away to boarding school."

"Ouch."

"And it still stings. All signs point to my going back in the fall, even though I deserve to come home for senior year. My track record over the last twelve months has been spotless."

Marcus sat up straighter and pushed his shoulders back. "Just tell your dad that. Easy."

If only. "It's more complicated than that." I had never *just* told my dad anything—any words I had for him were carefully selected, after mentally weighing all possible reactions.

Marcus shook his head. "It's not. You want something. You demand it. You get it. You just have to believe it will happen." It sounded like something my dad would say. Marcus was so self-assured. I could tell he *did* believe that. I doubted he'd experienced much rejection in his life, besides the aforementioned internship.

I sighed. "As nice as that sounds, I don't think I could ever demand anything of anyone. Like I said, it still stings."

Marcus put his hands on my shoulders, massaging them. "Anything I can do to help you heal?"

"You think you're smooth," I said, leaning into him just a bit. I couldn't deny that I liked the heat building between us from his touch.

"Am I?" he whispered in my ear.

I stood up, shivers running down my spine. "The jury is still out. I'll tell you when I've reached a verdict." I smiled sweetly at him and then turned to leave. In one swift motion, that was too flawless to not have been practiced, Marcus stood, grabbed my hand, and spun me around, like we were dancing, so I ended up in his arms. My heart beat faster as I realized we were so close I could feel his warm breath on my cheek.

"What do you think now? Did I convince you?"

Sometimes I hated that I was so transparent. Tatum used to roll her eyes at me for being a shameless flirt with boys at school, and sure, that flirting had gotten me into more than a little trouble with my parents, but I couldn't help it. I liked the way I felt when I did it. Like for once, I was in control. And I was never in control. So what if it was superficial? I wasn't planning to marry any of them. Marcus included.

"I may need just a little more persuading, counselor."

I knew he was going to kiss me. Boys like Marcus are like heat-seeking missiles. They see a friendly target and they launch. And right on cue, Marcus' lips landed on mine. It had been so long since I'd been this close to someone; I lost myself in the moment. His kiss was confident and I matched mine with his—strong and teasing. He knew exactly what he was doing and I knew exactly what he was doing too.

He pulled back and watched me, his skin alight in the flickering firelight. "You're something else, Ashlyn."

It sounded like a compliment, so I took it. "Thanks." I gently unwound myself from his embrace. "I need to go to bed. Lots of groups to check in tomorrow."

Marcus took my hand again, like he wanted to pull me back to him. "But I'll see you . . ."

"I'll see you," I said, purposely not committing. I could hear my dad's voice in my head telling me to watch myself, that this boy would distract me, that he only wanted one thing, that he would make me ruin everything that had been planned for me. I ignored it. I waved at Marcus and took off down the trail for my cabin, hoping Hannah would already be asleep so she wouldn't ask where I'd been.

On one of the benches on my path, far enough away that Marcus couldn't see me, I touched my lips, remembering how Marcus tasted like mint. Then I bent down and scribbled on the bench with the campfire pen,

Believe in kissing.
Eve Ensler

My good mood did not last.

"Ashlyn, where are the reservations for the March of Dimes group?" Deb asked accusingly, waving a piece of licorice in my face. "They're missing."

Deb was not a fan of technology. Even though retreaters were encouraged to book their stays on the Sweetwater website, she refused to turn her computer on most days—the only one on our "off the grid" campus hardwired to the internet. Deb liked to have me print the documents out for her, and then they'd inevitably end up in a chaotic pile on her desk. Mallory had mentioned her parents used to work together before their recent divorce—maybe her dad had been the detail-oriented one of the pair. I'd been seriously contemplating straightening up for her, but then decided against it. Who knew what else was in there? With my luck, some wild insect would crawl out of the abyss and bite me. And of course, when something went missing, though I knew logically it wasn't my fault, I inevitably second-guessed whether I'd made a mistake.

I waded into the sea of papers and folders and pulled out the reservation binder, only to have half the pages fall out onto the floor. *You were always so clumsy*, said phantom Dad. My cheeks burned. "Here," I said, handing it to her. "I'll check the ones that fell out."

"Thanks," she said dismissively and sat down behind the desk, flipping through the binder. "By the way, there's some mail for you."

"Mail?"

Deb waved her hand in the general direction of the folding table shoved in the corner that served as my make-shift desk. "Over there."

I stood in front of my little space and saw nothing that looked remotely like mail. I moved the chair and peeked under, but there were no stray envelopes. I side-eyed Deb's desk. If I were a gambling girl, I'd bet that my poor mail was somewhere in her mess. I sighed and gave up. I'd have to dig through it later on, when she left for her next cooking challenge—she was teaching cheese and chocolate soufflés later.

"Hey, Ashlyn?" Deb yelled. She was barely fifteen feet away from me, but from the volume of her voice you would have thought we were across campus from one another.

"Yes?" I said, moderately and professionally, modeling what an inside voice should sound like.

She drained the last gulp in her Styrofoam cup and crushed it in her fist. Gross. "Would you make me a cup of coffee? I'm just swamped over here."

More like in a swamp. Of papers. "Sure, Deb."

I walked down the short hallway, past the glass-walled classroom—the only other place on campus with technology—where Amos was guiding a group of lawyers through some kind of assessment results. There were pie charts up on the smartboard and ten heads were furiously taking notes on laptops and tablets. I wished I was in there instead of being Deb's errand-girl. When I entered the small staff breakroom and opened the cabinet to grab a coffee filter, two envelopes toppled out, bounced off the counter, and fell to the floor. When I bent to pick them up, I saw they both bore my name.

"Seriously, Deb," I groaned. She must have left them in the cabinet when she made her first cup of coffee. I stuck the letters in the back pocket of my jean shorts to read later when I wouldn't be infiltrated by the voice of Deb. Or my dad. I made her coffee as quickly as the machine would go and booked it back down the hall.

I handed the cup to Deb. "Here. I'm going to go make sure the gym is in good shape." *Ba dum ching,* I would've said, if I was talking to Tatum, adding in some air drums. Deb just waved, and I got the heck out of there.

Beyond the main lodge, in the opposite direction from my cabin, the firepit, and the lake, was the forest—tall evergreens as far as the eye could see and hills so far away

they looked purple. I followed the trail leading to the
ropes course and zipline for a bit, before ducking off the
path into the unmarked wilderness. I pulled the mail from
my back pocket and sat in a shady spot under a tree.

The first was greeting card–shaped and sealed in
a navy-blue envelope. Silver marker writing. Return
address: Tatum Elsea from Arlington, VA. I sliced it open
with my index finger, revealing a greeting card, with
two little girls making faces at each other on the front. I
laughed. They could've been us ten years ago.

> Dear Ash,
>
> Hope you're having a great time at your new job.
> No, I don't hope, I know. You're definitely having
> a good time. You're probably hanging by the pool
> with a hot mountain man by now, right? I'm totally
> right. Things here are fine. The step-monster and
> I are signing up for a photography class together.
> How's that for a plot twist? She's being surprisingly
> openminded. I'm going to have to check her kool-
> aid. I'm going up to visit Tilly in New York in a few
> weeks. I'll send you a postcard.
>
> > Love and ladybugs (the
> > best kind of bugs, right?),
> > Tate
>
> P.S. Have you heard from your parents?

I chuckled. Tatum and her stepmother got along only
slightly better than my dad and I did. The difference
was, they'd actually been working on improving their

relationship. I frowned at her P.S. Did my dad's prison phone check-in, aka the most pointless phone call in the world, count as hearing from my parents? I didn't think it did. I set Tatum's card down next to me and picked up the second letter. It was the kind of long, white, business-sized envelope I used to steal from my dad's office when I wanted to pretend I was the boss. I'd "send" letters to my employees—my dolls and teddy bears—telling them what a good job they were doing. And sometimes I'd tell them how terrible they were doing and fire them. *A chip off the ol' block.* This envelope had a return address I didn't recognize. I slid it open.

> Dear Ashlyn,
>
> I miss you very much and think of you every minute of the day. I want you to know that I'm feeling a little better and everyone here is treating me well. I should be able to make phone calls soon. Your uncle sent me the number to call and I can't wait to hear your voice. I know we have a lot to talk about and there's so much I need you to know. But for now, I love you more than anything.
>
> Love always,
> Mom

I didn't even realize I was crying until the tears hit her letter, smearing the ink. I wanted to talk to my mom more than anything right then.

"Hey, sad girl, what's wrong?"

Startled, I looked up. Bax hovered over me, a mess of cords and pulleys draped over him. I wiped my nose on the back of my hand and did my best impression of a girl who was definitely not sad, sitting under a tree. "Nothing. Nothing's wrong. I'm fine."

He looked at me. I couldn't read his expression, but in the sunlight streaming between the tree branches, his eyes were so pale blue they almost seemed colorless. And then he nodded, just once, and moved on as if nothing out of the ordinary was happening. "Tomorrow, Ruth and I are going to take some of the new staff up on the course. Through the ziplines. Do you want to come?"

Did I want to go on the zipline? Not only had I never done it before, I wasn't even sure whether I was afraid of heights. Right on cue, that familiar, cutting dad-voice invaded my brain. *Is it safe? Is this the best use of the opportunity I've arranged for you at Sweetwater?* But this time, instead of driving me back into my cocoon, my dad's phantom accusations gave me the push I needed to fly.

"Sure, why not?" And, he'd said *new staff.* Which meant Marcus might be there. And anywhere Marcus was, I wanted to be. Last night was the first time since my dad dropped his bomb that I felt, even for a moment, like nothing was wrong. Like my life wasn't in a tailspin. Like I could just . . . be. If flying through the air on a glorified rope swing with a boy who kissed me like I was the only girl in the world was an option, I'd take it.

Bax nodded again, adjusted the cords around his shoulders, and walked away. I turned back to my letters and reread both of them. It was nice to know that there were two people out there who cared about me, even if they couldn't be here with me.

Chapter 10

So what's the deal with your mom?" Hannah asked. She was seated at a long table in the cafeteria with Baxter, Ruth, Amos, and several others.

"What do you mean? Deal?" I set a platter of sandwiches on the table. It was the night off for a number of the serving staff, so, of course, Deb volunteered me to fill in. Nothing more confidence-boosting than the potential disaster of spilling a plate of meatball subs all over your fellow employees. I made sure to walk slowly and keep the water pitchers filled a few inches below the top.

Hannah unfolded her napkin and put it on her lap. "I saw she wrote to you. I was just curious if there was any news."

My cheeks flamed with rage and embarrassment. I hadn't told anyone at Sweetwater about my family situation and had no intention of doing so.

"You read my letter?" It came out loud. Deb-loud. The soft hum of conversation died down in an instant.

"Sorry," Hannah said, her eyes flickering around to the others at table. "Not on purpose. I wouldn't do that, Ashlyn, I wouldn't. You need to know that."

Everyone was looking at us now. And for a few terrifying moments, time slowed as I waited, on edge, to see if Hannah would blurt out my dad's legal status and my mom's stint in rehab in front of these people I barely knew.

"I don't think this is the time or place for this conversation, Hannah," I said, channeling my dad, using the tone and type of language he used when he was trying to coerce or intimidate someone. I took a step closer to where she sat, standing over her. Hannah, to her credit, didn't shrink back.

"Sure. We'll talk later." She took a giant bite of her sub and faced straight ahead.

Without saying another word, I went back into the kitchen and gathered another plate for the next table. I spent the rest of the shift going back and forth between the dining room and the kitchen, shuttling food and drinks, fetching extra napkins and wiping up spills. Although it felt good to stay busy, I couldn't get the looks of everyone around Hannah's table out of my mind. Pity? Curiosity? Judgment? Whatever they were thinking, I felt like an amoeba under a microscope, and I imagined that every conversation was about me. I liked attention when it was my choice, like when I was flirting for example. But this? Not a chance. And the cherry on top? I had no idea if Hannah was telling the truth.

Marcus and Mallory and the other lifeguards came in at the tail end of my shift. I smiled when I saw him, his brown hair almost black, still wet from the pool. Had he saved someone's life today? Had he taught someone to swim? A group of middle schoolers, a temple youth group, had arrived yesterday. I bet all those girls had enjoyed the view during pool time. I walked toward their table and casually put down the platter I was carrying.

"Hey, Marcus."

He gave me a lazy smile. "Hey, Ash. How's it going?"

"Not too bad. How's the pool today?"

"It's been really busy," Mallory answered for him. Even though I knew she was nineteen, her high-pitched voice made her sound like she was about twelve. "That new group of kids is so obnoxious. They splashed us all afternoon, didn't they, Marcus?"

He laughed like it wasn't nearly as annoying to him as it had been to her. I shifted my gaze between them and back again. Two things bothered me about what she'd said. One, she said *us*. Like she and Marcus were a team, or, perish the thought, something more. And two, she got wet. That kind of came with the territory of being a lifeguard, didn't it? Ugh. She seemed nice enough, but fussy. Just like her mother, actually. "Good thing your shift's over, huh?"

"Totally," she said, not detecting my sarcasm at all.

"So, *Marcus*," I said with emphasis, "did you hear Ruth and Baxter are taking the new employees on the zipline?"

"Hadn't heard that, but very cool. I did a zipline in Costa Rica a few summers ago. It's wild. Flying through the jungle like you're a bird."

"Or a pterodactyl," Mallory chimed in.

I didn't even look at her. "Right. Well, you should come."

"If I'm not working," he said, poking Mallory gently in the shoulder. "Boss Lady."

"Oh, stop, I'm not really your boss," she said, pretending to be embarrassed but so obviously pleased.

"Great, I'll see you tomorrow then." To the table, I added, "Let me know if you all need anything." I gave Marcus one more pointed look on the *anything* and walked away. Slowly. I knew he was watching.

It was late by the time I got back to the cabin. But not late enough apparently, because Hannah was lying on her bunk, reading, with all the lights on. When I came in, she sat up so quickly she hit her head on the bottom of my bed and yelped. I covered my mouth, trying not to let her see the laugh that was trying to escape. Hannah gave me a sheepish look and then her signature shrug.

"I'm glad you're back. Look, Ashlyn, I want to apologize for what I said earlier. Sometimes I just blurt things out without thinking and then later realize I hurt or embarrassed someone. I think I did both tonight. I'm sorry. I officially suck as a cousin."

The apology was unexpected, a pleasant surprise even, but it didn't take away from the fact that she'd read my letter. I wasn't prepared to let her off that easy. "But—"

"I know, but I read your letter. I'm the worst. But in my defense, I wasn't snooping. I sat down on the bed to tie my shoe and it slipped off your bed and landed face up. I picked it up and saw it was from your mom and, well, I have no excuse. But if it hadn't fallen, I would never have looked at it. I promise."

She looked sorry. She sounded sorry. And to be honest, if the situation were reversed, I probably would've read the letter too. Rarely had I forgiven someone so quickly in the past, but somehow, this situation felt different.

"Okay," I said.

"Okay what?"

"Okay, I believe you."

"Thank goodness. I thought you were going to set me on fire with the looks you were giving me in the dining hall. I told Bax I was afraid for my life after we left," she smiled. "He told me I should just talk to you about it, that it was terrible timing for me to ask you about your mom in front of everyone."

I sat down on her bed next to her. "He was right. I don't really want to share what's going on with my parents with the people here, you know? It's no one's business."

Hannah nodded and lifted her hand for a high five. "You're so right. So right." I left her hanging for a moment before tapping my hand to hers. Then she pinched her thumb and her forefinger together and mimed zipping her lips.

We sat there next to each other, quiet for a moment, me wondering what to say next. Hannah cleared her throat. "So. Okay, I know you don't want to talk about it, but my parents didn't really say much and this whole thing with your parents seems like such a mystery. Like, poof, here's the cousin you haven't seen in forever and, oh, by the way, she's coming to work with you this summer and we shouldn't pry too much, but we should also be supportive. And I don't know about you but it's hard for me to be supportive if I don't know what's going on. Maybe that makes me nosy. But I also think it makes me invested."

Invested. Like I was a stock or a bank account. I blew out a loud breath, my hair tickling my ears. I didn't think there was any way to get through the summer without telling someone, anyone, the truth. And it might as well be the one person I was related to. "My mom is in rehab. My dad's word was exhaustion . . ."

"Which is really just the old person's code word for depression."

"Exactly."

"I hate that. Let's not cover up mental health issues, you know? Your mom is a star for getting help. She shouldn't be made to feel like she's hiding something. If anything, she's strong. A fighter."

I liked thinking about my mom being strong. Maybe I could be too. One day. "Thanks for saying that." I crossed my legs beneath me, ducking slightly so I didn't bang my head on the top bunk. "So, she apparently can't call me until her therapist clears her, but you saw from the letter that she thinks that'll be soon."

"That's great news." Hannah smiled at me.

"And, well, my dad's in jail. Tax evasion."

She nodded, eyes wide. "My parents told me that part. And I saw the news articles. Some guy they went to high school with, and who lives in DC, clipped them out of the actual paper and mailed them to Dad."

"That's just wrong," was all I could say. Some friend that guy was.

"I know."

"So yeah, he's there. He got me this job before he left, through your mom I guess, and here I am."

Hannah studied my face. "And where would you rather be?"

I snorted. "That obvious, huh?" She smiled. "I was hoping to be at home. With my best friend. Doing normal summer things."

"I'm sorry you hate it here."

"I don't hate it here," I said softly. Sweetwater had its perks, namely Marcus. And it would be a cool experience to include in a college application essay. I didn't know anyone else who'd ever done a summer job like this.

"Good. So, are you going to write your mom back?"

"I probably should." But what would I say? *Hi, Mom, I'm sorry you're depressed and it's probably because Dad's a criminal. Wish someone had told me earlier. Get well soon! XOXO, Ashlyn.* Probably not. But, if she was getting help, maybe that meant that things might be different in the future. "What would you write?" I asked Hannah.

"Me? Well, my mom, the social worker and over-sharer, always says that honesty is the best policy. Cliché, I know, but she might as well have it cross-stitched over her bed. I guess I would just say that I miss her and I love her. You do, right?"

"Of course I do." My voice sounded so small.

"Then tell her. She probably needs to hear it now more than ever."

Hannah made it sound so easy. She had no idea we were not the type of family who shared our feelings. We had been going through life treading water in my dad's wake until near-drowning.

Hannah ripped a piece of paper out of a lined notebook and handed it to me. "Here. Just do it."

Reluctantly, I took the paper, crawled up onto my bunk, and used my quote journal as a makeshift writing surface.

> Dear Mom,
>
> Thanks for your letter. It was really nice to hear from you. I'm glad to know things are going well and that you're feeling better. Sweetwater is fun. I'm doing a whole bunch of jobs and staying busy. Everyone here is very nice and Hannah is showing me the ropes. I miss home. I'll tell you more when we talk. Here's the number, in case you need it again.
>
> Love,
> Ashlyn

I folded it up and hung my arm over the bed. "Here. I did the thing."

"Good for you." She snatched it and threw it on the dresser. "We'll mail it tomorrow." Hannah leaned her head out over the bed and looked up at me. "And for what it's worth, I *am* sorry. About all of it."

I offered her a weak smile. "Me too."

Chapter 11

My calves were burning by the time we got to the top of the hill. Well, Baxter called it a hill, but it felt more like Mt. Everest to me. The heavy harness Baxter had strapped each of us into before we got on our way didn't help. Now I knew what the cords and pulleys he was carrying yesterday were—a magical safety device that would prevent me from plunging to certain death. The harness wrapped around my thighs and waist, with an additional strap that would connect me to the actual zipline.

When I got to the top, huffing and puffing and ready to blow a house down, I was surprised to see exactly how high we were not.

Ruth chuckled at me. "Not much of an athlete are you, my dear?"

"Not at all," I replied honestly. Physical Education had been my least favorite subject in school. My dad, always nitpicking about my grades, even found fault with the time it took me to run the mile each year. Tatum and I first became friends because we were the last to finish our warm-up laps every day. That was about the only positive thing I had to say about the class. "I'm more of an academic, I guess."

"Then it's a good thing Deb has you working in the office and keeps the rest of us out in the yard," Ruth said with a twinkle in her eye.

"Oh, yeah, my four years of French and regional Quiz Bowl champion medal really help when I'm making Deb's coffee and refilling her candy bowls." I rolled my eyes, and Ruth cracked up. "The ridiculous thing is, my dad thought this would be a good résumé builder. That it might get me a good letter of recommendation for college. Pretty sure being an errand girl with a side of gym sanitation isn't going to look very impressive."

She patted me on the back in a maternal way that made my heart constrict. I'd sent the letter to my mother in between making copies of worksheets for Amos and wiping down the cooking competition kitchen after Deb's morning session—crème brûlée. I had no idea why she couldn't clean up after herself. Much like her desk, Deb left a trail of chaos behind her. I almost stepped on a knife that somehow ended up on the floor, blade up. Sweetwater had a shiny blue post box on site, near the admin office. I felt better as soon as I slid the letter through the slot. Just a little bit, but it was there.

Baxter stood in front of the whole group. "Each zipline consists of a platform you'll step off, the line you'll be crossing, and another platform where you'll land. Ruth and I will take turns hooking your harness on the line on the first platform and catching you on the second," he instructed, with an air of authority I hadn't heard in his voice before. "Never leave the platform unless one of us gives you the go-ahead." He demonstrated how to position our hands so we didn't get rope burn. "Just do what we tell you and you'll be fine. Safety is key."

"That's right," Ruth piped up. "No goofing off up there. One at a time. And watch your feet. Don't be the person who walks off the platform."

"Has someone actually done that?" Marcus asked, his hand in the air as if we were in a classroom.

"You'd be surprised," Baxter said. I pictured Deb, our careless leader, teetering on the edge, hands splayed and arms circling, trying to keep her balance. Maybe it wasn't a coincidence she had something else to do while the rest of us newbies were "taking the tour."

Besides Marcus and me, Mallory was there, of course, as were a cook, two servers, and the groundskeeper who didn't live on campus with the rest of us. Ruth and Bax double-checked our harnesses to make sure they were secure. Baxter jangled the latches on mine and tugged on the cords.

"All set," he said.

"Thank you." I met his gaze, which lasted a moment longer than it should've. Or maybe I was just self-conscious. In addition to the awkward contraption of ropes and metal on our bodies, we also wore helmets, bigger and bulkier than the ones worn to ride bikes or skate. I resisted the urge to push my hair behind my ears, certain I was sweating so badly under the helmet that it was plastered to my head. When I regained my composure, I noticed Marcus watching Baxter work on my harness. His eyebrows were practically touching. *Is he jealous?* I looked away, amused. Bax moved on to adjusting Mallory's harness. When he looped back around to Marcus, he had to ask him three times to relax so he could make sure the harness was fitted properly.

"You're too stiff, man. It won't fit right and you could get hurt going down the line." Marcus finally loosened up a bit. I hid a smile behind my hand, pretending to itch my nose.

Ruth lined us all up. "I'll go down first and catch the rest of you at the bottom of the first line. This is the shortest. It's just practice. There are four lines in all. The third one is the longest and the highest, so get ready." She winked, hooked herself to the line like the expert she was, stepped off the platform, and sailed off into the woods.

"Nothing to it," Baxter said with a reassuring nod. "Ruth will be at the next platform. Remember, don't move your hands out of position, okay? No one wants rope burn. When you get to the end of the line, you'll feel a jolt. Don't worry. That means we caught you." Baxter guided the first person, the cook, to the line and off they went, one by one. Waiting my turn, Marcus moved back a spot or two to stand next to me. He put his hand on the small of my back, almost possessively. I couldn't say I didn't like it.

"Do you want to go first?" he offered.

I looked down the line as Mallory whizzed away from us. "No, you go ahead."

"Want to watch the expert at work?" He winked.

"Something like that." *Coward*, my dad's voice

sounded in my head. He'd said that the first time one of my Quiz Bowl competitions was being televised live and I'd dared tell him I was nervous. *Don't be a coward. It's just local TV. It means nothing.* His words decimated me. I'd been so proud of getting that far in the competition. And when we won, he told me my collar had been crooked, instead of congratulating me.

It wasn't so much that we were high off the ground. It wasn't even a feeling of being unsafe—my harness had been checked and rechecked by Sweetwater's trained zipline experts. It was having the courage to throw caution to the wind after years of criticism and second-guessing. What I was about to do—walk off the edge knowing there was no ground under my feet—was in direct opposition to my dad's calculated, risk-managed, step-by-step way of doing life. I'd never been presented with such a situation before. My heart was racing, my palms were damp, yet a smile crept slowly onto my face.

The next thing I knew, Marcus was gone. I gasped. It was my turn.

"You probably shouldn't go down the line with your mouth wide open like that. You might catch a bug." The edges of Baxter's mouth quirked up.

I shut my mouth with a snap. "Sorry."

"Nothing to apologize for." He directed me to step up on the raised section of the platform so I'd be high enough for him to attach my harness to the zipline. Just then, Ruth's voice came crackling over Baxter's walkie talkie, giving me the green light to go.

"Ready to fly?"

"Fly?" My stomach dropped, even though I hadn't moved yet.

"Just let go, Ashlyn."

So I did. I stepped off the platform, and for one endless moment, I was falling. And then flying. The wind rushed over my skin as I soared through the trees, my feet dangling below me. I wanted to live in that feeling. Exhilarated. Unashamed. Free. And just as quickly as it began, it was over. After the aforementioned jolt, as Ruth caught me at the second platform, she reeled me in the last few inches by hand, and I put my feet down on solid ground.

"Did you like it?"

"Yeah. I did."

"Of course you did. How could you not?"

Seconds later, Baxter appeared on the platform next to us and we repeated the whole pattern, this time with him going first and Ruth sending us off. Again, I went last. Though my courage meter went up a few notches after the first trip through the trees, I wasn't sure I wanted the others to see me, just in case something went wrong or I looked silly. And just as before, a shot of adrenaline coursed through me. The combination of terror and excitement made my head spin. Now I understood, a little bit, why someone might want to skydive or bungee jump. I wasn't going to be trying those activities any time soon, but I got it.

On the third line, Ruth was sending again and Baxter was catching. Marcus was describing what it felt like to do this in the jungle in Costa Rica, but my mind was elsewhere. Waiting for the next ride. Waiting for the rush of wind in my hair and the moment of anticipation before the world fell away. For the third time, I was the last to go, watching my coworkers grow smaller and smaller as they flew away from me.

"This is the best one, Sweets. Long and high. And as soon as you get to the platform, Bax will send you down the last line right away, no waiting. Our colleague, Joe, is down at the bottom and will help you get this armor off." Ruth nodded and I stepped to the edge. Although I now had two zips under my belt, this felt much higher. Much . . . riskier. When my dad's voice tried to bulldog its way in, I just closed my eyes and tipped myself off the platform.

I couldn't bring myself to open my eyes and watch my flight. Maybe it was the residual fear. Maybe the flood of adrenaline. Maybe it was Marcus' recounting of a family vacation. Maybe it was the feeling like I was still so new and green and out of place here. I was never going to be the kind of girl who felt truly comfortable in the woods. Or, maybe it was the whole mess my family was in, hovering over me at all times. Whatever the reason, I started crying. Right there on the line, I let the floodgates open. As I approached the platform, eyes still closed, I forgot what I was supposed to do to be caught. And maybe my face startled Baxter as I approached the platform, because there was no now-familiar jolt at the end of the ride. Instead of getting reeled in like I had on the previous zips, I felt myself slowly sliding backward, and that's when I opened my eyes.

What just happened? Terror pierced my heart as I met Baxter's pale blue eyes.

The good news was he didn't look anxious so it was possible that I wasn't in mortal danger. My fear dissolved into confusion. *What now?* I finally slowed to a stop, hanging out several yards from the platform, at what felt like a thousand miles above the very safe ground. The awkward news was that we were all alone. Everyone else had gone ahead, as Ruth had indicated. Just me. And Baxter. And the rope between us.

"I'm so sorry," I called, my cheeks flaming with embarrassment.

"No, it wasn't you," he said, voice gruff, but not in an unkind way. "Totally my fault."

I drifted a few inches further away. I gulped. "It's fine. So now what? Do I have to pull myself in?" The gloves they gave us to wear so we wouldn't get injured were thick leather, I'd be protected, but I was almost a hundred percent certain I wasn't strong enough to pull myself along the line all the way to the platform. I made a silent commitment to actually use the gym next time Deb assigned me to clean it.

Baxter scratched his head. "I'm going to come out and get you." He told Ruth on the walkie talkie to wait until he gave her the signal, that he'd be just a minute, and began hooking his own harness to the line.

Get me? How the heck was that going to work? My science teacher in seventh grade had this fun contraption on her desk that demonstrated inertia. Little silver balls suspended on clear thread rammed into each other, transferring energy back and forth. If Baxter slid out toward me, would he slam into me and send me back the other way? He was a pretty big guy, muscular and solid, and I could stand to put on a few pounds thanks to the not-so-amazing Blue Valley cafeteria food. If he timed it right, I might make it to the opposite platform. "So. I should . . . ?"

He nodded. "I'll come to you. Just . . ." He blinked a few times like he was trying to work out a plan. "Stay there."

Where else was I going to go? I was grateful that Baxter seemed to know what he was doing, but it didn't take away the feeling of helplessness. There was nothing I could do but wait. *Of course you've gotten yourself into this mess. You're wasting everyone's time*, said invisible Dad. I winced, watching Bax, the expert, begin his rescue. Once he checked again that he was secured properly, he put one hand on the line, and slowly let himself down toward me. Overwhelming relief that there would be no slamming into me and sending me backward flooded my insides. He reached me in a few seconds, his gloved hand sliding carefully down the thick, metal rope, the muscles in his biceps flexing with the strain. His harness bumped against mine with a metallic clank.

"You okay?" he asked.

"Sure, just hanging out," I said. I tried to laugh but my face burned. With shame? Fear? Anger? It was exhausting feeling so much at once. All the time.

Baxter either didn't notice my emoting, or he was too polite to say anything and make it worse. "I'm just going to grab your harness here," he said, putting his hand below the part that connected me to the line, "and pull." With what had to be superhuman strength, one hand on my harness and another on the line, he tugged us both along with just one hand, inching us toward the platform. I was too stunned to speak, otherwise I would've complimented him on his abilities. Baxter was fascinating to watch—his face still and focused, like he had just one goal in life and that was to get us to safety.

When we were just a few feet away from our target, and the line actually began sloping upward a little, he cleared his throat. "So, I need to be able to use both hands now." His blue eyes searched mine. "Is that okay?" I didn't understand what he was asking. He blushed. "I need to wrap my legs around you."

Chapter 12

Tree trunks. A vise. A boa constrictor. Professional wrestlers. What are things that aren't as strong as Baxter Clark's legs, Alex? Ding, ding, ding.

I couldn't speak. I just nodded. Baxter wrapped his sturdy, muscular legs around my waist, crossing his ankles in their hiking boots and locking me in place. He was like a human harness.

"We'll be back in just a sec," he said, making me think he was just as uncomfortable as I was. "Don't worry."

"I'm not worried. You seem more than capable." If my hands hadn't been holding onto my harness, my way of preventing them from shaking, I would've covered my bright red face. He probably thought I was such a weirdo. I couldn't believe I'd just said that out loud. But again, either because of grace or indifference, Baxter didn't respond.

When Baxter, and his arms, had pulled us to the point where we were hovering over the platform, he set his feet down and, keeping one hand on the line, gently grasped my forearm and brought me in and over to the raised area so I could put my feet down as well. He wordlessly unhooked his harness and then mine.

"Thanks," I said, a little breathlessly, either from residual fear or the sheer strangeness of what had just happened. It wasn't every day that a certified mountain man, one who you hadn't noticed at first but now seemed more than a little attractive, used all his might to rescue you. My stomach began turning flip-flops. I couldn't even look at him.

"Not a problem," he said, as if he'd just mowed my lawn or carried my groceries.

"Does that happen often?" I asked. I wasn't sure if I meant retreaters getting stuck on the zipline or Baxter rescuing girls in need.

"Honestly?" The corner of his mouth quirked up.

"Yes, honestly," I said, my face flushing again. Was he making fun of me?

Baxter shook his head, his blonde curls bobbing. "I saw Joe retrieve someone once before, but that was my first time."

My eyes widened. "Seriously? I thought you'd done that a million times. You were so calm." And strong. And able. I blushed again.

"Nah. I knew what to do, thankfully, but I was just as scared as you were. But I knew I didn't have a choice but to get both of us back on the platform. One hand in front of the other." He smiled, warmly this time, forcing my own smile in return.

"One hand in front of the other," I echoed. "That sounds like a good life motto." I'd have to remember to write it in my quote journal once I was back on solid ground. Baxter nodded, his blue eyes on mine. "Well, thanks," I said, suddenly shy.

"You're welcome. Better get you back to the group." Into his walkie talkie, he said, "Ruth, all clear. She's on her way down." He put his hand on my waist, guiding me around him and into position myself to be hooked onto the final line. "You good?"

I didn't really want to get back on the zipline, but as there wasn't an easy way to get down, I nodded. "Sure."

Baxter's eyes met mine. "Are you really sure?"

No, I wanted to say. *I'm not really sure I want to be down there just yet.*

My stomach knotted again. "Yes," I said, in a near whisper.

He hooked me to the line. "See you on the other side."

Because I'd taken so long to finish the course, everyone else had already taken their harnesses and helmets off and returned them to the storage room. By the time I shrugged off the heavy equipment, Marcus was waiting to pick it up for me and carry it off.

"What happened up there? The group was getting really worried."

Were you *worried?* "I didn't make it to the platform somehow. No big deal."

"Did that Baxter screw up? He did, didn't he?"

Marcus's voice had taken on a tone of superiority that I definitely didn't like. Had it always been there or was it because he was talking about Baxter?

"No, nothing like that. It was my fault. But Baxter knew just what to do. It's fine. No big deal," I repeated.

Marcus turned around, scanning the trail we were walking on, and then pressed a quick kiss to my cheek. "I'm starved. Is it time for dinner yet?"

"I think we still have half an hour or so before they start serving."

"I'm gonna go take a shower then. See you later?" Marcus waggled his eyebrows up and down. I couldn't stop myself from laughing. He took off jogging and didn't look back.

I needed to process what just happened. Or not. I could probably benefit from not thinking about it too much. I started walking toward my cabin. As I was passing the storage room, I almost ran straight into Baxter on his way out.

We just looked at each other. Unsure of what to say, I opened my mouth, but there were no words. I could have said thank you again. I could have complimented him further on keeping his composure and getting us both off the line safely, told him how impressed I was that he stayed calm under pressure. I said nothing. Absolutely nothing. Feeling confused and strange for the millionth time in the last fifteen minutes, I walked away.

Hannah wasn't in the cabin when I got there, which was just as well. I crawled up on the bed and stared at the ceiling, reliving the most awkward zipline in history, my chest tight and heart racing. I heard my father's voice in my head. *Why didn't you pay closer attention to the directions? Did anyone see you screw up?*

I squeezed my eyes shut, hoping to turn him off. But it was no use. Once my dad wormed his way into my brain, it was impossible to get him to go away. I took a few deep breaths, practicing the stress relief technique of counting and breathing I'd learned in my psychology class. I hadn't used it much since it had been taught, but it now seemed appropriate. Unfortunately, it didn't work and I could see my dad's face in my mind, disgusted with me.

I pounded my palms on the bed in disgust and grabbed my quote journal, flipping to find something that made sense to me. Somehow the words and wisdom of others always seemed better than whatever was in my own head.

I LIKE DIGGING HOLES, HIDING
THINGS INSIDE THEM.
Alice Merton

Song lyrics. So deceptively simple. I leapt off the top bunk and landed on the cabin floor with a thud. I grabbed my pens and headed out the door, slamming it behind me. I jogged up the trail toward a patch of pine trees, choosing a tall, thick one off the path. I took the metal part of a pen cap and tried to carve into the trunk, but the metal broke off. I kicked the dirt and the metal went flying. I groaned.

Digging holes. I picked up a sharp branch lying nearby

and scratched into the ground, in letters as big as I could make them, Alice Merton's words. By the time I'd finished, my dad's voice was barely audible.

Only then did I feel relaxed enough to return for dinner. Hannah was waiting for me at our usual table, waving a little piece of white paper like a flag. "Two things. One, Deb wants you to do inventory with me tomorrow. Be prepared for the most boring day of your life. Or, as I like to call it, where did all the lifejackets go."

I rolled my eyes, but only half-heartedly. A day with Hannah, no matter how boring, would be better than another day fetching coffee and Swedish Fish for Deb.

"Sounds fabulous. I'll oil up my spreadsheet skills."

"Sold. And, number two, Dad called. He said to tell you he'll be here bright and early Saturday morning to pick you up. Six fifteen to be exact. And you better not wake me up when you leave. I'm not on the clock until eight, which means I can stay in bed until seven forty-five and still get to the kiosk on time."

"Hold up. What? Why is he picking me up?" Was I in trouble? Had my little mistakes somehow added up on a giant secret tally Deb was keeping and she was firing me?

Hannah's face blanched. "Um. He's getting you so you can go see your dad. I thought you knew."

I gritted my teeth. I should've guessed. Dad said I'd be able to visit him. It was weirdly convenient that he was only about an hour away from here. More than a coincidence that he chose Uncle Ed and Aunt Greta's house for my "supervision" this summer. Of course. This had nothing to do with me and everything to do with him keeping control. He could not have cared less if I was with family. He just wanted to be sure I was still within arm's reach of his control. One day, I promised myself, when he was giving me the lecture about following the rules and conducting myself responsibly, I would give it right back to him. Ask him if he was being responsible.

I shrugged, trying to take a page from Hannah's guide to nonchalant behavior. "Maybe I did. I might've just blocked it out. Maybe I was too caught up in all the millions of things I have to take care of here. You know, I'm so very busy." I waved my hands, imitating Deb.

Hannah laughed loudly. "You know, sometimes you're funny."

"I have my moments."

"Well, at any rate, Dad said to be ready down by the gate, he'll do a drive by. Six fifteen. Don't wake me up."

I saluted her. "I'll put my alarm clock under my pillow, how's that?"

"Perfect."

"Why are you setting an alarm on your day off, Hannah?" Baxter sat down next to my cousin, a glass of iced tea in his hand. He took a big gulp and looked at me over the rim.

"I'm not. Ashlyn is." Hannah eyed me. I eyed her back. She nodded almost imperceptibly. Was she telling me it was safe to tell him? Given that Baxter and I had shared one of the strangest experiences of my life thus far, maybe he was worthy of knowing what was going on. My dirty not-so-little secret. *One hand in front of the other.*

I sipped some ice water from my glass, cleared my

throat, and said, "I'm going to visit my dad in prison. Apparently, that means I need to wake up with the sun." Once it was out of my mouth, something inside me loosened. A little hole opened, like a cork was removed. And, contrary to what I thought would happen, I actually felt . . . better. Lighter somehow. Like letting those words trickle out removed a little bit of the metaphorical burden my parents had forced me to carry. Up to this point, Tatum was the only person I'd ever told anything so personal to. My fingers twisted the pearl at my neck, waiting for Bax's response.

Baxter took another drink, his face unchanged. "I've heard visiting hours are often at weird times. Sometimes you have to wait a while before they let you in. So, that makes sense. Waking up early, I mean."

A sob lodged itself in my throat. He didn't ask why my dad was in prison. He didn't make a sad or shocked or judgmental face. It was a small kindness, maybe not even one he did on purpose, but I was grateful to Baxter. For not prying. For not judging. For just taking what I'd said at face value.

Then, inevitably, my dad's voice showed up.

That was none of his business. You know nothing about him. We do not air our family concerns.

My appetite disappeared and my stomach began doing somersaults. I stood up and picked up my glass. "I'm not very hungry, actually. I think I'm just going to go finish up at the gym. I'll see you later."

Hannah's brows knitted together but she didn't press. "Want me to bring you something back to the cabin for later?" We weren't supposed to have food in our rooms, bugs and mice and whatnot, but it was nice she was willing to take the risk.

"No, thanks." I waved and walked out. The hole I'd opened earlier was beginning to close, the pressure building once again. *Why did I say that? He didn't need to know.* I took off down the dirt path, not caring where I ended up. Anywhere was better than here.

"Hey, where's the fire?"

I'd walked right past Marcus, swinging his keys on a Sweetwater lanyard. "Nowhere."

"Wanna come have dinner with me? I'm starving." I looked at him, his damp brown hair curling slightly from the shower, his eyes on me like there was no other girl in the world. And who cared if that was true or not. He made me feel good and that was something.

"I'm not really hungry." I met his gaze. "For food, that is." It had been a long time since I'd been so bold. But the emptiness inside me needed to be filled. Somehow.

As the sun began its descent, I held my hand out and Marcus, gaze never leaving mine, took it, smiling. I led him to a secluded spot under a circle of pine trees, where he backed me against a trunk and let me kiss him senseless.

Afterward, when he went to the cafeteria and I to my cabin, I couldn't help but notice that while the kissing was nice, the emptiness I'd been looking to fill was still there, and I felt exactly the same. Annoyed, I pushed into the cabin and called it a night.

Chapter 13

Williams Correctional Facility, the sign read. It was completely surreal. How had we gotten here? We had everything. Or, at least my dad did. Now, nothing. Not even his freedom. I felt as if I was walking onto a movie set or a simulation. There was no way this was real life, was there?

The officer who greeted me and Uncle Ed at the gate gave us a laundry list of what to do, what not to do, what to say, what not to say, what we couldn't bring in, what it would look like in the visitation area, how long we could stay, and how to leave the room and retrieve any items we'd left before entering.

What he didn't tell us was what to expect. He didn't tell us how it would feel to inhale the stale prison-scent for the first time. He didn't tell us how the person sitting across the table from us would look simultaneously like a stranger and someone you saw every day for the majority of your life. He didn't tell us how emotional we would feel. He didn't give us a heads up on how hard it would be—how heavy our bodies would feel, carrying so much. So much.

I sat in the chair, waiting for the guards to bring my dad in, my knee bouncing so fast I shook the table.

"It's okay, Ashlyn," Uncle Ed whispered, trying his best to comfort me, to make it better, but I think even he knew his words were pointless. There was no way to prepare for seeing your father locked up.

When they brought him in, I felt all those emotions that had been draped over me, a bulletproof vest of nerves and anger and anticipation, liquefy and drain all over the floor, leaving me completely exposed.

"Hi, Ashlyn," my dad said calmly, sitting down. Gone was the perfectly tailored suit, replaced by a bland khaki uniform that resembled hospital scrubs. "Ed." Dad nodded at his brother and extended his hand. They shook for half a second, both dropping their hands into their laps quickly "How are things?"

I tried to imagine we were sitting at the dinner table or in his office, instead of a federal prison, with the sickening fluorescent lights and reinforced windows. "Things are good. Work is really interesting."

"That's good. What kinds of tasks have you been doing?"

My jaw was stiff, my voice robotic. "I keep the gym clean. Sometimes I serve in the dining hall. I mostly work in the office with the director, though. Whatever she needs."

"Ms. Gress. Highly experienced woman according to your aunt. That's a position of power, being her assistant. If you do a good job for her, that can lead to a letter of recommendation. Hard workers who have the respect of their supervisors go far, Ashlyn."

There was no use telling him that working for Deb was just about the most useless, least rewarding position at the retreat center. I knew better than to tell him she'd practically dismissed me when I'd handed her the list of items that needed to be ordered for the equipment kiosk, including lifejackets, and compiled a list of repairs that needed to be made, notably patching holes in canoes and restringing tennis rackets. Nor did I tell him that when I'd also given her the printed list of safety regulations we were supposed to be following, she threw that down on her desk and asked me to make her another cup of coffee. No, working in Deb's office was not a position of power. It was the exact opposite.

"Ashlyn is doing a great job," Uncle Ed chimed in. I knew he had no idea if I was doing a good job or not, but I appreciated the support.

"Well, that's fine, just fine. I've got a job here too." Dad launched into an account of how he was learning the art of building maintenance. Though he made it seem like he was doing something really important and prestigious in the hierarchy of prison jobs, all I heard was mopping floors and cleaning toilets. He droned on about the importance of sanitation in an environment where "your proximity to large groups of people is inevitable." I laughed, on the inside, at the mental image of my father, on his knees, scrubbing a tile floor with a toothbrush. The perfect job for the man who hired a cleaning company to keep our house entertainment-ready at all times.

When he'd finally finished his story, Dad said, "Ashlyn, do you think you could give your uncle and me just a minute alone?"

My head popped up from where I'd been fiddling with the hem of my shirt. "Oh, sure."

Dad signaled to a guard to come escort me out of the room. As the uniformed woman approached, my dad rose and opened his arms. I didn't really want to touch him. In here, he wasn't my dad. Or, he was, but he was my dad in some alternate universe and maybe if I hugged him, I'd fall through some black hole and get stuck in that other world. But, guilt won.

So I hugged him. And despite the scratchy fabric of his uniform and the black scruff on his chin that he never would've allowed at home, he smelled exactly the same. Two years ago, when I was the youngest member of the Quiz Bowl team back at Henderson High School, before every-thing changed, I won the regional tournament for our team by answering a question correctly about humans being able to detect emotion through scent, notably anxiety. Perhaps it was because he wasn't allowed to wear his very expensive cologne here in the prison, and perhaps it was because, maybe, he was feeling nervous or scared today, but whatever it was, he smelled even more like Dad. I breathed him in. He smelled strong and clean and warm. He smelled like home.

I let go, mumbled, "See you next time," and bolted out of the room. I managed to hold my tears in long enough to collect my wallet from the entrance and duck into a bathroom. I clicked the lock into place, slid to the ground, and started sobbing. Scalding tears fell down my cheeks and ugly sobs erupted from my throat. I was cer-tain the guards on the other side of the door thought I'd unleashed some kind of wounded, wild animal.

I loved him and I hated him. And I hated that. I
felt like two people around my dad. Most of the time,
I wrapped myself in a cloak of silence and sneers. I
did as I was told, deflected his jabs, and kept my head
down, biding my time until I could legally cut ties. I
looked forward to the days when my only obligation
was to show up on Thanksgiving and Christmas. But
sometimes, I was the five-year-old little girl, riding on
Daddy's shoulders, waiting for the carousel in the park to
slow down so she could get on. Her daddy's hand holding her fast, protecting her from sliding off the painted
horse. I didn't know how to wrap my head around those
two Ashlyns. Or, even harder, those two Dads. Who
were we without the other? I had no earthly clue. But
it would be impossible to deny that my dad and I were
enmeshed—another handy vocabulary word from my
psych class—and if I wanted to go home, he would be
there too, even if he was still far away.

I sat on the bathroom floor, the tile cold beneath my
bare legs, until a soft knock came at the door. "Ashlyn?
Are you in there?"

"Yes, Uncle Ed. I'll be right out." I turned on the cold
water and let it run to peak iciness. I splashed my face and
patted it dry with the thin, brown paper towels that did
little to absorb the water. I stared at myself in the mirror,
just like I did the day Dad left to come here. My eyes
were bloodshot, my skin pale from days spent in Deb's
office instead of out in the summer sun. I sucked in a deep
breath, turned, and unlocked the door.

Uncle Ed and I walked to the car without a word.

As he turned out of the parking lot, I sat there, staring straight ahead, still smelling my dad's scent.

I turned to my uncle. "What did you talk about after I left?"

Even in profile, I knew he was smirking. "Money. What else?"

I snorted. "What? How we don't have any anymore?"

"No, you have money. Your father is bad at being a criminal, but he's good at earning money. There's more than enough to pay what he owes the government, all his fines and legal fees, your mom's treatment, and still be comfortable. He just wanted to make sure you were taken care of. That's all. He may not be Dad of the Year, Ash, but he loves you."

"I wish his love had nothing to do with money or appearing perfect." I'd never said that out loud, but I figured if anyone would understand, Uncle Ed would.

My uncle gripped the wheel a little tighter. "Me too. I miss my brother. He wasn't always like this, you know."

I had flashes of memories from when I was younger, but they never seemed real. "I guess."

"We didn't have money growing up. Your grandfather worked long hours in the hardware store in town. Your grandmother took in laundry to make a little extra. We always knew our dad wished he could be his own boss. He didn't like relying on someone else's decisions to put food on our table and he hated thinking that people were judging us for not having much. I think your dad, being the oldest son, took that to heart, maybe a little too much." Uncle Ed chuckled. "And then I went the other direction."

"I think what you and Aunt Greta do is great." Seeing how self-reliant and assured Hannah was, I wondered how I might've turned out if I'd grown up in a different sort of home.

"Thank you. We find value in helping others. It's more important to us than having a big house or the newest phone."

By the time we got back to Sweetwater, anger was brewing in me once again. Everything my dad did was a choice. He didn't have to commit tax evasion. He didn't have to criticize everything I did. He didn't have to pretend to be someone he wasn't, putting up a façade of perfection, and forcing Mom and me to do the same. I wished he'd chosen differently.

I hugged my uncle goodbye and stepped back into wilderness retreat land. Pushing into the lodge, I checked in with Deb, who was in the kitchen alone, covered in flour, food coloring staining her fingers.

She waved me over. "We just finished a cooking session. Those Patels are hilarious." I gaped at her. The Patels were here for a family reunion. There were forty of them according to the registration forms I'd processed. Had she had all of them in the kitchen at once? Somehow that didn't sound safe. "Can you clean this up for me? Wipe the counters and load the dishwashers?"

I opened my mouth to protest, cleaning up after Deb was almost as bad as making her coffee all day long. But then it dawned on me that I could take my frustration out on the kitchen surfaces. I shrugged and nodded.

Deb stretched a hand out to me, offering me a piece of

black licorice. It was my favorite, but my stomach protested. "Thanks, maybe later." She sniffed and walked out of the room.

When I looked more closely at the state of the competition kitchen, my mouth pressed into a firm line so hard it hurt. There was flour everywhere. Candy pieces and chocolate chips all over the floor. And two enormous gingerbread houses at the front of the room—not nearly as lovely as the one Deb had made herself, but it looked like the Patels had had a good time making them. Which only made me clench my jaw tighter. There was no way my dad would ever participate in something like this. He hated looking silly.

A stray bag of white icing, piping tip still on, lay on the far end of the room. Without a second thought—a thought that would have been delivered in my dad's voice telling me otherwise—I grabbed the icing and went for one of the houses.

I WAS BORN IN THIS HOUSE AND
I'M BURNING IT DOWN.
Ghost Beach

I stared at the white words on the white-iced roof for just a moment, satisfied with my handiwork, and then smeared it away with a spatula. The Patels didn't deserve to be graffitied. And besides, my house had already burned down, metaphorically. No need to rub it in.

Chapter 14

I left the kitchen, sparkling clean and smelling deliciously of lemon, feeling completely and utterly exhausted. Not only was my body tired from all the scrubbing, wiping, and rinsing, but my mind was empty. All the mixed-up and warring emotions I'd felt earlier were gone. I knew they'd come back. I wasn't naive enough to think that one spin around a kitchen and a little manual labor would beat the confusion, sadness, nostalgia—and love—out of me. But for now, I was pretty sure I'd sleep well tonight.

Just as I turned the kitchen lights off and pulled the locked door closed behind me, Mallory appeared. She practically skipped down the hall, serene smile on her face. "Hi, Ashlyn, how's your day been?"

I stared at her in disbelief, wondering if she could see, one, the sweat trickling down the sides of my face, and, two, the way my whole body drooped with fatigue. "Fine. How are you?"

"I had a great day, thanks for asking." She sounded one octave shy of Minnie Mouse. "Marcus and I threw a pool party for the Patels. They are such a great family. Have you met them yet?"

"Haven't had the pleasure." Was she just passing by or did she need me for something?

"Maybe tomorrow," she said brightly. "I came to find you to deliver a message from my mom, actually."

Let me guess, Deb has another giant mess for me to clean up. No, wait, she's switched to decaf now that it's almost dinnertime and needs a fresh cup? "What's up?" I asked instead.

She held out a tiny slip of paper. "Your mom called. This is the number you can use to call her back. It looks like," she paused to inspect her mother's writing, "you have about fifteen more minutes to reach her today, otherwise it'll have to be tomorrow."

I snatched the paper from her hand and sprinted to Deb's office, yelling, "Thanks, Mallory," as I ran. My middle school gym teachers would've been very impressed, and shocked, by the speed at which I reached the phone. Deb was conveniently elsewhere, so I closed the office door, pulled a chair over to the dinosaur of a telephone, and dialed the number Mallory had given me.

"Hart Canyon Ranch, how may I direct your call please?" The voice on the other end was pleasant and soft. Exactly the kind of calm, reassuring voice you'd expect in a treatment facility.

"May I speak with Celine Zanotti, please? She's a patient. I was told she'd be available at this time." I drummed my fingers on the desk.

"May I tell Mrs. Zanotti who's calling, please?"

"Yes, this is her daughter. Ashlyn."

"One moment, please."

There was a click on the line and then classical music filled my ears. I held my breath. The hold music was a solo cello piece, beautiful and haunting. I smiled to myself—Tatum's boyfriend played the cello. Maybe it was a good omen.

"Hello? Ashlyn?" My mother's voice was frantic. Desperate. A flutter of anxiety rose in my chest.

"Hi, Mom. How are you?" The words stuck to the roof of my mouth.

Her breath crackled into the receiver. "I'm fine, sweetheart, just fine. How are you? I only have a few minutes before my break is over and I want to hear everything about your job."

My shoulders relaxed and I slumped back in the chair with relief. She sounded okay. "It's good, Mom. I'm not doing anything particularly meaningful, but I'm filling in when I'm needed. Mostly cleaning up the gym and filing papers for the director."

"Well, that's alright. Even small tasks can be useful and make a difference in someone's day. That's one of the things I've learned in my time here, actually." I wished I felt useful here, but it made my heart happy to know Mom was finding the positive in her rehab stay. "It is so good to hear your voice. I can't even begin to tell you how much I miss you."

"I miss you too."

"I talked to Greta earlier. She said you visited your dad." There was a pause. "How was that?"

It was terrible, I didn't say. *It scared me*, I didn't say. "It was fine."

Another pause, longer this time. "That's good," she said, finally. "I haven't been able to make phone calls until today. The people here want to make sure you're settled before you introduce other factors. I'll probably talk to him this week." She called me first. It was then I knew my mom and I were more on the same page then I ever realized. "How is he?"

I gave her my honest assessment. "He's the same old Dad. He said he's getting along okay. They have him mopping floors. He sounded kind of happy about it actually."

Mom laughed out loud. I couldn't remember the last time I'd heard that sound. "Your father is mopping floors?"

I laughed too. "Right?" It was an amusingly ironic plot twist for a man who hadn't lifted a finger other than to sign his name on checks and documents in years. "I think he's proud of himself. Said something about making sure germs don't spread."

"Sounds like something he would say." And then, more to herself than me, "He's trying to convince himself he's okay. It's how he copes." Mom's voice faded. They were words of pity. As if she was saying Dad screwed up, and screwed us both up, but I still love him.

I knew from her wistful tone that she'd already forgiven him for landing us in these places we hadn't chosen for ourselves. I wasn't quite sure how I felt about that. I hadn't gotten there myself. Wasn't sure if I could.

She cleared her throat. "So, they're treating you well, there?"

"Yeah, Mom. Everyone's great."

"That makes my heart happy. I know this summer isn't what you hoped it would be, but I'm glad there are friends for you to lean on. The people here believe in a strong support network as part of your toolbox full of healthy coping mechanisms, that's what they call it. It's scary knowing that I'm going to have to build that from scratch when I get back home."

"We have each other," I said, my voice cracking. Was this the time to ask her if I could come home? If she needed support, she had me. We'd figure it out together. But would it push her in the wrong direction if I said I wanted to join her? I didn't want to add to her burden. Maybe it wasn't the time. Yet.

"We do, honey, we do. I am so grateful for that. One of the other things I've been talking about with my therapist here is a real-world plan. What I do when I get home. It's hard to admit, but my knowledge of how our household was run is practically nothing. That's shameful, I know, and it's on me. I'm going to do better, honey, for both of us." She sniffed and I knew she was crying. And of course so was I.

"I love you, Mom."

"I love you too, baby." A soft chime sounded in the background on her end. "I need to go. I have art therapy. But I can call again soon."

"Art therapy?"

"Yes, I've been working with clay. Sculpting a bit. More kneading than anything else, really. But it helps on the angry days."

"Is today an angry day?"

I could tell she was smiling into the phone. "No, sweetheart, today is a grateful day. Talking to you makes me feel stronger. Like I can dig myself out of this hole and rebuild. You are my purpose."

"Do it for yourself too," I heard myself say.

"Working on it."

Me too. "Okay, well, have fun. Make me a pot or something."

"I definitely will."

"Make it purple."

"Is there any other color for you?"

"Nope."

Mom air kissed, said goodbye, and that she'd call again as soon as she could.

After we hung up, I wiped my own face, ducked into the bathroom to see how bad my mascara had run, and looked at Deb's wall clock. Dinner had already started. I turned off all the lights except for the small one on Deb's desk and went to the cafeteria.

Sitting at my usual table were Hannah and Baxter on one side, Marcus and Mallory on the other. I sat down at the head of our table, between Hannah and Marcus.

"How was your phone call with your mom? Mine always jabbers on and on when we're apart for any reason. And, she's been even more clingy since the divorce. That's why I'm *slightly* glad we're working here together this summer." Mallory giggled and took a bite of her pizza.

Hannah's navy-blue eyes widened. She looked from me to the others and then back to me. "You talked to your mom?"

"Yes, and everything is fine." I said, keeping my tone casual. "She was just checking in."

"Parents are the worst, right? My mom called the other day to ask if I wanted her to pick up my laundry," Marcus said, rolling his eyes. "Like I'm not a legal adult who is fully capable of doing his own laundry."

"Yeah, but do you actually do it?" Hannah asked, pointing the tip of her slice of pizza at him.

Marcus turned beet red. "Well, I save it for breaks. It's not my fault if she empties the hamper before I can get to it."

"You don't do laundry at school?" I playfully wrinkled my nose. My red flag alert sounded, but I ignored it.

"My clothes are clean, thank you very much." Marcus winked at me. I already knew that. The scent of his laundry was pressed into my mind. "There is, however, this kid in my dorm who reeks. Like, you can smell him a mile away. My roommate and I nicknamed him Bo. Get it? B.O. Bo?"

Marcus was the only one laughing at his terrible joke. I just stared, his cruelty hitting a little too close to home. It was the kind of cutting comment my dad might make. Baxter shook his head and Hannah pointed her pizza, now just a crust, back at him.

"You really think that's funny? First of all, it's not. It's incredibly rude. And second of all, you're a terrible human being for calling him a name. Did you ever think about subtly telling him he might want to think about changing his personal hygiene routine? It would suck, sure, but he'd probably be grateful in the long run." Hannah took a bite of her crust, chewed, swallowed, and narrowed her eyes, watching Marcus intently the whole time. "I wonder what his nickname for *you* is."

Marcus said nothing. Neither did anyone else. Hannah had a special way of punctuating a conversation and shutting it down. And I was pretty sure Marcus was now going to go out of his way to avoid her the rest of the summer. We all ate our pizza quietly, and quickly. Marcus claimed he needed to go test the chlorine in the pool, Mallory offered to help him, and they practically ran out of the room.

"Well, that was delightful." Hannah dusted her hands off. "I'm out too. I have to set up a midnight lawn bowling game."

"Have fun with that."

With Hannah gone, that left me and Baxter at the table. We sat there in awkward silence while I chewed the last of my pizza and he took sip after sip from his water glass. When he wasn't looking, I stole glances. His nose was sunburnt and the ends of his blonde hair had gone practically white from the bright sunshine. His expression was calm and focused. I still couldn't get a read on him. He definitely wasn't much of a talker. What was going on in his head?

I pushed my chair out rather than sitting there another moment in the weirdness. But maybe it was just me. It usually was. "See you later," I said.

"See you, Ashlyn." Baxter smiled and a little bit of the weird drifted off. Yep. It was probably me. And that was it. So I left.

The bonfire was crackling when I passed. A group of

Girl Scout leaders were adding more logs to the pile. One of the adults had a handful of the same little slips of paper Ruth had given us at our first staff fire.

"Could I borrow one of those?" I smiled sweetly at the woman, who handed one over.

I sat down on the same log seat I'd used before and pulled out the purple pen I'd learned to always keep with me. I wrote, *I wish to be seen and heard*. Then I balled it up, tossed it into the fire, and kept on walking.

Chapter 15

Hey, where in the process are the repair requests I made a while back?" Hannah appeared in the doorway of Deb's office while I was sorting through the reservations for next week. Deb had turned over the schedule-making to me. I wasn't sure what skills I'd demonstrated that told her I'd be good at that, but I was glad for the change. At least I felt useful. And, I was an excellent agenda maker. The clients listed their goals on their reservation forms and, with just that little information, I could put together a few days of programming to meet their needs. Dare I say it was even fun?

"Umm, I gave them to Deb. Let me look on her desk." It was still my go-to when something was missing or delayed.

The piles were now so high, and in such disarray, that I considered just taking a hand and swiping it all to the floor in one giant snow pile of papers. It probably would've been better organized if I did.

Hannah stood there with one eyebrow up. "How do you even work in here? It's such a mess."

"No kidding." I counted back the number of days ago that Hannah and I had done inventory, estimated how many papers a day were tossed onto the desk, and grabbed a stack that looked about the right height. I lifted up one more, a list of meal requests from a group that came in last week, and, finally, there was Hannah's list of repairs. "Here it is."

"So now what? I needed those boats repaired yesterday. I managed to squeeze an extra kid in each boat with today's youth group, but there's no way I can keep that up with adults. Plus, we're short lifejackets. It's totally unsafe." Hannah's face was red, both hands on her hips.

I put up my hands in defense. "Don't look at me. I am just the errand girl." Hannah snorted. "But you're right about the safety. I'm sure there's some kind of code this breaks, right?"

"Many codes," she said in a huff.

"Well." I looked around the office. Deb kept all the important phone numbers in an old-fashioned rolodex. I'd never seen one; she had to explain to me what it was. "What if I called? Could I do that?"

"You mean pretend to be Deb? I mean, I guess you're just calling to make repairs. She can't object to that. You'd only be saving her butt."

Hannah made a good point. I certainly didn't want retreaters in sinking boats—or worse—and if it happened because I could've prevented it but didn't, I could never live with myself. I flipped through the weird little files in the circular rolodex until I found a phone number for a boat repair company. My hand was reaching for the phone when Deb blew through the door.

"What's going on, ladies?" she asked, oblivious to what I was about to do. *Saved.*

"Hi, Deb, we were just looking for the phone number for the boat repair company," Hannah said, smiling. "You know, for the repair list I gave you the other day."

"On my to-do list for today, in fact. Ashlyn, get me the phone number, it will save me from searching." Deb smiled back, unaware that before she entered the office, I was not only about to save her from searching, I was about to *be* her.

"Whatever we can do to make things easier for you." I handed her the phone. "Would you like me to dial?"

Deb eyed me cautiously. Too far. I took it too far. "I can do it. Thanks."

I handed her the receiver, looking for a way to get the heck out of there. "I'm just going to help Hannah in the kiosk. Wipe down the equipment." Deb nodded and waved her hand at me—her signature move. "The list of repairs is right on top of that stack by the phone. And there are some items that need to be ordered. Do you want me to look up the websites for those items when I get back?"

"No, no, no need. I'll just leave you the credit card and you can get what's needed." Deb seemed absolutely unconcerned that she was trusting me, an underage, temporary coffee maker, with the retreat center's financials.

"Um, okay. I'll take care of that in a bit. Thanks."

With another wave of her hand, she sat down at her desk and began to dial. Whether she was actually calling the boat repair place or ordering Chinese takeout was anybody's guess. Hannah and I bolted.

"Did that just happen?"

"You mean the part where Deb practically handed you the Amex black card? Yeah, that happened. Joan would have *never* done that. She kept that thing under lock and key, and only a few people had the privilege of being able to use it. She also had a whole system for making sure every area of the center had what it needed. Like, those boat repairs would've been taken care of in a few hours, not days. I'd have more lifejackets than I needed. Deb is so . . ." she searched for the right word, "careless."

It was totally the right word. *Deb is so unlike my father,* I thought. I knew from his many lectures over the years that to be successful managing others, and managing a business, you had to pay close attention to detail. Never mind the fact that he was also obsessed with the details of *my* life and making sure I did exactly as he expected. At. All. Times. The reality that my father himself had missed a few details in his grand scheme to fake out the government was neither here nor there.

"Good thing she has us." Hannah shrugged at my response. "Maybe we should keep an eye out. You know, in case there's more stuff."

Hannah nodded. "Probably a good idea. My mother says you have to document everything when you want to make a change. You need evidence."

"Is what Deb's doing actually wrong, though?"

"Not sure. But it doesn't hurt to keep track of stuff if we notice it."

"True."

I was making a list of the things I'd noticed about Deb so far, in the back of my quote journal where no one would look for it, when a large man in a Hawaiian shirt knocked on the office door.

"Hello there, young lady. Might I bother you for a quick minute?"

I couldn't help but smile. If the word jolly had an illustration on webstersdictionary.com, it would be this man's picture. "What can I do for you?"

"Well, my name is Harish Patel and my family is staying here for a few more days."

I grinned wider. "Oh! The Patel family. Everyone has been talking about you all."

"All good things, I hope." Mr. Patel winked at me from behind thick glasses.

"Definitely. The staff is glad to have you here."

"Well, that's wonderful. We're glad to be here. Listen," he said, looking at my nametag, "Ashlyn. We're not from around here and we'd love to see some local attractions off site. We've heard good things but we are unclear on what the possibilities are. Is that something you or Ms. Gress could help us with?"

I knew nothing about this part of Pennsylvania, but I was a champion googler. "I'd be happy to help you, Mr. Patel. Let me talk to Deb and then I'll put some information together for you."

"That would be excellent."

He gave me the details of the number of people and ages in their group, thanked me, and said he'd see me soon. I checked the campus schedule and saw that Deb was signed up for back-to-back cooking challenges. She was doing a charcuterie-themed session followed by an homage to apple pie. "The firefighters are going to be so full by the end of the night," I said to the empty office. It also meant Deb would be occupied for a good long while.

With no one around to "supervise" me in the office, I turned on the computer. I could practically hear gears screeching from rust and misuse. When it finally finished booting up, I pulled up a browser and searched for tourism in this region of the Keystone State. It turned out there was a lot to do here. Who knew? I started making a list of activities and destinations that looked family friendly:

- *underground caverns with stalactites and stalagmites to explore*
- *a trip down the nearby river in an inner tube, complete with a tube for your cooler*
- *a visit to a local farm that has its own ice creamery*
- *a tasting at a winery that has a playground on the premises*

It looked like the Patels could stay in the area for an additional week and not run out of things to do. I checked their reservation in Deb's dog-eared binder and saw they had one afternoon and one morning free before they departed. I opened the spreadsheet software and typed in the suggested destinations, included the estimated time to be spent at each option and cost per person, and added a link to the website for more information. And, for good measure, and because it was my brand of fun, I also included links to restaurant menus where social media users had left positive recommendations.

This is a terrible idea. You can't just do whatever you want. You're being reckless. What would your supervisor say? whispered my dad's voice.

I closed my eyes and shut him off, inhaling deeply to cleanse the negative energy he brought. For the first time since coming to Sweetwater, I felt like I was doing something useful. Meaningful. I didn't want him to ruin it.

I printed the document for Mr. Patel, intending to deliver it personally. Then I checked his family's schedule and saw that they were just about done with the ropes course. I closed the office door and headed out in that direction. When I got to the edge of the course, I could hear cheering coming from deeper in the woods. The last obstacle on the course, after crossing a bridge made of wooden slats that hung over a picturesque stream, was a flat, slippery wooden wall. The goal was to get all members of your party over the wall. The only help you had was each other.

As I approached to get a closer look, I saw Ruth standing on the front side of the wall, arms crossed over her chest. There were three Patels left to go over and eight already on the other side. Baxter was crouched down low to the ground, watching them. I walked over and stood next to him. A little girl, who had to be less than ten, dangled her legs over the top of the wall, trying to decide if she wanted to jump down.

"Sometimes it takes them a while to come down." Baxter spoke without looking up at me.

"Why's that? Fear?"

"Sure, some of it's fear. Also, a lack of trust. Which is interesting if you think about it. Kids her age," he nodded towards the girl, still waiting on top, "love their parents unconditionally, right? So, she should have no hesitation believing they'd catch her." A man and a woman on the ground were pleading with the girl, arms up, promising they wouldn't let her fall.

"So what stops her?"

"Not sure." He turned his gaze on me. "Would you jump down to your parents?"

It wasn't unkind or probing, but I shuddered to think, from the gentle pointedness, that Baxter knew more than the little bits about my family I'd let slip. "Did Hannah tell you about me?"

Baxter's ice-blue eyes were on me, making my cheeks warm. "Tell me what?" There was a certain authenticity to his words, and I immediately felt bad for doubting my cousin.

I sighed and turned my gaze back to the little girl, who had slid a few inches forward, her toes reaching for the ground. "No. It's nothing. Forget it." I expected him to push me on the subject, but he too turned his attention back to the girl, who I still wasn't certain was going to take the leap of faith to her parents below or hoist herself back up to the sure safety of the solid wall.

After a few moments, as the little girl continued to struggle with her decision, Baxter looked at me. "I guess there's not really a good answer to your question. Everyone's got their own reasons for not jumping." We watched as the girl finally slid off the wall into her father's arms while her mother embraced them both. "But I've found that when they do jump, they always land on their feet, one way or another."

Baxter stood up and walked to the girl to congratulate her on her courage. As he did, I couldn't help but wonder if we weren't talking about the ropes course anymore. I handed the list to Ruth to give to Mr. Patel and walked away, mulling over Baxter's words.

Chapter 16

I felt energized the next day. My feet moved a little faster as I walked to Deb's office—proud of myself and excited to tell her what I'd done for the Patels. Maybe, I could make this a regular thing, have more responsibility, actually help people at Sweetwater, do more than fetch coffee and shuffle papers. I imagined myself sitting down with the reservation-makers, discussing how much time they had for an excursion, the interests of the members of their group, if they had any goals to accomplish, if they wanted to eat, to adventure, to sightsee, all kinds of questions. Since Deb was such a fan of binders, I could print out brochures for the destinations and have it ready to show. It was the perfect complement to what she already had been doing with the agendas. *Unless she's angry you defied her*, my dad's voice reminded me. I twisted my pearl necklace between my fingers, shook him off, and continued on my route.

When I got to the office, the door was unlocked but the lights were out. I flipped them on and found a post-it note on my table that said, "running errands in town" in Deb's chicken scratch. The bad news was, I had no job unless she dictated it. The good news was, I could do whatever I wanted to fill my time until she returned.

I turned the computer on and scanned the software available. I opened one for cards and calendars, found a "flyer" template, and clicked. For the next three hours, while Deb was M.I.A., I went to work. I made a flyer to post in retreater guest rooms that showed all the off-site excursions they could sign up for. It was actually beautiful. Tatum, brilliant graphic designer that she was, would be proud of me. I added eye-catching fonts, selected enticing photos from each website, and included select quotes from online reviews.

I wondered if this was what it felt like to be a travel agent or an event planner. I made a note in my journal to investigate those career choices.

At the bottom of the flyer, I debated whether or not I should put my name, Deb's name, or just Sweetwater Overlook Retreat Center Staff, as who to contact to make your plans. In the end, I went with my name. *I did all the work, after all.*

I printed out enough copies to have one placed in every guest room and several extras to tape up in strategic places around campus. Then I set two aside, found two envelopes, folded the flyers, and slipped them inside. One I addressed to Tatum, with a post-it that said, "You're not the only designer now." And the other, I addressed to my mom at her rehab center, with a note:

Dear Mom,

Here's something I've been working on. I think the guests are going to be excited about it. Maybe when you leave, we can do some of these things together.

I love you,
Ashlyn

It wasn't a direct ask to come back home for my senior year. But it was close. I sealed the two envelopes and stuck them in my back pocket to toss in the camp mailbox.

I checked the clock. Literal hours had passed and Deb still wasn't back. I wanted to make the Patels' reservations but felt a little sneaky doing it—plus offering this whole new service, without Deb at least knowing about it, might blow up in my face, or so said Dad's voice in my head.

But Deb isn't here, I rationalized, before grabbing my flyers and heading out of her office.

I ran into Amos before I left the building. He was locking the door to his classroom, probably on his way to the cafeteria for lunch.

"Hello, Amos," I called from down the hall.

"Hi, Ashlyn, how's everything with you today?" He tipped an imaginary hat my way.

"Really good, I think."

"You think?"

I chewed on my bottom lip. "Well, I had what I thought was a good idea, but I haven't been able to talk to Deb about it, so I just . . . did it."

Amos chuckled, his laugh rough in his throat. "What is this idea of yours?"

I handed him a paper. "I want to help our clients do off-campus sightseeing. Mr. Patel asked me to put something together for him and I thought it would be good to offer it to everyone." I paused while he read over the flyer. "What do you think?"

Amos nodded slowly as he evaluated my work. He was the senior-most staff member, nicknamed "Teach" because of the way he made all the retreaters use their brains in his classes.

"I think this is a wonderful idea," he said to my delight. "Come to think of it, I have no idea why no one has put together something like this before. This is such a lovely area of the country, don't you think?" I nodded in agreement, even though I still hadn't seen much of it. "These folks should feel excited to be here. Good for you. Very enterprising, young lady."

I looked down at the chipping polish on my toes, not quite ready to celebrate. "Do you think Deb will approve?"

Amos lowered his head closer to mine and spoke in a loud whisper. "She has to be here to approve, doesn't she?" It seemed too easy, though. I pressed my mouth into a line and was ready to question him when he said, "Sometimes it's better to ask for forgiveness, not permission. And truly, if you're the one doing the hard work, it's no skin off her back, now is it?"

"No, I guess it isn't."

With Amos' blessing, I began posting my signs over

the water fountains and outside the mess hall. I was only a few feet past the doorway when I heard a bloodcurdling scream from inside. Without thinking, I raced in and found a small crowd gathered around someone sprawled on the floor. I jumped up on a chair to get a better look, and what I saw chilled me to the bone. A woman, around thirty or so, lay on the floor, her eyes closed, her lips blue. Her face was swollen, like she was part-balloon, and her skin was all blotchy. Baxter Clark, facing my direction, was on his knees, hovering over her, his fist raised with an object I didn't recognize in his grasp. He brought it down onto her thigh in a swift stabbing motion.

I startled, as if Baxter had stabbed me instead. "What happened?" I whispered loudly to the closest person to me, a middle-aged man in a Disney World T-shirt.

"We think it was an allergic reaction. Heather is severely allergic to peanuts. The cookies served for dessert may have had peanut butter in them."

On the table to my left was a plate with two cookies—one with a bite taken out of it. I broke the whole one in half and sniffed, then took a small bite. *There is absolutely peanut butter in here.* I clenched my jaw. Clients were asked to list any dietary restrictions on their reservation form. I'd seen it a bunch of times this summer. And I also knew that Deb, as manager, was supposed to deliver that information directly to the kitchen staff so they could make arrangements for that guest's food.

My cheeks warmed with shame. I knew Deb's hap-hazard organizational skills. I could've taken that list to the kitchen if I'd realized Deb hadn't done it. I should've assumed, given all the other evidence against her. *Was this my fault?* My breath caught in my throat. *My fault.*

"Thank goodness Heather carries an EpiPen with her at all times." The Disney man shook his head. "I guess when you're that allergic, you're never really safe."

A girl on my floor last year was allergic to shellfish. It wasn't a big deal, at least not at school; it's not like Blue Valley was serving us lobster and crab every night. She told us it was easy for her to just avoid eating it. But peanuts were everywhere. I felt horrible for this woman, Heather, who thought she was coming here to have a good time with her coworkers, learn a little about herself, and go back to the office feeling rejuvenated. Now, she was in serious trouble.

"Can someone call 911, please?" Baxter yelled.

"I will," I called automatically. I told myself I was contributing, being helpful, as I raced back to Deb's office and dialed.

"911, what's your emergency?" I'd never called 911 before. At the dispatcher's calm tone, as if she was asking me what time I wanted for my dinner reservation, was jarring.

I willed my voice to stay steady, though my free hand shook with all the nervous energy inside of me. "Hi, I'm at Sweetwater Overlook and we have a woman with a peanut allergy who just ate peanut butter."

The woman on the phone asked me a few questions about Heather's symptoms, which I answered as best I could. As I was giving her the address and directions to the cafeteria from the front gate, Baxter came in.

"Tell them she had one adult dose of epinephrine and she's sitting up and talking now. When they get here, give them this." He handed me the EpiPen, which had the time he gave it to Heather written on it in black marker.

"Okay," I mouthed, and repeated his instructions to the dispatcher.

"We'll have someone out there shortly," she affirmed, and we hung up. I didn't know how long shortly meant, but I closed my eyes and hoped it was short enough to help our guest.

Opening my eyes, I took a deep breath, exhaled loudly, and looked at Baxter. "That was terrifying." My voice cracked. At least I'd been able to hold it together on the phone call.

He nodded his blond head. "Yeah." He was so calm and unruffled, as if he hadn't just saved someone's life.

"How did you know what to do?"

He shrugged. "My mom is allergic to peanuts too. I've used an EpiPen on her more times than I can count." As he talked, I realized I knew nothing about him. And I wanted to know more. He was so quiet, yet his actions said so much. "Plus, the state requires all employees here to be trained in how to deal with anaphylactic shock." He looked at me, puzzled. "Didn't you complete the training?"

My mouth dropped open. "No one told me."

Baxter grimaced. "Figures. The same person who didn't train you also didn't tell the kitchen about the woman's allergy."

Baxter may have assumed this was all on our boss, but I still felt guilty. Maybe I could've prevented this.

"Hannah says there's a lot of stuff Deb does that Joan never would've let happen." I thought about the boat repairs I almost had to call in myself.

"Hannah is right. I don't think Deb's a bad person, but things aren't the same."

"I'm sorry I didn't get to meet Joan. She sounds like a great leader."

Baxter smiled a little half-smile. "Yeah."

"Well. You were great in there. You saved her life."

He blushed, and I couldn't stop myself from thinking it was adorable. "Thanks."

After the ambulance had come and gone, my guilt subsided a tiny bit. With Heather safely transported to the nearest hospital, I made my way back to what I'd been doing before the commotion—hanging flyers. When I approached the pool, Mallory spied me from her tall lifeguard chair. She waved at me and I reluctantly waved back. She looked so much more official than me, perched way up there in her blue racerback swimsuit. I continued on, taping a flyer on each of the locker room doors so clients would be sure to see it as they walked in.

As I lifted a flyer to the women's room door, an arm caught my waist and spun me around. My flyer—and all the other ones pinned under my arm—fluttered to the ground.

"What—" I began to protest, and then I felt Marcus' lips on mine. My shock and annoyance were overwhelmed by how good it felt to kiss him. Kissing Marcus was like a tiny little vacation. I didn't think about my dad or my mom, I didn't think about Deb or Sweetwater. I didn't think about school or my uncertain future. It was just him, our hips touching, his lips on mine, and me, lost in the moment. I melted against him as his hands caressed my back, sending shivers up and down my spine. I ran my fingers through his hair and pulled him closer, eager for more of him. More of this.

When we broke apart, I was breathless. "What was that for?"

Marcus smirked mischievously. "You were there." He planted a quick peck on my cheek. "Gotta get back to work before the boss sees me slacking. Mallory's a firecracker." Marcus ducked into the men's locker room and disappeared.

I bristled. *Was a firecracker a good thing or a bad thing? Does he like her too? But he's kissing me, so why should I care?*

I bent to pick up my fallen flyers and let out a little strangled cry. They were soaked, lying in a puddle of stray pool water tracked out of the locker room.

"One step forward, two steps back," I muttered to myself, and scraped the soggy flyers off the ground.

Chapter 17

*I*n an effort to do damage control, Deb comped Heather's room for her entire stay and offered the rest of her company a twenty percent discount on their entire package. If you asked me, which no one did, it was hush money. I was glad she was taking ownership and hadn't accused me of any wrongdoing, but I still felt bad about the whole thing. Not bad enough to not take advantage of Deb's "generous" mood, though. I made a point to check that she was okay with my offering a new service for the retreaters. She'd glanced briefly at the flyer, said, "Sure, why not?" and even said to let her know if I needed the credit card again to make it happen. Stunned at how easy it had been, I just nodded and thanked her.

After Heather returned from the hospital—totally fine, thank goodness—I went back through Deb's registration binder. There, in black and white, were the words "severe peanut allergy—cannot ingest" next to Heather's name. If anyone else saw this, Deb could be in serious trouble. The *fired* kind of trouble. Maybe even the *lawsuit* kind of trouble.

As if on cue, the next day, a registered letter, sent overnight, arrived for Ms. Deborah Gress. I signed for it and peered at the sender. It was from Heather's employer. The same company Deb had paid off in hopes of burying her mistake. Had they decided to press charges after all? I gulped and took it back to the office, where Deb was seated at her desk, funneling a handful of jellybeans into her mouth.

"This came for you. I think it's about the peanut incident." I held it out and willed my hand not to shake.

She accepted it wordlessly and set it down atop a particularly precarious pile. I resisted gaping. I didn't know what was in that envelope, but I'd seen ones just like it arrive at our house for my father. Rarely did they contain good news.

"Aren't you going to open it?"

She narrowed her eyes at me and then reached for the envelope, ripping it open at a snail's pace. I clasped my hands behind my back and rocked on my heels as she slid the contents into her hand. Deb skimmed the words on the page and breathed a heavy sigh. She glanced up at me, her stare searing into my forehead.

"Is it bad?" I whispered, unable to help myself. I held my breath, fearing the lawsuit I thought we'd dodged becoming a reality.

Deb folded the letter in half and tossed it on the desk. "No. It's just a summary of actions taken and confirmation of funds exchanged. For our records."

"Oh, thank goodness." I exhaled.

Deb raised one eyebrow. "Were you worried?"

I blinked. Was she not? "Of course. She could've sued

Sweetwater. They provided her medical information on the registration and it didn't make it to the kitchen." I chose my words carefully. I didn't want to sound as if I was accusing her or accepting blame that wasn't mine.

Deb folded her hands calmly in her lap. "Lucky for Sweetwater that they didn't." She popped another jelly-bean in her mouth and chewed slowly, still staring at me. "Are you enjoying your time with us, Ashlyn?"

Why is she asking me this? "Yes." *Mostly.*

"That's good." She pushed her chair out from the desk and kicked both legs up on top of the desk, crossing one ankle over the other. Papers fluttered to the ground. "Because the way I understand it, this job is a gift."

My heart skipped a beat. "Pardon?"

She nodded, a faint smile appearing on her face. "Your aunt mentioned some family trouble when she called to see if there was a place here for you—her reason for calling past the application deadline. So of course I googled and found out about your father's incarceration." Her smile widened. "I'm positive you aren't looking to go down that same path, correct?"

What is she implying? "Correct."

"Excellent. So we're on the same page." She stared me down again, as if she was trying to fire whatever point she was trying to make directly through my skull. I had no idea what page we were both on, but it certainly felt like Deb was accusing me of something.

"Same page," I echoed.

Deb nodded and rose. "I have class. See you later." The door slammed shut behind her.

Though she hadn't exactly accused me of anything, Deb's tone and choice of words, just as careful as mine had been, held a definite threat. I couldn't help but wonder how she would act if Hannah and I brought our other concerns to her. Would she fire us for being insubordinate? Would she find ways to blame her carelessness on us? What if she'd seen me as an easy scapegoat and purposely assigned me to the office with her? It felt like something my dad would do.

Goosebumps trilled up and down my arms in spite of the stale inside air. I just shook my head. How could we confront her now? I didn't want to make things worse for myself. On the other hand, if I kept my mouth shut, was I making things worse for everyone else?

Unable to shake it, I walked over to the kiosk and asked Hannah, "Have you noticed Deb is making a lot of mistakes? Like real ones now?"

Hannah thought for a second. "Well, there's the obvious one with the allergy."

"Which she just semi-accused me of."

"No!"

"Yep. I think it's okay, but I need to stay out of her way."

"I'm sorry, Ash. Clearly, not your fault."

I gave her a sad smile. "Thanks."

"So what else?"

"The boat repairs and lack of lifejackets," I said.

"That's been corrected. Thankfully."

"Thanks to me," I almost shouted.

Hannah nodded. "True."

I propped my elbows up on the window ledge and rested my head in my hands. "I just worry there's more. That desk is like a black hole. I worry about what else is buried under there. I mean, who knows what more could go wrong . . . has already gone wrong that we don't know about."

Hannah shook her head. "Joan was never like this."

"Do you think we should keep track maybe? Like, an actual written list? I feel like Mr. Allen would probably want to know." I looked to Hannah for agreement. She would know if the owner of Sweetwater needed to get involved. There wasn't exactly a law against being bad at your job, until that badness actually broke real laws. I couldn't help but wonder how Deb had gotten this job. She must have been exceptionally good at interviewing. Or somehow had glowing references. And if that was true, what had changed between those jobs and this one?

Normally so decisive, Hannah seemed stumped. I pulled out my journal to show her I'd already started. "I'll keep the list. You tell me if you notice anything new. Then, if we need to use it, we can. Sound good?"

"Sure."

Hannah and I went over the items I'd already recorded and added the latest mistakes. I silently hoped the list wouldn't grow any longer during our time here. But if it did, I hoped even more that I'd be brave enough to speak up. I wanted to believe that I would be, but my track record for letting people know what's on my mind wasn't exactly stellar.

When Uncle Ed picked me up for my second visit to see my dad, there was a plate of brownies wrapped in plastic on the front seat.

"Greta worked on those for hours for you girls," he said, pulling out onto the main road. "I know Hannah asked for cookies, but this was a new recipe someone recommended to her, so she went for it. Hope you like chocolate."

"Who doesn't like chocolate?" I said.

"I knew we were related," he said with a grin.

We chatted comfortably while he drove. Greta had reduced her hours at her agency for the summer so they could spend "quality old folks time" together. So far, they'd seen five movies, had three lunches out at new restaurants in town, and were planning a weekend trip to the beach and another to Philadelphia. It sounded nice. I couldn't help but compare that picture with that of my parents. I imagined when I was out of the house, they probably had most of their interactions at cocktail parties and business dinners. Before I'd left, they'd spent evenings in separate corners—Dad in his office working and Mom reading or watching TV, while I studied in my room. I couldn't remember the last time they'd gone to a movie together.

When we got to the prison, Uncle Ed decided to stay in the waiting area on this visit. Said he wanted to let me and my dad have some time alone. I wondered if he didn't want to see my dad or if he knew my dad had something to say to me. He patted my shoulder and said nothing more as the guard led me into the sterile white room.

When my dad came in, my breath hitched in my chest. Though he looked a little like my father, he was definitely not the father I had burned into my memory. His hair, normally black and shiny from expensive product, had grayed at the temples, and the lines in his forehead and around his eyes were deeper. He had actual crevices, not wrinkles that could be laughed off from too many years spent golfing in the sun—that hadn't been there during our first visit. There was silver stubble on his chin and cheeks. His face sagged; his shoulders slumped forward. My dad looked broken down. Gone was his easy confidence, his command of the room, his mask of perceived superiority. I barely recognized him. And this gave me hope. A kernel, a tiny flicker—maybe on the inside, he was tired too. Maybe he was exhausted from holding himself up, from clenching so tightly it hurt, like I was. He'd taught me to present myself to the outside world as if I had everything under control, and here he was, for the first time, looking completely out of control. He looked like I felt all the time.

"Hello, Ashlyn, how have you been?" Even his voice was depleted, like it took him every ounce of energy to produce sound.

"I'm fine, Dad. How are you?" He'd always put on such a good face; was this the moment he would finally tell me something true? It was too much to hope for a full-on emotional conversation—no one changed that quickly—but given his physical state, it would be reasonable if he slipped a little bit.

"I'm hanging in there. I keep mostly to myself and follow the routines."

I could read between the lines. He didn't have any friends or allies in here. He kept his head down and tried to not call attention to himself. I doubted prison was actually the way it appeared on TV, but I knew enough about psychology to know that humans struggle in stressful situations when they don't have other humans to rely on.

"Is your roommate nice?" *Roommate? Cellmate? Bunkmate?*

Dad nodded. "I share a bunk with a young man from Florida. He works in the kitchen. Sometimes he saves me an extra portion at breakfast."

I guess that was the definition of nice around here. "That's good." I shifted uncomfortably in my chair. His regard, harsh or accusatory like usual, was somehow muted. Diminished.

"Tell me about work." Dad looked me right in the eye and held my gaze. Was he actually interested in what I had to say?

I couldn't remember the last time he changed the topic from himself to me. It was always the other way around. "It's really good. I've started putting together tourism packages for clients who want to get out into the surrounding area." I tried to curb the growing excitement in my voice. My dad and I didn't do emotion. "I've already given some ideas to one family and I'm really excited to start spreading the word to the clients."

Dad's silver-tinged eyebrows knitted together. "What does Ms. Gress have to say about this?" Did he think it was a bad idea? My shoulders sagged. I knew he wasn't going to tell me he was proud of me for coming up with something new and useful, but my heart kept hoping. Over and over and over.

"She was fine with it." *When I finally got to talk to her about it,* I didn't say.

"Was?" Dad's tone cut through the stale air like a machete. "Did you get her permission before you did this?" There it was, the old dad, wounded but still dangerous.

My cheeks flamed. Of course he picked up on that. And assumed the worst. "She gives me autonomy," I said, backtracking. "And several of the senior staff members thought it was a fantastic idea." *Well, one at least.* "It's fine, Dad."

Dad put both hands down on the table and looked down at them. "As long as Ms. Gress has blessed it."

Wait, what? This was not the father I knew. Normally, after dictating something, he would try to intimidate me with a stare, but being here was chipping away at him little by little. If he retreated this easily now, it might not be as difficult as I thought to convince him I needed to come home. On the other hand, if he got worn down so much, if his hardened exterior shattered, who would he be then? The devil you know . . .

"I have a meeting scheduled with her to talk more about it later today," I lied.

"Good. You need to maintain a relationship with her. Ms. Gress' recommendation will really add a lot to your college admissions applications this fall. Have you been working on your essays?"

College is absolutely the last thing on my mind. "A little." *When does he think I have time for this?*

He shook his head. "You should've had a few drafts done by now. I know we discussed this months ago. You're going to have to have something ready before you start back at Blue Valley. Your lack of follow-through is disappointing. Abysmal."

It was the same old speech, but much of the bite was gone. Still, it stung. I pressed my mouth into a firm line and tried to ignore the feeling of shame that was trickling in.

Dad rubbed his palms against his bloodshot eyes. "What about the other employees? Are you making good connections?"

Connections, not friends. Other people were only good as rungs in the ladder to success. Whatever that looked like. I vividly remembered the day we drove to Blue Valley at the beginning of last summer, when my dad warned me to be careful whom I associated with. "If you spend time with trash, Ashlyn, you'll become trash." It was a knife through my heart. An equally harsh reminder of my bad choices—a criminal boyfriend most notably— and the fact that he only approved of my friendship with Tatum because her parents were educated professionals and, therefore, "acceptable."

Instead of shutting down, I tried an old trick—making it about him. "How's your job going here?" I would much rather listen to him talk about the merits of clean floors in a prison than my future, specially designed by him.

It worked. Dad launched into a monologue about how none of the inmates ever paid attention to the wet floors signs he put up after mopping, which was "quite the hazard" he wanted me to know. Always complaining, never about himself. He was just getting warmed up on how many guys had to go to medical after falls when the guards signaled that time was up.

"See you next time, Dad," I said measuredly.

He stood up and gave me a quick side hug. "Work hard."

"Always do," I said, with more ice than I normally would.

I pretended to be asleep all the way back to Sweetwater to avoid conversation with Uncle Ed. I knew he would listen to me, whatever I needed to say, but I just didn't feel like talking. It felt useless. When the car pulled through the main gate, Uncle Ed put a hand on my shoulder.

"Wake up, kiddo, we're back."

I opened my eyes. "I wasn't really asleep."

"I know. I've been a parent long enough to recognize when my offspring don't want to talk. And long enough to know not to push."

"I don't think my dad got those genes."

Uncle Ed chuckled. "No, subtlety was never Arthur's strong suit. There isn't a social cue he hasn't missed at least once."

This time I laughed and then the smile faded. "I wish I'd grown up around your family more."

Uncle Ed put a gentle arm around my shoulder. "We're your family too."

I managed a watery smile, grabbed Aunt Greta's chocolate brownies, and waved goodbye. I walked directly to my cabin, put the brownies on Hannah's bed, and headed out into the summer sunshine of the afternoon. I was off for the rest of the day, and I made a beeline for the pool. I knew Marcus was working this shift, but I was pretty sure I could find a way to convince him to take a break.

Chapter 18

Marcus was there, which was great. So was Mallory, which wasn't. The two of them were laughing side-by-side next to the lifeguard chair at the deep end of the pool. It must have been pretty funny, because she had her hand on his shoulder, doubled over at the waist.

Maybe she's planning to go headfirst into the deep end, and fake drowning, hoping he'll save her. I blinked at them. It sounded like something Tatum would accuse me of doing, actually.

I should go over there and get in the middle of their conversation. Or not. That would be petty. I could find something else to occupy my time. *Maybe I'll head back to the cabin and give myself a pedicure.* The green polish I'd applied a few days ago was starting to chip.

I had my quote journal with me, as usual, so I ducked into the women's locker room. It was empty. On the skinny edge of the door that swung back and forth as retreaters came and went, I wrote:

I DO LIKE NOT KNOWING WHERE I'M
GOING, WANDERING IN STRANGE WOODS,
WHISTLING AND FOLLOWING BREAD CRUMBS.
Tilda Swinton

I swished the door open and passed through before it could swish closed. I decided to take a loop around the property and check out whatever caught my eye. It was really a very pretty place—charmingly rustic. Dirt and gravel paths through tall pine and oak trees led me past the volleyball courts that overlooked the lake, an archery range where a group of high school principals fumbled with their bows and arrows, and near Hannah's equipment kiosk where all manner of sporting items could be borrowed.

As I approached, I spied Hannah backing out of the kiosk and locking the door.

"Taking a break?" I called.

She turned and grinned. "You're just in time. I've got the rest of the day off and so does Bax. So we're going to bike into town. Want to join us? You're off too, right?"

"Oh, I don't know, I don't want to crash your plans. I'm not really a very good third wheel." *Also, I don't know how to ride a bike.* But saying that out loud, at my age, was beyond embarrassing.

Hannah put both hands on her hips. "Please. If anything, you'll make it more interesting. When Bax and I hang out, it's me who does all the talking and he usually just nods or shakes his head. And as much as I like to hear my own voice, it gets old."

"How can I turn down an offer like that?" I joked. She made Baxter sound super boring, when, from my vantage point, he was one of the most intriguing people here. The words he spoke seemed to be chosen very carefully, which made me wonder which ones he was thinking, but didn't say out loud.

"We're meeting at the front gate in fifteen minutes." Hannah tossed me a ring of tiny gold keys. I surprised her, and myself, by catching it. "Take a bike from the rack. I'm going to get cleaned up, see you down there."

"Sure, no problem," I said to myself after she'd jogged off. Two bicycles, a red one and a black one, had already been unlocked. I released a purple one—if I was going to fall on my face, at least it would be on a bike that was my signature color. "Piece of cake. You can do this, Ashlyn. Little kids ride bikes all the time. If they can do it, so can you."

I did own a bike when I was younger, but never got past the training wheels stage. I preferred to be inside reading, and my parents never shoved me out the door so I could get fresh air. They were indoor people too. They never signed me up for soccer or gymnastics like the other kids I knew. I spent my free time after school working with tutors and doing extra math problems. The good news was that I genuinely liked school and found learning exciting, but there were times when I wished I was on a team. Not that I wanted to be running and jumping but being part of a team and working together was something I didn't really experience until high school and Quiz Bowl. But, even then, I don't think it was exactly the same.

"Hey."

I turned around to see Baxter a few feet away from the bike rack.

"Hey, yourself," I said, trying to act like I definitely knew what I was doing with the bike. "Hannah invited me to come with you into town. I hope that's okay."

"Of course." He smiled. It was genuine. There seemed to be nothing fake about Baxter.

He wheeled his bike, a red one, around to the road and swung his leg over. "Come on. Hannah is getting helmets on her way back from the cabin. We can go ahead, she'll catch up."

I slowly wheeled my bike to the road and stared at it. The tires were so much bigger than the little bike I'd had growing up. I imagined myself rolling along, losing balance, the wheels wobbling, and me ending up face down on the asphalt. I gripped the handlebars more tightly. *You're going to look ridiculous if you fall*, phantom Dad sneered. *You shouldn't attempt things you know you're not good at.*

"Are you going to get on?" Baxter teased.

"I . . . uh . . ." I started, as he raised a blonde eyebrow at me. "Maybe I'd rather walk."

Baxter's pale blue eyes studied my face. "Do you know how to ride a bike, Ashlyn?" I didn't answer. "Because it's okay if you don't. I can teach you."

I met his gaze, grateful that what was so embarrassing to me was, to him, no big deal at all. Baxter hopped off his bike and laid it on the ground. He walked over to me and put his hands on the handlebars, outside my grip.

"I'll hold it steady and you get on."

"Okay." I swung my leg over, like I'd seen others do. His arms must have been as strong as his legs, because the bike didn't wiggle or sway at all as I mounted my perch. "Now what?"

"Now you pedal." He said it like it was the most logical next step, when, in fact, the logical next step for me was panic.

"You say that like it's easy," I said, trying to gather my courage.

"It's easier than you think it is."

He sounds sure. I'm not sure. How is he so sure?

"And if I face-plant, will you scrape what's left of me off the ground?"

"Just pedal."

Maybe it was because Baxter's job was to help nervous retreaters conquer their fears, but the authority in his voice made me rethink staying still. So I pedaled. The pace of a tortoise.

"You have a greater chance of falling the slower you go," he said with a chuckle.

So I pedaled an infinitesimal amount faster and Baxter moved his grip on the bike from the handlebars to the back of my seat. "Don't let go," I cried, high pitched and screechy. Not unlike Mallory, but that was neither here nor there. I could no longer see Bax's hands steadying the bike, and that made my stomach twist into a knot.

"You're doing great. Go a little faster."

I pedaled a tiny bit faster, and then a tiny bit more. I made my way down the road to the gate while Bax jogged—like a sloth would jog if sloths jogged—along next to me, hand still on the back of the seat. I did my best to concentrate on pushing my feet down and around, keeping my hands steady on the handlebars, eyes on the road, all the while trying *not* to think about how close he was to me. It was the closest we'd been since we dangled, pressed against each other, in midair on the zipline.

I gritted my teeth and narrowed my eyes, focusing on the gate that was just up the road. Before I could convince myself not to, I pushed down hard with my right foot and took off. Up, down, up, down, I pumped my feet, flying down the road. The gravel on the road jumped out of my way, the wind ruffling my hair around my ears. When I reached the gate, I braked and skidded to a stop, panting, more from adrenaline than actual athleticism. But I'd done it.

"Yes!" I yelled to Baxter, who was strolling down the road toward me, his hands shoved in the pockets of his cargo shorts.

"You did it." He smiled at me.

"That was amazing." I'd only ridden about a quarter of a mile. Other people did it all the time; they went further than me, rode on more impressive routes than me. But there was something about doing a thing for the first time. It had been a really long time since I'd felt this way about myself, but I was proud.

Baxter nodded. "I've learned that the things we're afraid of are almost never as scary as they are in our imagination. And, if you're lucky, that scary thing turns out to be something awesome." He pointed. "Like riding this bicycle."

"Just like riding a bike," I quipped.

We smiled at each other, and suddenly I felt shy. A burning blush spread from my cheeks to my ears.

"Thanks for helping me."

"I didn't do much. And besides, I let go way before you decided to go all Tour de France."

"You did?"

"I did." His eyes twinkled. "You're more capable than you think. Don't psych yourself out too often. You might miss something."

This has nothing to do with riding a bike, does it?

Tatum was convinced there were people in this world who were part magic, put here to teach us lessons or watch out for us or make good things happen. I couldn't help but wonder if my path and Baxter's had crossed this summer for a reason.

"Hey!" Hannah was running down the road with three bike helmets on her arms like giant bracelets. "Thanks for leaving me, jerks."

"We didn't leave you. We were waiting right here. See?" Baxter pointed to himself and then me.

"Where's your bike?" Hannah demanded.

"Where's yours?" Baxter retorted.

"Ugh." Hannah stomped her foot and dropped the helmets on the ground. "Come on. Ashlyn, we'll be right back. Don't move." She and Baxter walked back toward the bike rack, leaving me there to wonder what kind of magic was in store for me next.

Chapter 19

I wobbled my way into town with Hannah and Baxter, having to stop a few times to center myself. But I did it. I wasn't on my way to the Olympic cycling team any time soon, but I did a thing I'd never done before and that counted for something.

The town, also named Sweetwater, was small. My mother would have called it quaint. It was the exact opposite of where I'd grown up. Sweetwater was basically a handful of streets making up the "downtown" area, with houses, schools, and businesses surrounding. There were trees everywhere, plenty of green space, benches for people to sit on, and a general warm and inviting feeling. In contrast, Arlington, which sits on the edge of Washington, DC, was urban and bustling, packed full of stores and restaurants, tall buildings and people. While the average speed in Sweetwater seemed to be somewhere between a stroll and a mosey, everyone rushed from place to place back home. Lining the main street, which was aptly named Main Street, was a drugstore with a doctor's office above it, a barbecue restaurant with a sign that proudly proclaimed: "THE BEST RIBS IN THE STATE," a coffee shop that doubled as an ice cream parlor, a law office, a hair and nail salon, and a used bookstore. Down the block, we rode past the courthouse, a statue memorializing town veterans, and a tiny used car lot. It felt right to be riding bicycles down the tree-and-flower-lined street.

"New girl gets to pick where we go," Hannah declared, as we racked our bikes outside the law office.

"Um, how about the bookstore?" My supply of paperbacks in my giant duffel bag was dwindling. I was going to need some reinforcements to carry me through the rest of the summer if Deb was going to keep assigning me to the gym, where I could only take so much sitting and watching lawyers and architects running on treadmills.

Hannah looked smug and poked Baxter in the arm. "I told you that's what she would pick."

Baxter put both hands up in surrender. "You win."

"Did you make a bet or something?" I didn't know whether to be flattered or offended.

"There was no money wagered," Hannah said. "But yes, we did each offer up a guess as to what you'd want to explore."

"What did you think, Bax?"

He grinned sheepishly. "I thought you'd want to go to the coffee shop for a triple shot almond milk latte with caramel foam or something equally as complicated."

I laughed so hard I felt it in my core. It was a good guess. "For the record, I like my coffee regular drip with hazelnut flavoring. No caramel foam needed."

Bax did a quick bow with a little flourish of his hand. "I stand corrected."

I curtsied. Hannah looked at both of us like we had lost our minds.

Island Book Shop was on the corner. A delicate bell tinkled as we passed through the door. A middle-aged woman, hair graying at the temples that reminded me of my dad on our last visit, stood behind the cash register.

"Hi, there, welcome to Island." She smiled politely at us.

"Why is it called Island? There's no ocean around here?" Hannah asked.

"It's a nod to the neighborhood where I grew up," the woman said, with a wink and a smile. "Can I help you all find anything?"

I glanced around. The shelves went on forever and were stuffed full of books upon books upon books. I could stay for days, just reading the titles. The store even smelled delicious—that musty, sweet smell only well-loved books carry. I inhaled, held it in my lungs for just a moment, and exhaled.

Hannah looked at me as if she were really concerned about my well-being.

"What? I like books. Always have."

"You look like you just got high off that sniff of the store."

I shrugged. "Books smell amazing."

Baxter put both hands on Hannah's shoulders from behind, as if he were going to leap frog over her. "She's right, Han."

She swatted him away. I knew Hannah was mostly just

playing, but there was something underlying. Like enjoying the smell of books was a club she wasn't a part of and she felt a little left out.

She stuck her tongue out at me and made a face. I did the same. Then we both giggled like little kids. Was this what family felt like? If so, I could get used to it.

"I'm going to browse," Baxter said, and walked down the closest aisle. I ducked down the next aisle over, while Hannah took the path farthest from the front of the store.

I found myself in the poetry section, which was definitely not a bad place to be. I'd spent enough time in used bookstores to know that certain kinds of books came with more love—lines highlighted, passages underlined, notes made in the margins. Poetry seemed to have that effect on readers. You wanted to record and remember the lines so you could experience what the poet made you feel over and over again.

I pulled a dusty, battered copy of *Leaves of Grass* off the shelf. I'd read it years ago and highlighted my copy—a hardcover special edition my dad said "belonged on every scholar's shelf"—within an inch of its life. When he'd discovered my "love," he'd pitched a fit. Told me I should take better care of my things, that I ruined this copy, and then threw the book away.

I looked over my shoulder to see if anyone was watching. When I verified I was completely alone, I wrote, very small, on the shelf where I'd taken the book:

> I AM NOT WHAT YOU SUPPOSED,
> BUT FAR DIFFERENT.
> *Walt Whitman*

It was one of those lines that stuck with me, that I repeated to myself from time to time. It was the lyrical representation of my father and me. I wasn't what he thought I was. In some ways, yes, I was the over-achieving daughter he wanted me to be, but I was also other things too. Not just that. Or, I thought I would be if he ever gave me the space to find out.

I tucked the book under my arm and moved on, flipping through the Pablo Neruda and the Emily Dickinson, the Li Bai and the Nissim Ezekiel. I slid a volume by Nikki Giovanni off the shelf and tucked that under my arm as well. I couldn't wait to pour over these pages and record the lines that touched my soul in my quote journal.

"Thought you might like this."

I jumped at the sound of Baxter's voice behind me. How long had he been standing there? My face heated, and I waited for it to cool before I turned around.

"What's that?"

He handed me a book. A huge book. Maroon with gold and white lettering on the torn dust jacket. *Bartlett's Familiar Quotations.* The 1980 edition.

"I know you like quotes. Thought this might be of interest."

My mouth betrayed me, popping open. "How?" I expected him to tell me he'd been following me around. That he'd seen me write on the door of the locker room, on this shelf, on the sign-in sheet at orientation, or any of the other places I'd left my mark. Those little acts of rebellion had always been my secret. Or so I thought. What if he had seen me? I suddenly felt exposed. Naked. Though I had no reason to think Baxter would judge me, his awareness of my covert habit made me feel more than a little vulnerable.

"Hannah told me you have a quote journal."

The sigh of relief that whooshed out of me was probably heard at the front of the store. "Oh. Yes. I do." I smiled at him and did my best to regain my composure. "Thank you. For the book. It's perfect."

"You're welcome."

We looked at each other for a second longer than two people who were just coworkers probably should. My toes wanted to curl, and I was glad I had sneakers on so he couldn't see.

And then of course, Hannah appeared and ruined the moment I suspected we were having.

"Come on, slowpokes, I'm ready for some ice cream. Or maybe a coffee. I'll decide on the way."

I paid for my books—Bax bought me the Bartlett's—and we left the store, bell jingling behind us.

The ice cream store was the most impressive business on Main Street. Twenty-eight different flavors, including ones the fanciest restaurants in DC might have dreamed up. Brown butter and fig jam, cilantro and lime sorbet, chèvre and blueberry, as well as all the traditional flavors, sat in the glass case, beckoning to sugar-hungry customers. My mouth watered just browsing.

"I'll have a scoop of chocolate and a scoop of vanilla in a waffle cone," Hannah told the man behind the counter.

"I would never have pegged you for a boring ice cream kind of girl. I'm kind of disappointed, actually." I smiled sweetly at Hannah.

"Yeah," Bax agreed, "I would've guessed Egg Nog or Pistachio."

I stood closer to him, conspiring, looking Hannah up and down. "Maple bacon perhaps."

He high-fived me and smiled; a rush of joy shimmered down my arm and through my body. There was nothing hanging over me, like my parents or school or work. I smiled back, and in a burst of spontaneity, I hugged him. I hugged Baxter Clark. And with that hug, I noticed a few things. One, he was just as strong everywhere as his legs had been on the zipline. The arms that enveloped me, the chest that pressed me close, the shoulders my cheek rested on—all rock solid. Two, he smelled like pine needles. And three, he hugged me back. A second later, I realized what I'd done and pulled away.

"Sorry," I said to his brown hiking boots. "I don't know what got into me."

"No apology needed." Baxter's voice was so warm that my insides went molten.

I took a small step back, my eyes darting away from his, and went back to the ice cream case. "Ready to change your mind, Hannah?"

"Not a chance. I know what I like." She already had her waffle cone in hand and immediately took a huge bite off the chocolate scoop on top.

Even when it came to ice cream, she knew exactly who she was. I envied that. Even if I wasn't sure about much else right now, at least I had a lock on my ice cream flavor.

"Mint chocolate chip in a sugar cone, please." When

the man handed it to me, I was pleased to see the ice cream was white. My favorite pint, consumed over many sad and angry nights, was the same. Not the fake green from food coloring. Each bite reminded me of Tatum and home and summer nights staying up late talking, but also of tears and exhaustion and defeat.

"Butter pecan with chocolate sprinkles."

I raised an eyebrow at Bax's order. "Really?"

He took his cup of ice cream, which had a mountain of sprinkles on top. "It's an underrated flavor."

You're underrated too, I thought as he took a bite, and instantly I blushed, probably just as pink as his spoon.

Chapter 20

We strolled down Main Street, eating our ice cream, slowly savoring it, peeking in the business windows. The drugstore display was especially entertaining. It had a mannequin in swimming trunks, goggles, and flippers, ready to dive into an ocean that was miles and miles away. We all laughed as we inspected the variety of different sun blocks and aloe vera creams spread around him, as well as colorful towels and a picnic basket.

Eventually, we sat down on the courthouse steps to people watch. Turned out, that was a favorite pastime of Bax and Hannah's. They liked making up stories about the passers-by, and I liked listening to them banter. Bax was different with Hannah than he was with anyone else. He spoke more frequently and at length, instead of the as-short-as-possible replies he gave most other people. I guess it made sense. I was kind of like that too. There were only so many people I felt comfortable showing the real me to. I also couldn't help noticing Bax had spoken a lot to me today too, like I'd passed some kind of test and proven myself worthy.

"What about him?" Hannah pointed to a man, in his late twenties or early thirties, walking a poodle. Not a golden doodle or a toy poodle that maybe he inherited from his grandmother, but a full-on standard-sized black poodle, complete with elaborate hairstyle and shave. I covered my mouth to keep from laughing as he passed by. The man didn't seem to notice the three of us watching him.

"Secret millionaire. Holds a patent for that gadget that spins water off salad greens. Breeds poodles on the side. That one is a Westminster champion." Baxter rattled it off like it was the truth.

"That is oddly specific," Hannah said, sounding impressed.

"My mom loves that salad thing. She says it gets her lettuce super dry, which I guess is one of the more important things in life," I said.

"Speaking of moms," Hannah said. My stomach fluttered, but she turned to Baxter instead of me, "How is your mom doing, Bax?"

He nodded. "She's getting along okay. Talked to her last night actually." He swung his gaze my way. "My mom had surgery last week. Hysterectomy. She's off her feet for a few weeks."

"That must be hard for her," I said. "Is your dad helping at least?"

"No dad. Just Mom and me. He left when I was little. It's always been the two of us." Baxter didn't sound bitter about it. Just matter-of-fact, the way he was about everything.

"Then it must really be hard for her if she's at home and you're here," I realized aloud. "Is someone else helping? A neighbor?"

Bax laughed. "She has a boyfriend, though Mom would never call him that. He's making her meals and keeping her supplied with books and magazines. She told me she's looking forward to binge watching all the TV she never has time to watch."

"Bax's mom is a nurse. She works all the time. Like, literally all the time." Hannah shoved the last of her waffle cone in her mouth.

"She takes off at least one day a week," Bax countered. And then to me he said, "She makes a lot more in overtime, so she tries to pick up extra shifts when she can. Any time someone's kid has an appointment or a school concert or something, she raises her hand."

"Does that mean she missed your school stuff growing up?" I asked. My parents came to every single event, competition, concert, and tournament. Which inevitably were followed by a list of things I should've done differently.

"Sometimes. But I understood. If she didn't work, we didn't eat. Pretty simple."

Is that how it would be for me and Mom? Would she need to find a job to support us? I knew my tuition at Blue Valley was already taken care of for the next year, and Uncle Ed said living expenses were covered, but for how long? What if my dad's business sunk for good?

"My mom and I are going to be in the house by ourselves too," I heard myself say before I could censor my thoughts. Hannah's eyes got bigger, just as surprised by my admission as I was. And maybe more surprising, I wasn't embarrassed. I didn't feel like clamming up, as I usually did. Maybe it was the afternoon spent together. Maybe it was being in the presence of family. Whatever it was, my skin wasn't crawling and there was no desire to dive behind a tree.

"Oh, yeah?" Bax said lightly. "That's probably going to be an adjustment."

Hannah eyed me. I knew she wanted me to talk, so I nodded at her. "My mom is in rehab right now. For depression," I clarified. "Not drugs or anything like that. She'll probably be home in a few weeks."

Hannah looked at me again before blurting, "And you already know her dad is in jail."

There they were. Both elephants in my life. Brought out into the open. To their credit, neither Hannah nor Baxter said anything after that. We sat there letting the slowly setting sun warm our skin. I ate the last of my ice cream cone while Bax scraped his spoon along the sides of his paper cup, getting every last sprinkle. I inhaled, exhaled, inhaled again. There was no reason to keep quiet about any of this really. Talking to Tatum was my go-to when things were rough, but she wasn't here, and these two were the next best thing. Tatum's voice in the back of my head whispered, *Trust them.*

"My dad was sentenced to prison for tax evasion. He'll be there just over a year. That's probably what sealed the deal for my mom and her depression, though I think she's been struggling for a long time and tried to cope by just ignoring it." I put my elbows on my knees and rested my face in my hands. "And because I've been away at school for most of the last year, I missed that all of this was happening. It's not exactly a great day when you find out your family is falling apart via social media."

"Ouch," said Baxter. "I'm so sorry, Ashlyn."

"Me too," Hannah said in a very un–Hannah-like muted tone.

"It is what it is. My mom is going to be coming home at some point soon, and I want to go home too, but I don't think they'll let me."

"Why wouldn't your parents let you come home?" Bax asked. "I mean, where have you been?"

I winced. I didn't want to tell him that part. I was pretty sure Hannah already knew, but who knows what version of the story she had heard. It was embarrassing to have to admit your mistakes. Especially in front of people who had just accepted you into their circle of friendship. Then again, *not* talking to people about what was going on hadn't exactly been helpful. And it definitely didn't make me feel any better.

I recounted the same shoplifting story I'd shared with Marcus, way back during the first campfire, tears pricking my eyes as I mentioned being sent to Blue Valley. "My dad saw it as an opportunity to teach me a lesson, to assert his power over me, but the only thing I learned from him sending me away was that he didn't want me around."

A fist squeezed my heart. I had never said that out loud before. Maybe never even fully admitted it to myself. I struggled to breathe, somehow managing to get a few shallow breaths in before the sobs came. Hannah scooted

over and put her arm around me and hugged me so tightly
it hurt.

"I didn't know that part," she whispered in my ear.

She let me cry for a few minutes, rubbing small circles
around my back. It reminded me of how my mom would
put me to sleep when I was little. She always promised to
check on me after I was asleep. I'd drift off, feeling safe,
knowing she was coming back. Now the question was,
would *I* come back?

Baxter cleared his throat and looked at me before he
spoke. "Speaking from experience with my own mother,
I would be really surprised if she didn't want you to come
home. You know, to be there when she gets herself back
together. After my dad left, at least from what I remember, my mom was kind of a mess. We both were. But we
figured it out together."

Hannah shook her head back and forth, like she was
trying to dislodge a thought. "I don't get it. Why do you
even want to go back to her? To them? Because your dad
will be back eventually."

I took a breath in, held it, and let it out slowly. That
was a really difficult question to answer. There was an
ocean's current tugging me back to the house where I
grew up, where all my memories began. But now, what
was there for me? Home was supposed to be a place of
comfort, right? I may not have gotten it all the time, but
there was something about the sanctuary of my room,
my mom, the routines that made us who we were, and
even the reliability of my dad's judgments, that brought
a prickly kind of comfort. "Because. They're mine. And

maybe it's hard for you to understand that because your family is amazing, Hannah, but it's not so black and white. A family isn't only good or only bad."

Hannah crossed her arms and huffed. I thought for a moment about how to convince her, then pulled the tiny pearl necklace out from the collar of my shirt. "My dad gave me this when I turned thirteen. It's one of the few presents he ever picked out on his own. And for whatever reason, he was insistent that I needed to have it."

Hannah stared at the milky white pearl between my fingers for a moment before speaking. "Our grandmother had one just like that. It's in every photograph of her. Always around her neck."

"I didn't know that. He never speaks about her." I shivered, even though it was still warm outside.

"Sounds like there's a lot he didn't talk about," Hannah said under her breath. Baxter smacked her on the arm and she turned to him. "What did I do?"

Baxter inhaled loudly, caught between the weight of my sadness and Hannah's vitriol for my father. "Ash," Bax said to me, "it sounds to me like you and your father are going to have a lot to discuss. Your mom too. When everyone is back under the same roof."

"If we ever are under the same roof again."

"Don't even ask. Tell them you're coming home. Demand it." Hannah's voice was rising with emotion. "Ashlyn, you should fight back more."

My mouth popped open, unsure of how to defend myself. Hannah's frame of reference was so different from mine.

"I don't think it's that easy, Han," Bax said quietly. "Families are complicated." He gave me a sad smile.

"Well, thank goodness mine isn't." She threw up her hands and stood, clearly done with the conversation. "We should get back."

"To avoid the rush hour traffic?" I gestured to the completely empty street.

"You're being funny again," Hannah said, pointing a finger at me.

She took off in the direction of where we'd left the bikes, leaving Baxter and me to follow. I dusted off the back of my shorts, balled up my napkin, and stuffed it in my pocket.

"Ash?"

"Yeah?" We made it to the sidewalk, standing side by side, both facing forward.

"If you ever want to talk. About your family. Or anything else. I'm a good listener."

But not today. I felt depleted, but it was a good emptiness. The emptiness after a good cry when you're ready to start fresh and move on. "I'll think about it. Thank you."

"Anytime."

Chapter 21

*B*ack at the retreat center, the sun had just dipped below the horizon and the sky was an inky purple. I racked my bike, gave Hannah back the helmet, and thanked her and Baxter for including me in their outing.

"You're not a guest, Ashlyn," Hannah said. The feeling of belonging to anything that even resembled family was still foreign.

As nice and peaceful as the evening had been, my mind was spinning. It was a strange thing to have new allies after being isolated for such a long time. To be accepted, and allow myself to accept in return, threw me off. And the fact that I shared what I had, and made myself vulnerable? I knew without a doubt I'd be up all night, Bax and Hannah's words playing around and around in my head. Dad's phantom scolding would probably show up too, reminding me to keep my cards closer.

I decided to go for a walk. There was a chill in the air now, so I walked quickly up the hill to stave off goosebumps. The moon rose, half bright and half in shadow, over the lake, illuminating the ripples cast by the slight breeze. I rubbed my bare arms as I walked past.

"Cold?"

His voice was like honey. I turned and saw his almost-feral grin, lips curling upward.

"Hi, Marcus." I remembered how, earlier that day, I saw him laughing with Mallory. Somehow that seemed like weeks ago, instead of just a few hours.

"What have you been up to?"

"Went into town with Hannah and Baxter."

"Oh yeah? The boring twins?" He chuckled.

I gritted my teeth. "You know Hannah's my cousin, right?"

"Sorry, sorry. But you have to admit, she's super uptight. Am I wrong?"

"She's just . . . focused."

"Is that what the kids are calling it these days?" I crossed my arms, leaning backwards to give him a hard stare. "Hey, hey," he said, putting his hands on my arms and tugging me closer. "I didn't mean to hurt your feelings. I guess I'm just confused why you're hanging out with them. That's all. Doesn't seem like a good fit. Especially when you could've been hanging out with me instead."

Before I could respond, fully prepared to tell him how I'd found him *occupied* earlier, he smiled at me. Against my better judgement, I smiled back. Marcus lowered his head to mine and I let him kiss me. He held my face in his hands gently, like I was more than a girl he kissed a few times at his summer job. His lips on mine, I tried to imagine what it might be like if we kept talking after he went back to school. Maybe started dating. Would he invite me to see him at college? Introduce me to his friends as his girlfriend? Would he meet my mother and send me letters at school? I couldn't picture it. I pulled away.

I hadn't started kissing Marcus because I thought he would make a good boyfriend. I had liked his confidence, his ease in navigating a room full of strangers, his magnetism. But I wasn't the same girl who had thought those things anymore. Though I was still a work in progress, I could see cracks in his façade. *Not unlike my dad, actually.* The little jabs at Hannah and Baxter. The joke about his roommate. Having his mom do his laundry. The flirting with Mallory. Perhaps I'd been able to ignore them a few weeks ago, but I wasn't the same girl who would settle for those things now. Whatever was in that kiss, even though it felt nice, was no longer what I wanted.

I put both hands on his chest and pressed lightly. "Good night, Marcus."

He looked confused, wounded almost, like he'd never had a girl say good night to him before he was ready, but he nodded and let me go. "Good night, Ashlyn."

Those things I liked about him tasted sour on my tongue now; Marcus was all smoke and mirrors. And maybe, just maybe, I deserved something more.

I went back to the cabin. Hannah's shower stuff was gone, so I knew I had at least a few minutes alone. I dashed off a quick letter on a Sweetwater postcard to mail in the morning.

Dear Tate,

    I think I may have just lost my taste for boys with polos. What do you think about hiking boots?

        Love,

        Ash

"Ashlyn, I need you," Deb bellowed from the office door as I walked into the lodge the next day.

I hurried to her, afraid there was another emergency. "What's going on?"

"Well, nothing good. We have a group arriving today and we are short staffed; there's some kind of summer flu going around. I'm going to need you to cover the morning shift."

"Sure, where do you need me?"

"Volleyball courts. It's the Springville Methodist Church's Sunday School group. They need to be supervised while the adult leaders go through the ropes course. You can play games with them. Red rover and that kind of thing, okay?"

Ugh. Kids. I was not a kid person at all. And all morning in a pit of sand? "Okay," I said, though, because I had no other choice.

"They'll be there waiting for you in about fifteen minutes, so get a move on."

Aye-aye, captain, I didn't say.

When I got to the volleyball court less than five minutes later, a large group of kids and one harried-looking adult, who was tapping her foot and staring at her watch, were already waiting for me.

"Oh, I'm so glad you're here." The woman squeezed my shoulders like we were long-lost friends. "I don't want to miss the directions. We'll be back when we've mastered the course," she called, already starting to run up the hill toward the zipline.

"Okay," I said, mostly to myself. I surveyed the crowd and then counted. Twenty-nine, thirty, thirty-one, thirty-two. Thirty-two children, and from the looks of it, none of them were much older than twelve. Some looked as small as kindergarteners. They were running in circles, throwing sand in the air, tagging each other and darting away, turning cartwheels and being louder than a rock concert.

"What am I supposed to do with them all?" I asked no one.

The ropes course took what? Two hours? More? I felt the first threads of panic rising in my throat. *You're in over your head. This is beyond your capabilities*, Dad's voice said in my mind. I clamped my jaw tight and ignored him.

Back in control of my thoughts, I tried to form a plan. *Think. What did I like to do when I was younger?* That was ridiculous, I liked to stay indoors and read, play with makeup, and watch TV. Not options there. I spun in a slow circle trying to get ideas from my surroundings. And then it hit me. I was standing smack dab in the middle of a teambuilding retreat center. For weeks now, I'd been watching groups of all kinds go through exercise after exercise, learning about one another and themselves. I pulled out my quote journal and ripped out several pages. I quickly wrote down some information on the sheets and smiled to myself.

"Hey!" I called as loud as I could. Approximately two kids turned and looked my way and then went right back to their friends. "Hey!" I tried again, waving my arms in the air like I was trying to land a plane.

A small girl with glasses, who was about ten or eleven years old, came up and tapped me on the shoulder. "You need to put your hand up like this." She held her hand up high in the air, as if she were ready to receive a high five.

"Oh. Thanks. What's your name?"

"Avery Chen," she said, flipping her dark pigtail over her shoulder.

"Thank you, Avery."

"No problem. What's your name?"

"Ashlyn Zanotti."

Avery nodded and walked back to her group of three friends. I thrust my hand into the air, my fingers splayed, and waited. Avery did the same, and her friends followed suit. One by one, the other members of the Springville Methodist Church youth group raised their hands and stopped talking.

Why hadn't that woman told me about this magic trick before she'd rushed off? When I had their attention, I cleared my throat and smiled. Oddly, I enjoyed public speaking. There was something much less threatening about talking to a group of strangers. It was just talking to people I knew that scared me.

"Hi, everyone. My name is Ashlyn. I work here at

Sweetwater. And we're going to do something fun today. Has anyone ever been on a scavenger hunt?"

A few kids raised their hands. "This is going to be boring," a little boy said out loud. I didn't let it derail me.

"I want you to count off by fives and you'll be matched up by your numbers. You'll need to work together to find all the items on your list." I held up the papers I'd written on. "Everyone has the same things to find but you won't all have the same answers, and that's okay. When you find an item, describe it as carefully as you can. First team to come back here with a completed list wins."

"What do we win?" An older girl raised an eyebrow at me.

I blanked, but only for a moment.

"Do you like Swedish Fish? Jellybeans?" There was so much candy in the lodge, in all of Deb's stashes, she would never miss it.

The kids cheered.

"Alright, get with your teams and remember to stick together. If a team comes back without all their members, they're disqualified. Go!"

They all ran off. As I watched them study their lists in their small groups and chatter, presumably about the best way to go about ticking off all the items, my heart warmed. I'd done that. They were happy because of me. And I'd done it all by myself. I couldn't help the wide smile that broke out on my face. Maybe I wasn't a one trick pony after all.

Avery's group paused near the entrance to the locker rooms right by the pool. I knew what they were looking for, the one I had listed as "one item that gets you wet." At that location, they could choose the pool, the showers, the sinks, or even the hose used to wet down the pool deck and chairs. I smiled and moved on.

I found another group pointing to the archery range, most likely searching for "something sharp." The smile stayed on my face as I kept walking the trail, by the edge of the lake, and towards the lodge. Occasionally a group would run past me, making a beeline for whatever they'd identified. I spotted the equipment kiosk up ahead and decided to tell Hannah about my great idea.

Chapter 22

I raised my fist to knock on the frame of her open window when I heard her groan from inside.

"Hey, what's wrong?"

Hannah popped her head up to the window and rolled her eyes. "There are kids running rampant all over the campus. Unsupervised. Two little packs of them have already come over here asking if I have anything round. I told them to go jump in the lake."

"You did not." I gave Hannah my best stern look, and she rolled her eyes again.

"I did not. I showed the first group a bocce ball and the second group a Frisbee. They said thanks and ran away. Do you know what's going on?"

"Yes, yes I do. I'm in charge of them and they're on a scavenger hunt. I'm pretty proud of myself for thinking of it, especially since Deb told me I was watching them, oh, about thirty minutes ago."

Hannah shook her head. "Deb is the worst. I'm sorry she stuck you with them. That totally sucks."

"Once I figured out a plan, it didn't suck that much. I'm guessing they should be occupied for at least an hour or so, and then we can share what they found. And then . . . who knows?"

Hannah put a hand in the air. "Back up a minute. How many kids are you talking about exactly?"

"Thirty-two."

I thought her eyes were going to fall out of her head. "Deb left you in charge of thirty-two children? Has she lost it? There are ratios to maintain, and one adult to thirty-two children is way over the acceptable limit."

My heart started to race. "What do you mean? What ratios?"

"There are very strict guidelines for how many children can be supervised by one caregiver. Unless they changed the laws since last summer, it should be no more than fifteen school-aged kids per legal adult. That's why last year I was an assistant lifeguard and couldn't supervise any kid groups on my own. I wasn't eighteen yet."

"I'm not eighteen yet," I whispered.

"Oh, my gosh, I forgot. The ratio is totally off *and* you're not a legal adult?" If Hannah had punctuation floating above her head, it would've been an exclamation mark followed by a question mark, and repeated about a hundred times. "If someone were to come inspect right now, we would be in so much trouble."

"So what do we do?" My knees quivered. This was *exactly* the kind of thing I was afraid of—some kind of huge disaster that my dad would assume was my fault, sending me back to boarding school for another year. If

Sweetwater got written up for these violations, I would never hear the end of it.

"I don't know that there's anything we can do right now," Hannah said with a concerned look. "You can't abandon the kids in the middle of an activity. Plus, we don't want them to think something is wrong and alert their parents or whoever they're with. That would be bad too. I'll close up the kiosk and supervise with you until the adults come back, and then we'll figure out what to do next." She looked at me and realized I wasn't breathing. "Ashlyn? It'll be fine. Take a breath." I did. My heartrate slowed a tiny bit. "We can handle this. Sorry I went off the rails there for a second. It's just one more thing with Deb, you know?"

"I know."

We agreed to take opposite routes around campus, keeping an eye out for the teams, and planned to meet back at the volleyball court. I went toward the lodge while Hannah went uphill in the direction of the ropes course. I spotted a group making their way out of the lodge's front doors with huge grins on their faces.

"Ashlyn! There are gingerbread houses in there!" a tiny boy exclaimed.

"There sure are, buddy. *Handmade*," I said with a smile.

"Is that where the candy is coming from? Are you stealing it from the kitchen?" A girl, maybe nine or ten, gave me a skeptical look.

I laughed. I was pretty sure I'd used that look a lot at her age too. "I'm not stealing." I leaned closer to the kids. "I bought that candy."

One boy shoved another with his elbow. "Come on! One more thing to find and then we win." The whole team dashed off, cheering. Despite my growing anxiety over the situation, at least the kids were having a good time. And, up to this point, nobody had a clue that anything was amiss.

I took a lap around the lodge and then walked through the main hallways. I noticed Deb's office was now dark. *Now where did you go?* What if there was some kind of emergency again and she wasn't there to report it? I didn't want to have to call the paramedics again, and I definitely didn't want to have to try and explain why a minor like me was in charge of a huge group of other minors.

I suddenly regretted putting "something sharp" on the scavenger hunt list of items to find. I could just see the little boy who called the hunt boring looking for ways to make the game more interesting. *Irresponsible*, my dad's voice scolded. My hands began to sweat as I speed-walked to the competition kitchen to make sure none of the knives were out of place. There, I saw the lights were on but the room was thankfully deserted and untouched. *Phew.* Before locking the door behind me, I snagged a few bags of candy to take with me back to the kids and tried not to think about other potential dangers.

Miraculously, everyone made it back to the volleyball court in one piece. When I got there, Hannah was tossing a tennis ball back and forth in her hands while a bunch of the younger kids were making snow angels in the sand. It appeared a group had brought back a broken branch, as "evidence," and another team had started making a daisy chain out of the weed flowers that grew on the edge of the sand. I counted and breathed a sigh of relief. Thirty-two.

"Good work, everyone. Welcome back. Who would like to share their lists?"

About half the kids raised their hands. Hannah and I called on group after group as they read their descriptions for each item found. I was impressed with their creativity and how they defended some of their finds. Two boys, I think they must have been brothers, successfully convinced us that the shoes they were wearing counted for something that gets you wet "because you run and you sweat." I told them they should become lawyers when they got older.

Hannah and I made a big show of deciding who won. A lot of the groups had the same items—the pool for wet things, a ball for round things—and we ultimately decided, after much exaggerated whispering to one another behind our hands, that every team would win.

"You all did such a good job so . . . you all get candy!" I threw my hands up in the air like a gymnast after sticking a landing.

"Participation trophies," Hannah said to me, shaking her head, while the kids all cheered.

"We're trying to call as little attention to ourselves as possible, remember?" I said into her ear. She groaned.

When all our charges were in a bona fide sugar coma, the adults appeared. They looked just as exhausted as the kids, but at least everyone was smiling. Hannah and I told them how well-behaved they'd all been, and then pointed them in the direction of the lodge so they all could get lunch. We waved goodbye until the last of them disappeared down the path. Once they were gone, Hannah grabbed my arms.

"Go get whatever list you've been keeping on Deb. We need to make a plan."

"Yes, ma'am." I grinned at her and pulled out my journal. "List is right here actually."

"I still can't believe you're keeping a blackmail list in your quote journal."

Was she impressed or horrified? "Better to keep it close. Also, would we call this blackmail? We're not going to go wave it in Deb's face, are we?"

"No, I guess not."

"You should probably lay off the espionage movies. Let's go."

In the equipment kiosk, Hannah turned on the laptop she used for checkouts and inventory and pulled up a blank email. "Okay, hit me with your list."

I rattled it off.

1. Disappears for hours at a time without notifying staff of her location
2. Improper food allergy communication with kitchen staff
3. Not enough lifejackets for boats
4. Slow to repair boats
5. Improper staff-to-kid ratios
6. Allows minor to do things only permissible for a legal adult
7. Competition kitchen safety concerns

"There also aren't enough bike helmets," she added. "And the signs in the parking lot indicating a crosswalk and the speed limit are covered by tree branches. I almost got run over by a guest the other day."

I read over what she'd typed. "This is a long list. All these violations . . . we should tell Mr. Allen, right?"

Hannah nodded. "I think it's time."

"Wait, I just thought of something. What if there are more things? I mean, this is only what we've observed, and there are tons of other things that could go wrong here. So many moving parts. Should we scout around some more first?"

"We do want to make sure Mr. Allen takes us seriously." Hannah scratched her head.

This is your supervisor you're about to implicate, said my dad's voice. *What a lack of loyalty.* A wave of guilt hit me. "Before we go to Deb's boss, don't you think we should talk to Deb first? For all we know, there's a perfectly reasonable explanation for her behavior."

Hannah put a hand on her hip. "A perfectly reasonable explanation for violating multiple state laws?"

"Well, she did say we were short staffed this morning. That's not her fault, right?"

Hannah gave me an eyebrow. "A perfectly reasonable explanation for endangering the life of a woman, who paid good money to be here, with a peanut allergy?"

I looked down at my feet. "Maybe you're right. But I do feel bad about the idea of blindsiding her. Don't you?"

"A little," she sighed. "Do you think she's back now?

We *could* go talk to her." I didn't even have to answer, my face said everything. "Come on."

I followed her out of the kiosk, waited for her to lock up, and trudged slowly to the lodge. I wasn't good with confrontation. I'd experienced enough harsh tones, firm lectures, and disappointed stares in my life that I did anything I could to avoid them. I hoped Hannah would take the lead. Especially given what happened last time Deb and I talked.

The office was still dark when we arrived, and the coward in me, who had endured years of criticism, felt overwhelming relief. Hannah and I walked away from Deb's office, past Amos' classroom full of people—bariatric surgeons this time—past the entrance to the cafeteria, and out the back entrance. No Deb in sight. We checked the parking lot. Nothing. It was as if she'd gone up in a puff of smoke.

"Well, we tried. Should we wait for her to come back, or should we go straight to Mr. Allen?" Hannah rocked back and forth on her heels.

Think of your recommendation letter, Ashlyn.

"Let's wait," I said, the guilt tightening my chest. "What else can happen between now and when she gets back anyway?"

And then, in some kind of epic grand gesture, maybe in the universe's evil way of proving me wrong, someone began to scream.

Chapter 23

I have never run so fast in my life. I ran like my feet were on fire while simultaneously being chased by a wicked witch. Tatum wouldn't even recognize the Ashlyn who made it from the lodge to the pool in fifteen seconds flat. Hannah got there just a moment before me and flung open the gate. In the deep end of the pool was the little girl from this morning, Avery Chen, flailing and bobbing up and down in the water between screams. One of the other little girls from Avery's scavenger hunt team stood on the side, screeching, but paralyzed by fear. I understood the feeling.

Without a word, Hannah dove straight into the water, clothes and all. I watched, frozen in place, as my cousin drove her arms into the water in long, confident strokes. My hand covered my mouth when, still inches apart, Avery's face dipped even lower as Hannah reached out for her. She grabbed Avery, just as it seemed she would sink and not resurface, and swam with her in long, strong, confident strokes to the edge of the pool.

"Help me get her up," Hannah called to me, and I

sprang forward. She pushed and I pulled and we got Avery onto dry land. She had gone limp and silent. Hannah climbed out of the pool. "She isn't breathing. I'm going to do CPR. You go call 911. There's a phone in the pool office."

My feet seemed made of lead as I made my way to the office. I couldn't get there fast enough. My brain knew there was only so much time Avery could go without oxygen before she would suffer permanent damage, but help seemed so very far away. My heart beat wildly in my chest, a bass drum booming an ominous rhythm. With shaking hands, I finally reached the door and flung it open.

There was no more time to freak out or think about how small and scared I felt seeing Avery's tiny frame come out of the water, not moving. I ran into the office and snatched the phone and dialed 911 for the second time this summer.

"911, what's your emergency?"

"There's a child who almost drowned here. She's not breathing." Panic zipped through my lungs as I gave the dispatcher the address. *Not breathing.* He took some information on how long Avery was in the water and recorded that a certified lifeguard was performing CPR. I told him how to direct the ambulance to the pool and hung up. The tightness in my muscles released a tiny bit. *They'll be here soon.*

Before I left the office, it dawned on me—where was Mallory? She was the head lifeguard. Shouldn't she have been the one to intervene? I left the office and headed back to the pool. I was elated to see Avery with her eyes open, talking to Hannah. I gave a thumbs-up and went to look for the missing lifeguard.

I went into the women's locker room. "Mallory," I called, my words echoing on the concrete walls all around me. I checked every shower stall and found no one. I went back out and did the same in the men's locker room. Again, nothing. *Weird.* I walked around the perimeter of the locker room building, and as I rounded the last corner, in a shaded area, I heard giggling. I inched closer, my stomach practically in my throat. If Mallory was out here on a contraband phone, or just chatting with another coworker, I couldn't stop myself from getting angry. Somehow confrontation seemed easier when a child's life was in danger.

Another few feet and Mallory's cloud of hair came into view. And just below that hair was a pair of hands, roaming up and down her back. It didn't take a genius to figure out whose hands they were.

"Hey," I said, as sharply as I could muster.

Mallory and Marcus broke apart. Marcus' face went from stunned to annoyed to ice. Mallory at least had the grace to blush.

"Hey, Ash," Marcus said, completely unfazed. He looked at me and licked his lips. Gross. The face I'd once thought handsome and confident just looked entitled and creepy now.

"Hi." Mallory's voice was barely audible. She took a step away from Marcus and looked at her bare feet. I felt a little sorry for her.

"Yeah, so while you two were sucking face, a little girl almost drowned." Mallory gasped. Marcus remained a statue. "I'm not sure how you missed the screaming, but Hannah jumped in and saved her." I stared at them. "You're welcome. An ambulance is on its way. I would suggest you get back to your chairs. We wouldn't want any other kids to go unsupervised." There was bite in my words. I wanted to make them feel bad. I may have spent a fair amount of time this summer kissing Marcus too, but at least I was professional enough to not do it while I was on the clock.

Mallory smoothed her hair behind her ears and rushed off around the building. Marcus and I just stared at each other, waiting for the other to back down. It was clear that any affection I had for him was gone. And if I had to guess, I would say by the lock of his jaw and squint in his eyes, the feeling was mutual.

He broke the chilly silence first. "Look, Ash—"

I put up a hand to silence him. "No, Marcus. Whatever you're going to say is not necessary. If you want to be with Mallory, you don't owe me any apologies or excuses or lines. I don't need them. I just wish you had waited until your shift was over. That little girl could've died."

"Yeah, but she didn't," he countered, so incredibly sure of himself and his safe place in the world. I wanted to punch him. It was the same feeling I got when my dad did things like ordering for the whole table at a restaurant, signing me up for classes or tutoring without asking my interests, or making plans without consulting my schedule. They were small things individually, perhaps, but each one was like a tiny stone that built the pedestal he put himself on. I was nauseous just thinking about it and comparing the two of them.

"But she could've. And that would've been your fault."

"Au contraire. I am not on the clock right now." Marcus was almost smiling.

"But Mallory is. And you distracted her. Which makes you just as culpable as she is."

"Fine," he said taking a step closer. "I didn't hear you complaining about my distracting you last time we were alone."

"Emphasis on the words *last* and *time*."

"That's okay. I typically don't spend time with felons anyway. But you're cute, so I made an exception." Marcus' voice dripped with cruelty as he threw the secret I'd trusted him with in my face. My jaw dropped. Maybe I'd known this was who he really was all along. Surface-level conversations only, even the ones that appeared deeper. Rude, judgy comments. Acting like the world was his for the taking. *Just like my dad.* I knew better than to stick around this time.

I turned on my heel, physically unable to look at his smug face another second. I raced to the pool deck where a group of paramedics were hovering over Avery. I joined Hannah who was standing by, cool and composed, while Mallory bawled and wrung her hands.

"I'm going to go find out if Avery's parents are here. I'm not sure if they came with the group or not," I said to Hannah. There was an incident report to fill out as well and, knowing Deb, I was better off getting it started myself.

"Good call. I'll find you, okay?" Hannah's eyes were dark with worry. "We should probably make another phone call tonight too, yeah?"

I didn't have to ask to whom she meant. We needed to call Mr. Allen. It was past time to tell him what had been going on. "Definitely."

I sprinted back to the lodge and Deb's office. The lights were on, but our manager was nowhere to be seen.

"Shocking," I muttered to myself. I opened the filing cabinet next to the desk and flipped through the folders until I found one labeled "Incident Reports." I pulled out one form and laid it on the desk. As I was shutting the drawer, I saw another folder labeled "Résumés." I pulled it out and opened it, not feeling even a little bit guilty. I knew Hannah had been furious when Mallory had been given the head lifeguard position, and here was my chance to see if she really had more experience. I flipped to the G section and found Mallory Gress—printed in some ridiculous font, triple-spaced, with huge margins. *Does she turn in essays like that too?* My dad, who always insisted on proofreading my work, would've handed it back to me and said, *Make it longer.*

Mallory had graduated from high school two years ago with a middle of the road grade point average and was currently attending a nearby university. She'd spent her summers in high school working at a popular clothing retailer that was in every mall I'd ever been to and served as secretary of the German Club. She'd listed typing and social media as relevant skills. That was it. No mention of swim team. No lifeguard training. Not even first aid. I blinked a few times, just in case I'd missed something, but no. Mallory had absolutely zero qualifications for the position she held. Had she wanted it just so she could look cute in a swimsuit all summer?

I shook my head and put the file back. I pulled my quote journal out and quickly updated the list:

1. Disappears for hours at a time without notifying staff of her location
2. Improper food allergy communication with kitchen staff
3. Not enough lifejackets for boats or helmets for bikes
4. Slow to repair boats
5. Improper staff-to-kid ratios
6. Allows minor to do things only permissible for a legal adult
7. Competition kitchen safety concerns
8. Parking lot signage concerns
9. Hired head lifeguard with no qualifications or certifications
10. Unavailable during crises

Hannah barreled through the door a moment later. "Where's Deb?" she asked.

"Who knows? Where is Deb *ever*?"

"Ugh."

I sighed loudly. "How's Avery?"

"She'll be okay. The other girl, Jasmine, said she and Avery were playing tag and Avery slipped and fell into the pool. Neither of them could swim, which I find odd for girls their age, but at any rate, it was the perfect storm. Non-swimmers plus no lifeguards. Where the heck was Mallory anyway?"

"Kissing Marcus behind the building. Apparently, they were so focused on each other, they didn't hear Jasmine yelling. Which is just ludicrous. We heard her a mile away."

"Are you serious? Whoa. No wonder Mallory wouldn't stop crying. She couldn't even talk she was so upset."

"Wouldn't you be upset if you'd almost let a kid drown and you didn't actually have any lifeguard experience?" I raised one eyebrow at Hannah.

"Shut the front door. For real?"

"For real. I just found her résumé. Mommy hired her daughter who probably hadn't been in a pool since swimming lessons fifteen years ago."

Hannah slowly shook her head. "Deb is in so much trouble." She leaned over to get a better look at my open notebook on the desk. "Wow. This just gets better and better."

"Or worse and worse," I said wryly.

Hannah looked over her shoulder to the door and then back to me. "Do you think there's a file on Deb too?"

My eyes flew open. I locked gazes with Hannah and reached for the drawer where I'd found the résumés. With a shaky hand, I pulled it open and sifted through the files.

No "Deborah Gress," but there was one titled "Manager Candidates." I pulled it out and held it up.

"Here it is," I whispered, holding it up.

Hannah hovered over my shoulder as I opened the folder and flicked through the contents until I saw Deb's name.

Hannah ran a finger down the three most recent positions listed. They were all brand name hotels with references provided. She flipped the page over to find a very complimentary letter from Deb's previous supervisor.

"It all looks fine," I said.

"Maybe." Hannah grabbed the papers, picked up the phone, and dialed. She waited for a moment and then hung up. "Out of service."

Why would a major hotel's number be down? A horrible thought crept over me. "What if she faked this letter?" If she had, what would have made Deb do such a thing? Was she desperate for a job? Did she have something to prove? Maybe this was all just a misunderstanding.

Hannah shrugged. "I think anything is possible at this point. Either way, we have to stick with the facts. Snooping doesn't help our case."

"True. Do you know how to get a hold of Mr. Allen?"

"I'm sure it's in that giant rolodex thing," Hannah said, plucking it off the desk. She flipped through the awkward little cards until she found Fred Allen. She picked up the phone again and held it out to me. "Do you want to call or should I?"

"You go ahead. He knows you. But tell him we need him to come here. This is probably a conversation better had in person."

If I'd learned anything from my father over the years, and that was a short list to say the least, when it came to business, he told me, "You should look someone in the eye when you're giving them bad news. It makes them trust you because it appears like you care, even when you are destroying them." The master of all things fake. Except in this case, I *did* care. Hannah and I both did. I wasn't sure if revealing this news to Mr. Allen would destroy Deb, but it was the truth. And that was one thing my father never taught me.

Chapter 24

Hannah dialed the number and waited while it rang.

"May I speak to Mr. Allen, please?" Pause. "Yes, this is Hannah Zanotti over at Sweet—I'm fine, thanks for asking. Well, that's actually why I was calling. I'm so sorry to drop this on you, but we're having some trouble with Ms. Gress and I was hoping you'd be able to stop by and chat about it. My cousin and I have some information to share with you." Hannah nodded a few times at whatever Mr. Allen was saying. "Great, see you soon. Thank you so much." She dropped the receiver into the cradle.

"Well?"

"Well, he's on his way. Said he'd be here in about thirty minutes." She checked her watch. "We haven't had lunch yet. We should get something now, before he comes."

I wasn't really hungry after what just happened, or what might be yet to come when Mr. Allen got here, but Hannah was right. We hadn't eaten anything since early this morning. We walked to the cafeteria, grabbed two of the few remaining sandwiches, and took a seat at a corner table. I took a reluctant bite of my turkey and cheddar. I wasn't looking forward to throwing Deb under the bus. While she hadn't been the ideal boss by anyone's standards, she'd given me autonomy, and that counted for something, didn't it? She hadn't shot me down when I wanted to add a whole new service to the retreat center. And yet, somehow those small kindnesses for me, which probably weren't intentional, didn't take away the mountain of carelessness she'd shown for everyone else, her own daughter included. I could barely swallow the one bite I'd taken.

"You look like you're going to throw up," Hannah observed.

"I'll eat after we talk, I guess. I don't like confrontation." Understatement of my lifetime.

"Well, good. Because I have no problem with it." Why was I not surprised? "Besides, we're not confronting Mr. Allen. We're just delivering a set of facts. He's the boss, he'll be the one doing the confronting."

"What do you think he'll do?" My voice had shrunk, like it always did when I was scared.

Hannah swallowed a huge bite of her ham sandwich. "I'd like to think he'll fire her. I would." She took another bite, washing it down with a sip of her water. "The thing about Mr. Allen is, he thinks we should provide excellent service to the clients. They pay to come here and, except for when they're with Amos doing some personality test, they shouldn't have to think about anything. We should have it at the ready, he likes to say. The way I see it, Deb's made that harder for a lot of people.

Also," she said, pointing a finger in the air, "some of the stuff she's done is illegal."

I snorted. "True."

"So, I guess we'll see what he does. This place is his baby. I'll be surprised if he doesn't make some kind of move to protect it."

I nibbled the edges of my sandwich, admiring how factual and unemotional Hannah was, while my heart was beating like a rabbit racing from the jaws of a fox. I hoped Mr. Allen wouldn't ask me to talk much. Maybe I could just slide him the list and let Hannah do the rest.

I ended up dumping my sandwich in the trash as Hannah polished off the last crumb of hers. We walked to Deb's office, me like I was on my way to the guillotine, Hannah like she was the superstar attorney about to deliver the evidence that would make the courtroom gasp. Thankfully, the lights were off and Deb was still absent. Hannah took a seat behind Deb's desk, spinning back and forth in the big chair. I slumped in my chair in the corner of the room, trying to make myself so small no one would notice me.

A few minutes later, there was a loud knock at the door. Mr. Allen, looking tanned and summery in a T-shirt and sandals, stood in the doorway, filling most of it with his tall frame.

"Hi, kids. Is this a good place to talk?"

Please, Hannah, take the lead, was my first thought. And then, immediately after, *What if Deb shows up?*

"Why don't we go down to the classroom? This needs to be a private conversation," I suggested.

"Lead the way," said Mr. Allen, stepping aside and gesturing for us to go first. When we were all in the hallway, I reached back inside, turned off the lights, and shut the door.

I didn't do anything wrong, so why does it feel like I'm closing up the office for the last time?

Luckily, the classroom was empty and we each took a seat at one of the desks, which had been arranged in a circle. I pulled out my quote journal, laid it on the desk in front of me, clasped my hands on top of it, and waited for Hannah to begin. Then she looked at me pointedly, waiting for *me* to start. *The list*, I thought. I would just read him the list and Hannah could take it from there.

"Well, Mr. Allen, sir, we asked you to meet with us because we've noticed a number of things Ms. Gress has done this summer that don't seem to be in line with regulations."

"And she definitely doesn't keep things in shape the way Joan did," Hannah added, a note of defensiveness in her voice.

Stick to the facts, keep emotions—and loyalties—to a minimum. For once, Dad was exactly right. "Sir, Hannah and I have compiled a list of items we feel . . . you will also find troubling once you consider the larger picture. In isolation, each one perhaps is not so egregious, but together, well . . . take a look." Hannah mouthed "egregious?" as if she'd never heard the word before, while I passed my notebook to Mr. Allen. Hannah and I held our breath. When he finished, he closed the notebook with a heavy sigh.

"Thank you for bringing this to my attention. I will certainly investigate this matter to the fullest." We exhaled. "Ashlyn, may I make a copy of this?" He held up my notebook.

"Of course."

He nodded. "I'll bring it right back."

While Mr. Allen was gone, Hannah and I said nothing. The anticipation was almost too much to bear. He would investigate? Did that mean he believed the things we told him or not? And if he didn't believe us, what would that mean for the rest of the summer? Suddenly I felt a rush of fear ripple through me. Two employees had the nerve to accuse their boss of wrongdoing. I could kiss my college recommendation letter goodbye. I picked at the new pink polish on my fingers and sent a huge piece spiraling to the ground.

"Hey," Hannah said in a low voice. I looked up and met her eyes. "It's going to be okay. You know that, right?"

I shook my head. I didn't know. It wasn't like I had a great track record of things in my life going right. My dad's face flashed in my mind, stern and disapproving, but silent.

"Mr. Allen is a good owner. He cares about this place. I trust him." Her eyes searched mine. Pleaded. "Do you trust me?"

Did I? Hannah had done a good job of showing me, and everyone else, exactly who she was, at all times. She didn't always think before she spoke. And there were times she spoke her mind when she probably shouldn't.

But she tried to do the right thing. She hadn't judged me or picked on me, which would've been easy to do. And she let me into her world.

"Yes," I said.

"It will be fine. We did the right thing."

Mr. Allen returned my notebook, thanked us again, and assured us he would take care of the situation. As Hannah and I left the classroom, my stomach dropped. Deb was coming down the hall toward us.

"Hello, Fred, what a pleasant surprise." Deb smiled in a way I hadn't seen all summer. Was that her professional smile, reserved just for her superior?

"Deb, let's go into your office. I've got a few things I'd like to discuss." Mr. Allen's voice was curt, but not unpleasant. If it had been me he was talking to, I doubted I would've suspected I was about to be pushed into an oven and covered in flames.

"It would be my pleasure," Deb said, looking me and Hannah up and down suspiciously, before turning and walking away with Mr. Allen trailing behind her.

I gulped and looked at Hannah, who pushed me lightly away from the train wreck we were leaving behind.

Early the next day, we got word that all morning activities would be postponed for an emergency staff meeting in the cafeteria. A skeleton kitchen crew would serve bagels and fruit to the guests out on the lawn and everyone else was to meet with Mr. Allen. It was the first time we'd all been together in a big group since the bonfire our first week here. I perched on the edge of my seat, hands folded in my lap to keep them from shaking.

I'd barely slept the night before. I tossed and turned so much that Hannah finally smacked the bottom of my bunk in the middle of the night and told me to be still because she felt like we were on a boat rocking back and forth. I tried counting sheep, but their faces kept turning into Deb's face, and then my dad's. So, when I heard Hannah snoring gently, I got out a tiny flashlight, something Aunt Greta had hidden in my suitcase, and the *Bartlett's* Bax had bought for me. I passed the hours writing down the lines that gave me hope.

> HOPE AGAINST HOPE, AND
> ASK TILL YE RECEIVE.
> *James Montgomery*

> THE UNIVERSE IS CHANGE; OUR LIFE
> IS WHAT OUR THOUGHTS MAKE IT.
> *Marcus Aurelius*

> HOPE, LIKE THE GLEAMING TAPER'S LIGHT,
> ADORNS AND CHEERS OUR WAY.
> *Oliver Goldsmith*

> AWAKE, MY SOUL! STRETCH EVERY
> NERVE, AND PRESS WITH VIGOUR ON.
> *Philip Doddridge*

Because, this was about more than Deb and the job. This was about me. As much as I didn't want to admit it, I was always going to be trying to meet my dad's expectations, no matter how high they were. He'd made me believe that I wasn't there yet, but maybe? I hated myself for thinking that way, but it was hard to change what you'd been taught to believe your whole life. I finally fell asleep around four or so, but Hannah's bouncing out of bed at six woke me, my mind and body detached from sheer exhaustion.

I searched the cafeteria for the usual suspects. Baxter had joined me and Hannah, while Ruth and Amos sat in the back, sipping coffee with confused expressions and talking in anxious whispers. My skin crawled with anticipation. The majority of the kitchen staff, the grounds crew, and the athletic instructors were all there. But there were three faces noticeably absent from the group—Deb, Mallory, and Marcus.

Mr. Allen walked out of the kitchen to address the group, a clipboard in his hand. "Hey, everyone. Thanks for joining me this morning. I'm sure you're wondering why I've assembled the staff, so I won't beat around the bush. Deborah Gress will no longer be with us at Sweetwater. It was brought to my attention that a number of important regulations were violated over the course of the last several weeks and, while I certainly understand human error, I cannot, and will not, put the safety of our guests or this staff in danger. I will serve as manager for the remainder of this season, with Amos as my backup, and will work on hiring someone for the fall." He looked out over the crowd, his face still as granite, giving away nothing. "We've also had a handful of other jobs become vacant, so I'll be shuffling positions and asking some of you to cover them. Please know that I value the hard work you've done thus far. The care you've given to our guests has not gone unnoticed. It's difficult to serve well without good leadership, and I'm proud of the way you've given it your all. Does anyone have any questions before I read out the new assignments?"

The crowd was silent. The lack of questions made me think that I must not have been the only one who had noticed Deb's missteps. And that realization felt like relief. Like I hadn't screwed up. Like maybe I'd made their lives a little easier too.

Chapter 25

Mr. Allen assigned Hannah to the head lifeguard position. *Poetic justice.* He promoted one of the junior lifeguards, who had turned eighteen two weeks ago. Hannah was elated, her chest puffed up like a rooster. And although it was the job she should've had since the day we got here, I was glad she hadn't. Otherwise, she and I would have never bonded like we had. I was happy for her, but it also meant less time to hang out now since she would be much busier. Still, she deserved it and I wouldn't want it any other way.

I, somewhat predictably, had been reassigned Hannah's old job at the equipment kiosk. I didn't really mind. It would give me time to think, time to breathe now that I wasn't worrying about Deb. It would also give me a quiet space to put together sightseeing packages for any retreaters who might want one.

"Ashlyn, I've gotten so many compliments from our guests. I don't know why I never thought about adding offsite excursions to our packages, but I'm certainly glad you did. You're quite the creative thinker," Mr. Allen said with a smile as he handed me the keys to the kiosk.

I beamed. It had been a long time since someone complimented my work, or anything about me for that matter. "Thank you, sir. That means a lot to me." My dad's voice was suspiciously quiet.

Mr. Allen nodded. "Maybe you have a career in tourism."

It wasn't something I'd ever considered, but if it allowed me to make people happy, I wouldn't rule it out. It seemed to work for Uncle Ed and Aunt Greta. "I'll consider it, sir."

After the rest of the staff had started their shifts, Mr. Allen asked me and Hannah to follow him to the office. He closed the door behind us and motioned for us to sit down.

"I want to offer my deepest gratitude." His lip quivered with emotion. "When I followed the leads you gave me, I found many other distressing things about the way my retreat center had been run this summer, and I am grateful to you both for documenting what you observed and bringing it to me. Obviously, the two 911 calls are at the top of the list of things that should not have happened, but the overall neglect and lack of care was pervasive. The absolute worst thing you can be, as the manager of this type of operation, is careless, even if you're the nicest person in the world. So, I thank you for speaking up."

Deb definitely wasn't the nicest, but she wasn't the most evil either. I was glad Mr. Allen pointed this out. His opinion lessened the guilt that was slowly fading. It did, however, remind me that lying and lack of attention to what was happening around you, despite your demeanor, landed you in hot water. It did for my dad, and for Deb.

He continued, "Now, normally I keep hiring decisions confidential, but I discovered Ms. Gress had not been truthful about her previous employment." *I knew it.* "Also, I thought you deserved to know that not only did I let Ms. Gress go, but also her daughter, Mallory, and Marcus Toft. I've been around this place long enough to know that staff romances are inevitable." I blushed and hoped he didn't notice. Not that a few kisses with Marcus counted as a romance, but still. "But it is unacceptable to leave your post and create a dangerous situation." He shook his head. "We're lucky that girl's parents aren't pressing charges." Then Mr. Allen smiled. "You two are heroes. Plain and simple. Thank you."

I blushed again, this time with pride. I couldn't wait to tell Tatum about all of this. And my mom. And, if I was being totally honest, I really wanted to tell my dad. Maybe he would be proud of me. Maybe this time I would be enough.

I spent my first day in the equipment kiosk handing out tennis rackets, soccer balls, and lifejackets. It was quite the change from the empty office and the nearly deserted gym. I didn't have to shuffle through piles of disorganized paperwork, and I didn't smell like disinfectant. What I did do was work on my project, in between equipment handouts and returns, that is. I made phone calls to wineries and scenic caverns, working them into packages of varying prices and lengths of time. I connected with the owner of a charter bus company who offered me a discount for our retreaters because she worked for Mr. Allen years ago and wanted to pay it forward. Which gave me a great idea. I could use my new connections to pay it forward too. I started formulating an idea—my way of saying thanks to the people here at Sweetwater who had made my summer, whether they realized it or not, more bearable than I ever could have hoped for.

It was amazing how much my mood had lifted with the removal of Deb and her chaos and a few positive interactions with other people. And, when I'd done all those things and there was a lull in the requests, I pulled out my quote journal and reread the lines I'd copied last night. I looked back at some of the ones I'd recorded years ago, the song lyrics and wishes of a girl looking for something. Anything.

Near the end of my shift, Bax knocked on my window. "Hey there." His smile was easy, and I couldn't help but smile back.

"Hey, yourself."

"I just stopped by the pool, and Hannah's tied up for another few hours. Pool party. Want to join me for dinner? I was thinking of roasting some hot dogs at the firepit."

"Yes," I said, probably a little too quickly. I looked away, in case he noticed how eager I was.

"Great. Meet you out there when you get off?"

My heart began to flutter. "Sure, do you need me to bring anything?"

"Nah, I'll take care of it." He waved and headed toward the lodge.

I watched him walk away and smiled to myself. Dinner with Baxter. Alone. So what if he stopped to ask Hannah if she could join in first. And so what if she was only not coming because she had to work. It would be the first time we'd been alone since he taught me to ride a bike. And before that, the zipline. My heartbeat drummed with anticipation that was pleasant, and also terrifying.

The seconds ticked by like hours, and I felt silly for being so nervous. Who got nervous about eating hot dogs? Me, apparently. When it was finally quitting time, I closed up the kiosk, fumbling with the keys, dropping them twice before I managed to get the door locked. I dropped them a third time trying to open my cabin door so I could change into a clean T-shirt. *Get it together, Ash.*

I considered stopping by the pool to see if Hannah had any advice for talking to Bax, but then I stopped myself. I knew how to hold a conversation. I'd talked to plenty of people—and many of them boys—in my lifetime. And still, there was something about anticipating small talk with a boy who was so careful with his words. And bonus, he knew my secrets, and he'd offered to talk if I wanted. Did I want to talk? I wasn't sure yet. I figured I had approximately two minutes on the walk over to the firepit to figure it out, though.

When I got there, the fire was crackling in the nearly setting evening sun, but no Baxter. I settled myself on a tree stump and, partly out of habit, partly out of the nervous need to have something to do with my hands, I pulled out my quote journal. It fell open on my lap and my eyes landed on a quote I'd written several years ago.

SET YOUR LIFE ON FIRE. SEEK THOSE
WHO FAN YOUR FLAMES.
Rumi

It felt like a sign. I slid my purple pen out of the spine of the journal, stood up, and wrote Rumi's words on my log seat, waiting a moment for the ink to dry before sitting back down.

A moment later, I heard the crunching of footsteps on gravel and fallen leaves. Without announcing himself, Bax sat down and methodically put two hot dogs on the metal rods he'd brought. He handed one to me, and we leaned over together, sticking our dinners into the flames.

"So, that was pretty brave what you did. Talking to Mr. Allen about Deb, I mean," he said.

I shrugged. "I didn't think there was any other choice. People were getting hurt."

He looked at me and smiled, his crooked tooth visible. A cute flaw. "Are you a superhero in disguise?"

I scoffed. "Hardly. That was probably the first brave thing I've ever done, actually."

"I doubt that. Most people are braver than they think. I see it every day. With the ziplines and ropes course. They almost always jump down from the wall." Baxter turned his hot dog, and I did the same.

"Is that your metaphor for life?"

He laughed. "I guess it is."

"And what about the people who don't jump? What does that say about them?"

Baxter thought for a minute, his elbows resting comfortably on his knees, hot dog almost crispy from the fire. "I think they aren't ready. They always have the choice though. One time, this woman who decided not to jump with her group came back a few hours later and told me she wanted to try again."

"And?"

"And she did it. She just needed a little more time."

His story reminded me of something I hadn't ever told anyone before. And because there was no reason not to, I jumped.

"Once, in eighth grade, my parents took me to therapy. It was really out of character for them, because my dad is so concerned with what people think of us and how a mental health incident"—I made air quotes—"might follow me for the rest of my life. I'd had a really rough month. I'd come in fourth place at the regional spelling bee, which sent my dad over the edge, which spiraled into me getting a couple of Cs on tests, and that just made it worse. I wasn't sleeping and was almost always anxious. I'm pretty sure a teacher tipped off the school counselor that I might be stressed and then the counselor made a referral. Not wanting to look like an uncaring parent, my dad made an appointment to check the box."

"So what happened?"

"I sat down with this guy who asked me about my life and I talked. I didn't spill my guts but I was honest enough." When he asked me how I got along with my parents, though, it was like the dam broke. I could still feel the ghosts of scalding hot tears from that day on my cheeks. "I told him how my dad was constantly picking at me, that his expectations were too high, that there wasn't a ladder on the planet tall enough to even get close to reaching them. I said I'd probably fall off and break into a million pieces before I could get halfway."

"Impossible."

"But it felt true. Still does. And when I'd left four tissues, completely shredded, on the floor at my feet, he looked at me thoughtfully and asked if I wanted to change the relationship. I remember looking back at him like he was from outer space."

"And then?"

"He told me something I will never forgot. I think about it all the time, actually. He said I had a choice. I didn't *have* to change my relationship with my dad. I'd been enduring it my whole life, so if I thought I could continue to do that and live with the results, that was fine. Or, I could choose to speak up and try to change it. But he made sure I knew that it was a choice. He said sometimes accepting status quo is the right thing to do and perhaps that was the right thing for me at the time."

Baxter slid his hot dog off his rod and onto a paper plate. "Was it?"

"Maybe. Because that's what I did. I never went back to see that therapist. I told my father afterward that it was a waste of time and he said he knew it would be. But he sure as heck emailed the school counselor to say he had taken me so she would get off his back."

Bax took my hot dog from me and put it on another plate. "So you thought the therapist was wrong?"

I paused. I'd sat in that office so many years ago, completely convinced that keeping my head down and plowing through until I could leave the house for good was the right thing to do. It had been a relief to hear him say I could carry on as is.

"Maybe not wrong, but it was more familiar. It was easier to believe my father's opinion that therapy wasn't something I needed to think about. So, in some ways, that was my choice too."

Baxter waited a few beats before speaking again. "And do you still think it was the right choice?"

I was quiet. Heat crept onto my face, down my neck, and to the tips of my ears. I was glad for the darkness of the setting sun and only the flickering light of the fire. "Maybe not."

Chapter 26

I went to therapy too," Baxter said, after we'd both finished our hot dogs in comfortable quiet. His words broke through the sounds of crickets and the distant laughter coming from the pool. "I was acting out a lot in elementary school. Knocking over chairs and yelling at other kids for no reason."

I couldn't picture perpetually-calm Bax yelling at anyone, let alone being violent. "Not you."

"Oh, definitely me. It was hard to be a little boy without a dad. My mom tried her best, but she couldn't be both parents at the same time, and I think I was still struggling with my dad's leaving."

"Well, it must have worked," I said.

He laughed softly. "Hard work. I drew a lot of pictures of my family and role-played with a lot of stuffed animals. And I eventually learned how to control myself and my feelings. I think that's partly why I do this job. You have to be in control of yourself to help others take on new challenges."

I mulled over what he said. Was I in control of myself?

"Are you trying to say I need to be in control of myself to talk to my parents?"

Bax gazed at me, the flames making shadows on his face, highlighting his strong jaw and turning his hair to gold. "I don't know that I was talking about you specifically, but I think it could apply to your situation."

I opened my mouth to talk, closed it, and opened it again. "I want to go home. I miss my own bed. I miss my best friend. I miss my old high school. I miss my life, as uncomfortable as it is. I feel like my whole life has been on pause for the last year and, just when I was about to press play again, I fast forwarded to some weird alternative universe I don't recognize."

"Tell me about home. The parts you miss."

No one had ever asked me that before. Not Hannah. Not Uncle Ed or Aunt Greta. Not the girls at Blue Valley who looked at me curiously and wondered why I was suddenly at school with them. "My best friend Tatum and I like to have dance parties. We close my bedroom door and turn on terrible old disco music and sing into our hairbrushes like they're microphones."

"My mom does that in the kitchen, except she sings obnoxious country music into a wooden spoon," Bax said with a grin.

"I like your mom."

"I do too."

"And I love trivia and collecting facts. I was on the Quiz Bowl team and did spelling bees and geography bees my whole life. The teachers and coaches were always kind and encouraging to me. I collect words too, but you already know that." I held up the quote journal that had been resting in my lap. "I guess that makes me a bit of a nerd."

"Hey, I'm a nerd too. Nothing wrong with that."

"You graduated really early, right?"

"Yep. That came out of my therapy, I think. I got really involved in school, realized I was good at it, skipped a grade, and voila. Working full time has allowed me to save a lot of money. If I ever decide I want to go to college."

I resisted raising my eyebrows. "That's kind of a given for me."

"Do you want to go?"

I'd never really thought about it, but it was something I'd always assumed I would do. At any rate, I definitely looked forward to being out on my own. This summer had proven to me I could survive, even if my dad wasn't convinced. "Yeah, I think I do. I have no idea what I want to major in or do with my life, though." I laughed. "Mr. Allen suggested I go into tourism."

Baxter nodded. "The retreaters seem happy with your plans. Were you happy making them?"

"Yeah. I was." I'd had a purpose, making those plans. There wasn't anyone pressuring me to win an award or be the best. I'd done it solely to make someone else feel good. Which made *me* feel good.

He nodded again. "Do what makes you happy."

I smiled. "My best friend says that a lot."

"One hand in front of the other," Baxter said. It was hard to believe the first time he'd said that to me, on the zipline when I was so awkward and embarrassed, was just a few weeks ago. We'd come a long way since then. I'd come a long way.

We were both quiet for a moment, lost in thought.

"What would you do if you had nothing else to do?" Baxter asked, breaking the silence. "Your perfect day?"

If someone had asked me before I got to Sweetwater, my answer would probably have involved something like going to a movie or maybe a trip to the salon for a fancy pedicure. Or, if money was no object, traveling—maybe to Paris to practice my French. But now? With the stars beginning to wink and a full moon rising overhead, I didn't really want to be anywhere but right here.

"Actually, this is good."

"Me too," Bax agreed. "This *is* good."

I was laying on my top bunk reading from the *Bartlett's* when Hannah burst in, towel wrapped around her waist, still in her navy tank suit. A whistle dangled from her neck.

"Gosh, I missed that." There was a smile in her voice.

I closed the book and sat up in bed. "Missed what?"

"Lifeguarding. It's so fun. I love sitting in that chair and watching everyone splashing and doing handstands and playing Marco Polo."

I snickered. "You like being in charge and having power."

She shrugged her Hannah-shrug. "Maybe. I also

like knowing that if something goes wrong, I can fix it. Unlike some people we used to know. What have you been up to? Shut up in here?"

I hesitated. "I had hot dogs with Baxter at the firepit."

"Just the two of you?" She didn't really sound surprised. Had she known he was going to ask me?

"Yes." My face warmed, as if I was still sitting by the fire.

"Did you have fun?"

Fun wasn't exactly the right word, but I'd definitely enjoyed myself. There was something about Baxter that calmed me. And made me talk. I liked how he never pushed and didn't offer too much advice or force his opinions on me. "We talked about my parents. And home."

"Did he convince you to talk to your dad yet?" Hannah's voice took on a defensive edge.

Was she mad at me now? "I'm still thinking about it." The idea of having a choice had been hovering over me since I left Baxter by the fire and returned to the cabin. Realistically, there was no reason not to shake things up, but in my heart? I wasn't sure. The idea of letting the words I'd said in my head over and over actually come out and be heard by the person with all the power was scary. I was still sitting on the fence, looking over. Or the wall, I guessed.

"Do you think you'll have a decision soon? I mean, you're kind of stuck with me now and I would like to have my cousin around for holidays and stuff. I feel like your dad robbed me, you know?"

I smiled at her unexpectedly kind words. "I'd like that too, Hannah. That really means a lot."

"I think *my* dad would probably like having his brother back too. I know he misses that relationship."

I had no idea how my dad would feel about patching things up with Uncle Ed. I didn't even know why they stopped talking. But I wanted to believe my dad missed his brother, even if he was too proud to say so. "I'll add it to the list of things to bring up." If I ever brought them up. I knew my mom would be coming home soon. The clock was ticking. My time was limited. And I knew it was my decision to say something or not.

"Here's the part I don't get," Hannah said abruptly. "Why aren't you angry? Your dad has totally laid out your life for you, stomped on your preferences and choices, and trained you to think he's right." The look on Hannah's face said she was willing to be angry for the both of us if I wasn't.

"Who said I'm not angry?"

"Well, you never say so. You never look like you're angry. I see you look sad and disappointed, and sometimes wistful or even scared, but never angry."

Years of cultivated suppression, I could've answered. Some by my father's reaction to things I would do—towering over me after I brought home a B on a test, telling me to change my outfit, commenting on my choice of friends, boyfriends, school activities, etc. Some by me. My choice. *Self-preservation.*

Hannah charged ahead. "If it were me, I would be smashing things. I would be sending angry letters to my dad, telling him I refuse to be treated this way."

"You have to feel brave to do stuff like that, like

your effort would matter," I said. "Other than talking to Mr. Allen this week, I've never felt brave." Despite what Baxter said, I couldn't believe it about myself. Not yet.

"That's crap. You are brave. You took charge of the off-campus tours here. That was brave. You collected evidence on Deb and presented it to Mr. Allen. That was brave. You told Marcus to take a hike. That was brave. Don't tell me you're not brave."

"It's a lot harder to stand up to the person who taught you to keep your mouth shut and do as you're told. Not everything is black and white. Most things are more complicated and gray. At least for me." I tried to think of an example that would make sense to my emboldened cousin. "Do you know the term *learned helplessness*?" She shook her head. "We talked about it in psychology class last year. It's the idea that when you are constantly shut down and told, or shown, that you can't or shouldn't do something, you learn and begin to believe that you can't do it. When in fact, you can. There was a famous experiment that used dogs and electric shocks. The dogs became conditioned to think they couldn't get away from the shocks. So they just laid down and accepted them. Even though they were in pain."

Anger clouded Hannah's face. "That's horrible. Inhumane."

I nodded. "A lot of older experiments would never be performed today. But the point is, we adapt to our environment, and if part of your environment is teaching you to lay down and take it, many times you do. Why do you think victims of abuse frequently don't leave? It's hard to believe in yourself when someone is constantly telling you that you're nothing."

Hannah got quiet before speaking again. "Would you call what your dad does abuse?"

"I don't know. Emotional abuse maybe." I'd looked up the definition once. A lot of what my dad had said over the years fit, but it was hard to admit it. "He's manipulative, that's for sure. But you're wrong. I *am* angry. I am filled with white-hot rage a lot of the time. I've just learned from a lifetime of being in my family, from being me, and from observing his interactions with my mother, that he wins no matter what." My shoulders sagged with the burden of the pain. "I learned that I have a choice. I made the choice to be quiet and bide my time." I looked down at my hands in my lap. "It's hard. Knowing exactly what you are and hating it. When I read about learned helplessness, saw the pictures of those dogs, it hit me as hard as if someone had punched me in the stomach. They were me."

Hannah eyed me. "But?"

I sighed. "But what?"

"But I don't think you can stay quiet anymore. And you know it too. You're not that helpless dog now. At some point, it has to hurt more than speaking up, doesn't it? You want to go home. You want to be with Tatum. You want to be with your mom. And really, what say does your dad have in any of this right now? He's in freaking prison. He can't physically stop you from moving back into your house. He can't unenroll you from your high school. This sounds like the perfect opportunity for you and your mom to empower each other." She paused and inspected my face. "Right?"

It sounded so good. I wanted this picture Hannah was painting to be my life. "Maybe you're right. Maybe I'm ready to say something." *Maybe.*

Hannah put her arms around me and hugged me tight. "I'm gonna quote you on that."

I put my head on her shoulder, like I'd done with Tatum so many times. "Okay."

Chapter 27

A few days later, I returned to my cabin after my shift at the equipment kiosk to find a package and a letter sitting on my bed. Had Hannah picked them up for me? I doubted it; she'd become so busy lately that she was rarely anywhere other than the pool. Could it have been Bax? I grinned to myself at the idea that he'd been thoughtful enough to retrieve my mail and leave it for me here.

I looked at the letter first. It had a return address of Williams Correctional Facility, complete with a stamp in angry red ink as if to say, "Make no mistake, this was sent from a federal prison." A brick dropped into my stomach. I hated that the very thought of my father made me anxious. Somehow, it was worse now as I was getting closer and closer to D-Day. Decision Day.

Reluctantly, I slid a finger in the seam and ripped it open. Inside was a piece of lined notebook paper, the kind I had taken notes on at school for years. My dad's handwriting, predictably neat and uniform, spelled out the date, which was ten days ago.

Dear Ashlyn,

How are you? I'm writing to you on paper I bought at the commissary with the money I earned mopping the floors. I also bought packages of ramen and spices and stamps. My friends gave me a tip that these things can be used to barter with other inmates, so I took their advice. I haven't had to use them yet, but every day is different here, so better safe than sorry.

I dropped my hands for a moment and stared out into the empty cabin. *Unbelievable. Dad never takes advice from anyone.* I continued reading, shaking my head.

The food leaves a lot to be desired, so it's understandable that spices are in high demand. The stamps, obviously, are for writing to friends and family. I hope you're continuing to work hard. I know you're doing a good job. Write if you get a minute.

Dad

In many ways, it had all the hallmarks of any conversation with my dad. He talked about himself. He showed zero emotion. He reminded me to work hard. And yet, that line near the end gave me pause. *I know you're doing a good job.* Did he? Did my dad *know* I was doing a good job? Despite so many years proving otherwise, I hoped in the very recesses of my heart that he did. That he knew I tried my best. Always. That, somehow, he realized that I needed to hear him say so. It was just a crumb, but it was something. I read it again. And again. And again. Until I finally had to shove the letter under Hannah's pillow because I couldn't breathe.

Only after I had regained my composure did I pick up the package. The address was written in sparkly green marker, my first clue to the sender's identity. The second clue was the stick figure drawing on the back of the package—a girl I assumed was supposed to be me based on the very long lashes drawn on her face—in front of a giant house that looked vaguely like mine. A speech bubble next to stick-Ashlyn's face said, "Home sweet home!"

"I hope so," I said to the drawing. It felt so close. I just needed to ask. No big deal. And if my dad *knew* I was doing a good job here . . . I ripped open the top of the package and turned it over on the bed. Out slid a small, square hardcover book. It was purple, of course, and on the front was a photograph of me and Tatum from Homecoming our sophomore year. I smiled at the memory it ignited. The picture was one of a series taken that night at our local department store. We hadn't actually made it to the dance, mostly because of my terrible radar when it came to picking dates, but instead had capped off our evening with an impromptu photo shoot as a way to make ourselves feel better about the crappy evening. This photo was the twin with the one that had sat, framed, on my dresser at school last year. Tatum and I were posed as if we were each other's date for the dance. A hand on a shoulder, an arm around a waist, stiff smiles. I laughed, remembering how much fun it had been after realizing our Prince Charmings were actually charmless.

And, bonus, it was a nice memory to hold onto the next day when my dad lectured me about making good choices and spending time with "quality people," which was an obvious implication that my date was not.

Also on the cover, in a swirly font, it read, "Dear Ash, Love Tate." I ran a finger over the words. We'd spent this summer and last, plus the year in between, writing to each other more than actually being in the same room. I wondered if this was how our relationship would always be—lived more in writing and on screens instead of in person.

The next page was the dedication: *For my best friend who is on her way home*

Ever the optimist, I thought. And then out loud, "It's so far from a done deal, friend." I flicked through the rest of the pages. Tatum, genius that she was sometimes, had made an album of hope for me. She put in photograph after photograph of our childhood memories, combined with ones from the past year and this summer. There we were in seventh grade, wearing the gym uniforms we hated so much that we often talked about burning them and anonymously sending the ashes to our gym teachers. There was one of Tatum, her boyfriend Seamus, and her friends Abby and Hunter, at Seamus' high school graduation this past June. Seamus looked handsome in his cap and gown, his arm snugly around Tatum's waist as she kissed his cheek while Abby and Hunter smiled happily at them. Tatum's stepsister, Tilly, dancing across a stage at what I guessed was her final high school performance. Tatum and me in ninth grade rocking out in my room in our pajamas, lip-syncing into our hairbrushes. Seamus and Hunter's band, The Frisson, performing last summer on a stage covered in twinkle lights. Tatum and Abby working on the school paper. Tatum and Tilly posing over a mixer in the kitchen, waving spatulas. Entwined around the pictures were graphics of flower garlands, stars, geometric shapes in patterns—all things I knew Tatum had designed herself.

There's more of this waiting for you when you get here.

The last page of the magical little book was the one that made me cry. I'd cried an awful lot this summer. I'd cried an awful lot in the last year, actually. I'd been upset at what had become of my life, and rightfully so. But this time, it was the possibility of what *could* be that started the waterworks.

Tatum cleverly chose a photograph from my family's annual Christmas party a few years ago. Every December, Mom and Dad had the house decorated with glitter and snowflakes and lights and at least five trees throughout the house. Though the party was for Dad's clients, this was Mom's baby. She was in her element, choosing the food from the caterer's menu, selecting the perfect outfit and jewelry, checking off the RSVPs. I had to admit, I loved it too. Getting ready for that party—when I was small, with Mom, when I got older, with Tatum—was so special. It was the first time I was allowed to wear makeup. It was the first time I was allowed to wear shoes with heels. Sometimes I was allowed to carry drinks or trays of appetizers to the guests. There was always an overwhelming feeling of being almost an adult at that party. It was the most special night of my year.

In the photograph, I stood at the bottom of the curved stairs in our foyer. The railing was decorated with pine boughs, red velvet ribbons, and white lights. I was wearing a navy-blue dress; my dad's pearl hung, floating on its silver chain at my neck. Tatum, in a white and gold sweater dress, stood next to me, our elbows grazing, with Tilly on her other side in a pale pink dress. Behind us, up the staircase, were our parents. Moms in the middle, dads at the top. My dad's hand rested on my mother's shoulder and her face was turned, just a little, to the side, as if she were trying to catch a glimpse of him. Around us, all over the foyer, were guests holding champagne glasses, raised in a toast. We were smiling. Our cheeks were pink. We looked happy. We looked like a family. The family I always hoped we would become.

Sneaky Tatum. She knew exactly what she was doing by making this photo the grand finale of her little book. This photo was hard evidence that we'd been that happy family, even for the half a second it took for the flash to go off and capture our image forever. It happened once, it could happen again.

I turned the last page over and noticed there was more. Written on the jacket page were messages. Handwritten. There was one from Tatum, of course, telling me she was counting the days until I got back and she'd have a pint of mint chocolate chip ready and waiting. I loved her for knowing just what I needed.

But it was the messages that followed hers that left a lump in my throat. One was from Abby telling me she was going to recruit me to write for the paper next year. One was from Seamus telling me to hurry home so he didn't have to listen to Tatum say how much she missed me all the time. Another was from Hunter, which wasn't actually a message since we didn't really know each other, but song lyrics from Edward Sharpe and the Magnetic Zeros.

Home is wherever I'm with you.

There was even a note from Tatum's step-grandmother, Blanche, whom I'd met last summer and liked instantly. She wrote a phrase in Spanish and then translated it for me.

¡Levántate! ¡El sol sale para todos! Get up! The sun rises for everybody.

They were more Tatum's support network than mine, but there was the promise that I would be welcomed into the fold when I got home. Goosebumps ran up and down my arms as I closed the book and hugged it to my chest. It was enough—just the thing I needed to push me over the edge and leap. Hannah and Baxter were right. I needed to find my voice and use it. I'd spent so much time saying things in my head, never letting those thoughts come off my lips. I'd used the words of others to express myself, protecting myself. I wrapped myself in an armor of silence and the written words of other people. But now? I could draw strength from those words in a different way. I could use them to give me courage to break out and say what I needed to say.

> Dear Tate,
>
> Thank you for the book. It's the nicest thing anyone has ever given me. I'm lucky to have a friend like you in my life. Please thank the others for their

messages as well. I'm looking forward to seeing them. And because I know you're wondering, I'm going to ask. Soon.

Love always,
Ash

I picked up the envelope to throw it away and heard something rattling. I shook it and a pen fell out, along with a tiny folded piece of paper.

Give this pen to Hannah and your friends from work. They need to sign this book too.

XO, Tate

My breath caught in my throat as I gripped the pen. There was only one way to repay her kindness. Call my mother and tell her I was ready to come home.

Chapter 28

*I*t took a few days of missed messages before I finally connected with my mother. In that time, I had reserved new touring packages for a group of local school board members, the employees from a restaurant supply company, and another family reunion, though not quite as fun as the Patels. I also went on another bike ride into town with Hannah, this time to get souvenirs—a fridge magnet for my mom and a package of soup mix for Uncle Ed and Aunt Greta. A thank-you gift, really. I had no idea what to get for my relatives who had taken me in, no questions asked. Nothing quite said, "I appreciate you more than I can say, and I hope you invite me back soon because I need more family," but I hoped it was a start.

I had also spent a lazy afternoon with Baxter, just lying on the bridge at the ropes course and listening to the stream burble beneath us, reading—him, a biography of Theodore Roosevelt, and me, the copy of *Leaves of Grass* I'd bought on our first trip into Sweetwater. It was nice to just sit near someone and say nothing and feel no pressure to fill the space with small talk. It was more than nice, actually. I tried not to steal glances at Baxter, but I know he caught me more than once. Which meant he was watching me too.

As I was walking into the office to print out an itinerary for the family reunion's day trip, the phone rang. Mr. Allen, looking much more authoritative than Deb ever did sitting at the big desk, now cleaned off and organized, held the phone out to me.

"Your mom," he mouthed. He got up to let me sit down in his place and left to give me some privacy.

"Hi, Mom," I said, a little breathless.

"Hi, Honey, I'm glad I caught you," Mom said, sounding clear. Mindful. Energized. I felt like the woman from earlier in the summer—the one who couldn't get out of bed to pack a suitcase—had vanished. I knew enough about depression to know that she wasn't gone forever, that she'd put in an appearance from time to time, but it was comforting to know that my mom would be prepared for the next time she showed up.

"You sound good," I ventured.

"I feel good. I feel like me again. Isn't that amazing?"

"I'm glad," I said, smiling into the receiver.

"And how are you? Work still going well? Are you getting along with Hannah?"

I smiled again. I hoped she could hear it in my voice. "Yeah, everything is good here too." And it was the truth. Everything at Sweetwater, for once, was great. My side-gig as our guest's local travel agent had been well-received. Hannah and I were not just cousins, but real friends. And now that Deb was out of the picture, and I was no longer sneaking around with Marcus, I felt a little more like me again too. The me I wanted to be anyway. Hanging out with Baxter didn't hurt either.

"I'm glad. I know this hasn't been the summer we wanted, but maybe it was the summer we needed."

It felt like there was more she wanted to say. "What do you mean?"

"Well, that's partly why I wanted to talk to you today. My therapist has been helping me formulate a plan. For when I get back home, which should hopefully be soon." My heart leapt into my throat. Did that mean I would be going home soon too? I hoped, I hoped, I hoped. "She's already got me connected with a therapist not far from our house."

"That's great, Mom."

"Yeah, I'm looking forward to meeting her." I was so proud of my mom, putting herself out there in such a vulnerable way, without pride or shame. "Your father will be gone for some time still." I knew. I was painfully aware of that fact. "And while there's money for me to live on and for your tuition . . ." I winced. ". . . I've been learning a lot about how to be self-reliant. I've depended on your father, and the people he hires, for entirely too long. If I had been more involved or aware, I might have been able to prevent what happened. So, I've made appointments with our bank, our financial adviser, our realtor, and a number of other professionals so I can understand more about running our family."

"That makes sense," I said quietly. I was still stuck on the word *tuition*.

"And, here's the big news. I'm getting a job." Her voice rose with excitement as she said it.

"That's fantastic," I said, making sure I matched her tone. My mother hadn't had a paying job my entire life. She had a degree in something like communications or English, I wasn't exactly sure, but hadn't used it. Mom spent most of her spare time getting her nails done, having long lunches with friends, going to yoga and spin classes, organizing open houses for my dad to drum up new clients—her ways of comforting herself and trying to tune out the bad moments like I did with quotes and ice cream. Occasionally, she assisted with charity events, which I'd always thought was to send some good out into the universe to counteract Dad's awfulness, but maybe it was Mom's way of staying connected to her skills and strengths. "What are you going to do?"

"I think I want to be a librarian."

"Really?" I couldn't hide my surprise. It was so different from the mother I'd had in the last several years. And yet, when I gave it a little more thought, I realized my mom had just as much influence on my love of learning as my dad did, she was just subtler about it. She took me to the bookstore and the library when I was little. She shared her favorite books from childhood. And, on my eleventh birthday, she bought me my first diary, which evolved into my quote journal.

"Yes. I already have a lead as a library assistant and I'm thinking about going back to school. Librarians need a master's degree and there's a good program nearby." I pictured my mother at the rehab center, sitting at a computer doing research on grad school. It made my heart swell.

"I think that's amazing, Mom. Really and truly."

"Thanks, Ash. I'm hopeful." I could hear her sniffle a little on the other end.

"Will you still work when Dad comes home?"

"I think so. Part of what I've been talking to my therapist about is building my self-confidence. She says I need to believe that I'm useful and that I have a purpose. I think I had convinced myself that helping out with the occasional charity luncheon was good enough."

Or Dad convinced her, was probably more like it. But I knew exactly how she felt. Until I decided to be brave and plant that seed here at Sweetwater, helping guests plan excursions and standing up to Marcus, I too had convinced myself that my old way of life was good enough. "But what about Dad?"

"What about Dad?"

"Well, I think he likes having you and me behave a certain way." I was trying to be diplomatic. "Dad feels pretty strongly about what behaviors are acceptable and which friends are worthwhile." I was choosing my words carefully. I didn't doubt that Mom would agree, but she *was* married to the guy after all. She picked him, whereas I'd had no choice.

Mom paused long enough for me to wonder if I'd hit a nerve. "We talk about that too. In therapy, I mean."

"And?"

"And your father is a very proud man. It's much easier for him to focus on what he sees as faults in other people than on his own faults. I think it's painful for him to look inward. He doesn't like what he sees, so he steers clear."

"That doesn't make it right," I muttered. I pinched my pearl necklace between my thumb and forefinger, making two pink indents.

"No, absolutely not. And some of that is my fault too. It has always been easier for me to just accept that's the way he is and be glad he comes home to me every night and isn't out drinking or flirting or who knows what else. And that he provides."

Provided, I didn't say.

"But I've realized that a lot of things have to change if we're going to be a fully functioning family. I've been told family therapy is commonly recommended to help reintegrate loved ones back into the home after they've been to prison."

I gulped. It wasn't the first time someone had told the Zanottis they might want to talk to a professional. "Like, all of us? In one room? Together?"

Mom chuckled a little. "That's generally how it works, yes."

"Okay." I'd do it for her. For us. For the family in that Christmas party photo. And, if Mom was expecting all of us to make some changes, maybe this was the time to ask for the one I wanted most of all. I knew without question that home was where I wanted to be, even if what that meant, with Dad still gone and Mom taking on new roles, was still a little murky and uncertain. Would she enforce Dad's rules? Would she go the other way and have no rules? I couldn't even imagine what that might be like. Logically, I couldn't see either option becoming a reality. Mom would be somewhere in the middle. And we could figure out what *home* was together.

"So," I started, my hands sweating and my throat dry, "what about me?" My voice cracked. "About school this year, I mean."

Mom paused. "What do you mean, sweetheart? Dad took care of it already."

"I know," I said, dragging out the O, like a little kid might. "But I was hoping I could come home. I was planning to ask before everyone . . . left. And then Dad mentioned tuition was paid for and I felt guilty and I didn't ask. But I really want to come back. I miss my friends. And I miss you too. Even Dad." *Just a little.* "I've done everything you asked. My grades are perfect. I made good choices. I think I deserve it."

There it was, poured out of me. It was the most I'd said to my mother about how I was feeling in a long time. A really long time. All the words I'd kept hidden inside fled my mind, leaving it deliciously free and empty. It felt *good* to let it out. *Good* to tell my mother how I'd been feeling. *Good* to trust her.

Mom was quiet for several beats. I clasped my hands to keep them from shaking. She finally sniffed again and said in a tiny voice, "It would be nice to see your face every day again. Especially since you're going to be in college so soon." Her voice trailed off. "I had no idea, Honey."

"So, is that a yes?" I sucked in a silent breath and held it tight. That breath was hope, hanging in the balance, like that little girl deciding to jump from the wall.

Mom sniffled twice and then spoke again. "Yes.

You've more than proven you deserve it. And, I wasn't exactly looking forward to living in an empty house, I must admit."

My heart exploded. If a human being could burst into confetti, my whole cabin would've been covered in bits of red and yellow and blue. If there was room to do backflips in the office, I would've done so many, I'd have been dizzy.

When the tears came, there was no anger or fear or shame. Only hope. For so long, longer than the last year, I'd felt unwanted. And here was my mom, admitting that she needed me. She wanted me. It was almost more than I could bear.

"We'll have to say something to your father," Mom said.

"I know," I said through hitching breaths.

"But," she said, a slight smirk in her voice, "he's not really in a position to argue now, is he?"

We both laughed. Knowing that my mom was on my side, and that we were going to move forward with changing our family dynamics—hopefully for the better—was empowering. I felt powerful. I felt strong.

Mom sniffed. "How about I come pick you up on your last day? We can go see Dad together."

"Sounds like a plan. I love you, Mom."

"I love you too, baby."

Chapter 29

Planning a sunrise hike was something I never imagined I would do, but I also never thought my dad would go to prison, so never say never. I originally hoped to keep my plans secret but trying to get every single employee at Sweetwater Overlook Retreat Center to agree to wake up before dawn on the last day of the season, for some unknown reason, was nearly impossible.

Hannah's little alarm clock went off at four in the morning. She banged on the bottom of my bed with her fists.

"Why are we doing this again?"

"Because it'll be fun. And because it's my way of saying thanks."

"You couldn't thank us with a cake or coffee delivery like a normal person?"

I slid off the top bunk with a thud. "Nope."

I picked a hike because I knew it would push me out of my little indoor box. I thought it would make all the people who lived in an outdoor box—Baxter included—happy. And, if I was being really honest, I knew it would make an amazing photograph. Because I wanted that one in a frame, to prove that I'd done it and to remind myself that I could do it again one day. Whatever the challenge. With any luck, everyone else would want to be in the picture too and they'd be part of my memory. And with a little more luck, I'd be able to put that framed photo on my dresser. At home.

Hannah and I dressed quickly, and I slid my feet into the brand new, unused hiking boots I'd bought at the beginning of the summer. The boots hugged my feet and ankles. I felt a little like I was wearing a costume, something someone who wasn't Ashlyn would wear. And I didn't hate that. This signified both my last big hurrah of the summer, and the new beginning of my senior year at home. I made sure to put on my old Henderson High School sweatshirt—a sign of where I'd come from and where I would return.

The guide from the touring company I'd hired, with Mr. Allen's blessing and his checkbook, met us outside the lodge at four-thirty sharp. His name was Glenn and he was wearing the same brand of hiking shoes I was. I took that as a good omen.

"Good morning," Baxter said, a travel cup of coffee in his hand. "Awake yet?"

"Getting there," I said, with a smile.

"Maybe this will help?" He reached behind himself and handed me a second cup. "Sugar and hazelnut creamer."

"Perfect." I took a sip, flattered that he remembered. "This is the appropriate hiking fuel?"

"It's appropriate for anything that takes place before the sun comes up."

"Fair." I took another sip. He'd made it exactly right. "Did you get some for Hannah too?"

"Of course I did. I value my life."

"I hope it's black," Hannah interjected, grabbing the third mug that was still sitting on the table. She took a long swig. "Good memory, Bax. Not like most guys," she said, eyeing me. Was that for my benefit? Even if it was, I'd definitely already figured that one out.

"I do my best," he said, taking her sideways compliment with a grin.

Three sharp claps sounded from nearby, and we jerked our heads. "Is everyone ready?" Glenn asked.

"Let's get this show on the road," Ruth said, with a wink in my direction.

We loaded into the shuttles and headed toward the base of the trail, where we would begin our climb to the top of what locals affectionately called Owl Hill. Glenn narrated the short drive with facts about what kind of trees and other birds and animals we might see on the hike. He told us to keep an eye out as we went, since we might still be able to see some owls before the sun came up. Glenn then assured us that it was an easy hike, "perfect for beginners," which I already knew because I'd triple checked that part when I booked the tour. He said there would be breakfast waiting for us at the summit and someone from their company would take our picture. I'd triple checked that part too.

During the ride, I zoned out a little, the nervous anticipation building inside of me. I wasn't afraid of the hike itself, but the closer we got to the trail and this hike, the closer we were to the end of the season at Sweetwater. And that meant the closer I also got to having *the* conversation with my dad. I shouldn't have been afraid. My mom was on my side. I was going home, no matter what. But some part of me still longed for his approval. I'd been searching my whole life for my father's "good job, Ashlyn," and an, "I'm so proud of you," or even better, "I'm so proud to be your father." I didn't expect it now. Mom had said this was going to be hard work, fixing the things that needed repairs. So maybe one day . . .

I practiced the things I wanted to say to my dad in my head until we arrived at the trail. Glenn unloaded us and led us up the hill. I looked around for owls, but only saw a handful of sparrows and some very tall evergreens as we started up the rocky trail. My boots were covered in dust within minutes.

An hour later, my sweatshirt was tied around my waist, my feet were sweating inside my boots, I was panting, my stomach was growling, and my calves were burning. Beginner trail had been a bold statement. But, I'd done it. I hadn't stopped. I just kept putting one foot in front of the other until I reached the top.

At the summit, the sky had just begun to lighten from the dark indigo of early morning. Another member of Glenn's company was passing out bags of hard boiled eggs, apples, and granola bars. I took a bar and sat down on a fallen log to catch my breath. Hannah plopped down next to me.

"That was awesome, cuz," she said, a bite of apple stuck in her cheek like a chipmunk.

"Cuz?"

"You know. Short for cousin." She elbowed me in the ribs.

The nickname felt strange in my ears, but I flushed with pleasure.

"Nothing like a good stroll up a mountain at the crack of dawn." Hannah side-eyed me and then laughed.

I elbowed her back. "One, it's a hill, not a mountain. And two, the good part hasn't happened yet. I have it on good authority that the sky is about to put on a pretty spectacular show." I'd been nervous about this part too, but I'd checked the weather numerous times over the past few days, including right before leaving the office that morning, and the forecast called for clear skies all day. I pointed up, as, right before our eyes, the sky went from dusky purple to pink and then orange and finally a brilliant gold as the sun made its appearance. The trees around us were silhouetted against the beautiful back-drop as the whole group fell silent and just took it all in. I inhaled deeply, the fresh green scent of the leaves and the earthiness of the ground and the wood filling my lungs. Here, I felt like anything was possible.

When Hannah got up to get another apple, Baxter took her place. We sat side by side on the log, legs gently touching, an electric charge buzzing between us. I tried to ignore it. I knew I liked him. He was nothing like any other guy I'd ever had a crush on in the past, and I was quickly realizing that wasn't a bad thing. Baxter was smart and thoughtful and respectful and probably parent-approved. In fact, if I were ever to bring Bax to meet my parents—in some alternative universe where my dad wasn't in jail right now—he'd probably fall over from shock at my choice of date.

"You did good. With this, I mean." Bax gestured to all our fellow employees milling about, chatting and laughing, still marveling at the beauty of our surroundings.

"Thanks. I'm glad everyone likes it." I smiled at him. My uncle had told me that's why he does what he does. Not to make money. Not to build the biggest house or hold the most power. To make others happy. I understood why it was so important to him. It was something I could definitely get behind.

"Actually, you did good with all of it. The job. Deb. Handling your parents' situations."

"Yeah?" Coming from Bax, who'd had his fair share of tough life situations, that meant a lot.

"I think whatever happens from here on out, you'll be able to handle that too."

"I think so. One hand in front of the other." I looked at him through my lashes and nibbled on my granola bar. "My mom is coming to pick me up tomorrow. We're going to see my dad together and we're going to tell him I'm coming home for good."

Baxter nodded. "How do you feel about that?"

"Scared out of my mind," I admitted.

"But you're going to do it anyway."

"I'm going to do it anyway," I agreed. And in a moment of impulse, I leaned over and kissed Baxter softly on the cheek. "Thanks for listening to me."

"You're welcome," he said, looking straight ahead.

And I smiled to myself, seeing the faint blush appear on his cheeks in the golden sunlight.

Moments later, Glenn and his assistant assembled us for the summit photograph. The entire Sweetwater crew gathered together for one of our last moments together. With Hannah's arm slung around my neck, Ruth and Amos beaming behind me, Baxter's fingers threaded through mine, and the sun shining brilliantly above us, I smiled.

Sweetwater was closed for the rest of the day. When we got back after the hike, those of us who were leaving had time to finish laundry and pack, while those staying on for the fall season helped with inventory and other odds and ends to get ready for the next wave of retreaters. I folded my clothes slowly and placed them in my suitcase one piece at a time, stealing glances in Tatum's scrapbook every so often. I stared at the photo of us on the stairs at our Christmas party the longest. We looked so nice and normal. Happy. I couldn't help but be hopeful that we could be that happy family for real. One day. Mom and I had plenty of time to get ourselves together before adding Dad back in. And who knows? Maybe the prison had some kind of family therapy program we could start before he got out.

On the inside of my nightstand drawer, just as I'd done at Blue Valley two months ago, I left a note for the next occupant.

YOU CAN ONLY LOSE WHAT YOU CLING TO.
Buddha

I'd spent years clinging to a way of life that made me unhappy. But thanks to Baxter, for just being himself, to Hannah and my aunt and uncle, who introduced me to a different kind of family, and my mom, who had the courage to throw off the old way and restart her life, I knew I had the power to change as well. It was time to let it go.

At the final employee bonfire that night, I sat between Hannah and Baxter. When Ruth passed out the little slips of paper for our end-of-summer wishes, I took three.

On the first one, I wrote:

I wish to be strong.

I was a lot stronger than I was when I came to Sweetwater, and I knew I'd need to continue to be in the year ahead.

On the second:

I wish to use my voice.

While I knew I would always collect quotes, I needed to use my own words more often. Starting tomorrow, with my dad.

And on the third:

I wish for someone who sees me just as I am and accepts what they see.

I knew Baxter was just such a person. And it would be so easy to lean over and really kiss him, but there was something about the fragile possibility of him that I didn't want to break. I knew I had a lot of work to do in the next year, or longer, with my family, with myself. That wouldn't be fair to Baxter. I was also afraid that starting a long-distance relationship would destroy it before it even got to the good parts. But he'd shown me what was out there, and I knew I'd carry that with me.

I balled up all three wishes and tossed them into the fire.

Chapter 30

The hug I gave my mother when she arrived at Sweetwater the next day probably left her bruised and breathless, but I didn't care. It felt like I hadn't seen her in a year, which was kind of true. The mother I'd left at home when I went to boarding school last summer had changed so dramatically by the time I returned in June that she was unrecognizable. A shadow had replaced the beautiful woman I'd grown up with. And here she was, no longer faded but in Technicolor, back the way I knew her best, smiling at me with tears of joy in her eyes.

"Hi, Mommy," was all I could say through my tears. My heart was beating so loudly, I was sure she could hear it. I inhaled her scent—her signature perfume mixed with something new, something clean and fresh—and was instantly transported. This was home.

"Hi, baby, how are you?" Mom stepped back and held me at arm's length. She reached one hand out and ruffled my shorter hair. "This is nice. It suits you somehow. I can see your face more. No long hair to hide behind anymore."

Is that what I'd been doing? "Thank you." Another hint

that my mom had been much more observant than I'd realized.

"Will you show me around?" Mom asked. "I want to know everything you've been doing."

"I'd love to."

We loaded my bags into Mom's car and I led her on the unofficial Sweetwater tour, hand in hand—I didn't want to let her go. I took her to the top of the hill first, pointing out the ropes course and telling her about the little girl who couldn't decide to jump.

"Sounds like the same way I've been feeling for a long time," she replied. "Stuck between two decisions."

Me too, I almost said. And then I caught myself. There was no reason to keep quiet. "Me too," I told my mom. She squeezed my hand and we looked at each other for a moment. "What made you finally get help?" I asked quietly.

"You. I knew I needed to get myself together to be there for you. But also me. I wanted to do better and I wanted to be better. I wanted to learn what to do next time the depression creeps in." Mom stopped walking and turned to me. "Because it will be back. Maybe not so severe, but I have no doubt I'll need to use the skills I've been learning again. And now that I've started feeling like myself again, I'm in a better place to make other changes in my life. In our lives. It won't be like it was. Not anymore. Never again."

"I know, Mom. I've got your back. You don't need to keep things from me, okay?"

"No more secrets."

"No more secrets," I promised too.

I showed Mom the pool and the volleyball court, stopping at the firepit where I'd made my wishes for this summer and beyond. I pointed out the equipment kiosk, saying, "Staffed first by Hannah and then by me," and then I took her through the lodge. Deb's gingerbread house was still displayed in the competition kitchen, the icing chipped off and broken in many places now. It was a fitting end for the fake house that Deb had built.

We made our way to the office, where Mr. Allen was behind the desk.

"Ashlyn, is this your older sister?" He winked at my mom. We walked in, and my mother offered her hand.

"Celine Zanotti. And thank you for the compliment."

"Mrs. Zanotti, the pleasure is all mine. You have quite the remarkable daughter here."

"I do," Mom said, smoothing my hair back.

"I owe her a debt of gratitude for her courage this summer. Why, if Ashlyn and Hannah hadn't blown the whistle on the woman I hired to manage this place, who knows where we'd be right now."

Mom raised an eyebrow at me. "Oh?"

I cleared my throat. "I was just going to tell her about that, Mr. Allen."

"Humble, too, I see. I'll leave you ladies to it. Ashlyn, I hope you'll consider joining us again next summer."

"I'd like that. Thank you, sir." I walked into Mr. Allen's open arms, grateful that he'd taken a chance on me.

On our way to the car, I told my mom the whole story about Deb and the 911 calls and finally confronting

Mr. Allen with our list of evidence. By the time I finished, tears shone in her eyes.

"I don't know whether to be angry at her or proud of you. You should never have had to deal with that, sweetheart. Why didn't you say something earlier?"

"Probably for the same reasons you and Dad didn't tell me about prison and rehab. I didn't want to worry you. I didn't want my story to be a distraction. And really," I said, "I think on some level, I wanted to see if I could handle it by myself."

"Did you think you couldn't?" Mom asked. I gave her a look that said, "Are you seriously asking me that question?" She sighed. "It hasn't been easy for you, has it?"

"No, not really," I said to my feet. I'd put my hiking boots on that morning. Maybe I'd hoped they'd make me feel brave. I knew my mother was on my team and had already given her blessing for me to come home, but a small part of me was afraid my dad would still say no and she would allow it. It was a reasonable fear.

Mom pushed her shoulders back. "We're going to fix this. All three of us. Dad's not off the hook anymore. I know a lot of sweeping his words under the rug was my fault. I do. And I'm going to be better about that. I want you to do the same. With both me and Dad. If there's something you don't think is right or something you feel strongly about, I need you to say it. I can't help if you don't, deal?"

"Deal." Mom held her hand out to me and I shook it, like we were business partners.

When we got to the car, both Hannah and Baxter were standing there waiting for us.

"Mom, this is my friend, Baxter Clark," they nodded at each other amiably, "and you remember Hannah."

Hannah stepped forward and said, "Hi, Aunt Celine, it's so nice to see you." She and my mom exchanged a long, overdue hug. It was clear Mom had been missing the warmth and closeness of family relationships, *real* family relationships, as much as I had.

"Hannah," she said looking her up and down at arm's length, "you're so grown up. Last time I saw you, you were this high." Mom held her hand at her ribs. "How are you? Did you have a nice summer?"

"I did, thank you. It was really nice having Ashlyn here." Hannah chucked me on the arm. "She saved the day more than once."

"So I heard." Mom's face shone with pride. "How are your folks?"

"They're good, thanks. They should be here in a bit, actually. Be prepared. They're probably going to give you the strong-arm about coming for Christmas."

"I don't think they'll have to convince us," I said.

"If Greta is making her baked ziti, we'll be there with bells on."

My jaw dropped open. "You know about the ziti? How am I the only one who didn't know about the ziti?"

Mom put an arm around my shoulder. "There are probably a lot of things your father and I should've shared with you." Bax stood there, smiling faintly and taking all this family talk in.

Hannah looked from Bax to me and cleared her throat loudly. "Aunt Celine, do you want to come with me to get some drinks for the car ride? We can snag some from the kitchen. In the lodge," she said, not at all obviously.

Mom looked at her quizzically before catching on. "Sure, Hannah. Let's do that."

When they were several yards away, out of earshot, I turned to Bax, shyly.

"Are you glad to be going home?" he asked.

"Yes, though it'll be weird without my dad there."

"For sure. But you'll figure it out."

I smiled at him. I wanted to reach out and hug him, but I was afraid it would make it harder to say goodbye. "Are you looking forward to the new season?"

"I'll keep busy. But it won't be the same without Hannah here." He looked at me intensely, his pale eyes glittering. "And you. I'll miss having you around."

I clasped my hands behind my back to keep myself from launching myself at him. "I'll miss you too. Would it be okay if I write to you?"

Baxter's face broke out into a wide grin that I couldn't help but return. "Only if you promise to send me some new quotes."

"I think I can handle that. I actually have one for you now. But read it later, okay?"

"Okay."

I pulled a tiny, folded piece of paper from my back pocket that I'd torn from my quote journal that morning. It read:

> SOAR, EAT ETHER, SEE WHAT HAS NEVER
> BEEN SEEN; DEPART, BE LOST, BUT CLIMB.
> *Edna St. Vincent Millay*

I slid it into his hand, which was warm and rough and made me wish I could hold it, but I didn't let myself.

"I'll see you," Bax said, still smiling, though it had slipped a bit, and put the paper in his pocket.

"See you," I echoed. And I watched him walk away until he disappeared up the hill. I was glad we hadn't said goodbye. I truly hoped I'd get to see him again.

Mom and Hannah appeared a few minutes later, bottles of water in their hands. "Did you say goodbye to your friend?" Mom asked pointedly. Hannah stifled a giggle.

"Yep," I said.

"Well, I guess that means it's my turn," Hannah said, nodding toward the car that was pulling in next to my mom's. Uncle Ed and Aunt Greta.

"Celine!" my aunt exclaimed, climbing out of the car and making a beeline for my mother. "You look wonderful. Positively glowing." I was grateful Aunt Greta knew exactly what to say to make my mom feel good.

"A good long rest will do that for you," my mom said, returning her hug. "It's been entirely too long, Greta. Hannah tells me you've been making holiday plans already."

Greta actually clapped her hands like a little kid. "Yes! I hope you and Ashlyn will come and stay with us for Christmas. Dylan will be home, it'll be great. A regular reunion."

"I think we can arrange that. But only if you'll all come to Virginia for Thanksgiving."

Greta looked like she was about to cry. Uncle Ed rubbed her shoulders and blushed, smiling like he'd just won the lottery. "We'd love to," he said.

"Good. It'll be nice to have a house full of people for once." Mom nodded, pleased with herself. I was proud of her. She may not have been voicing her opinion in family therapy just yet, but enlisting allies was a good first step. She turned to me. "Ashlyn, love, we need to get on the road if we want to get there before visiting hours are over."

I nodded and kissed my aunt and uncle on the cheeks. "Thank you. For everything." I knew I didn't need to say anything more. They understood.

"Tell your dad I'll see him next week," Uncle Ed whispered in my ear. I pulled back a little, my eyes wide, and he smiled. "We've been talking."

"That's good," I whispered back.

"We'll see you soon, Ashlyn. Okay?"

"Yes, see you *very* soon," I said and gave Aunt Greta another hug.

And then there was Hannah. Only a few months ago, she was as good as a stranger, someone whose ease at life I envied. And now, we were a team. Hannah had helped me shrug things off a little more often and showed me how to be brave.

"Will you text me when you get home?" I knew we were both happy to be going back to the land of cell service.

I nodded. "And will you text me when you get to college?"

"You can come visit me any time. We'll go to a party or a concert or something." Hannah's voice cracked.

"You got it, cuz," I said.

We stared at each other, neither of us wanting to separate, but my mother gently placed her hand in mine to let me know it was time to go. I put my free hand up to wave and suddenly Hannah rushed at me. She hugged me so tight I could barely breathe. And I hugged her back, just as hard, glad to have family who would miss me.

Chapter 31

*I*t was different this time, driving up to the Williams
Correctional Facility, and not just because I was with
Mom instead of Uncle Ed. Mom hadn't seen Dad since
he left—they had only communicated through letters and
a few brief phone calls. Neither one of them was in an
emotional state, or physical place, to have deep discus-
sions. They probably hadn't been for some time. I knew
this visit was, in some ways, going to be harder on Mom
than it was on me. At least I knew what to expect when
we walked in. And I was no longer facing Dad by myself.
The few times I had visited, he was still in control, even
in here. But things had changed. I'd changed.

Right after I'd written Bax's quote last night, I'd written
one for me. It was folded up in a tiny square in my pocket.

> DO THE HARDEST THING ON EARTH FOR
> YOU. ACT FOR YOURSELF. FACE THE TRUTH.
> *Katherine Mansfield*

As we crossed the threshold and entered the building,

Mom shuddered next to me. She grabbed my hand tightly. "I'm not sure I can do this." I had no idea what it felt like to see your husband in prison, but I did know what it was like to see your father there.

"You can do it, Mom. He's the same person he always was." Although the statement wasn't exactly comforting, it was enough for her to release the death grip she had on my hand.

"Okay." She continued to cling to me as we followed the security procedures and waited to gain entrance.

When we were finally ushered into the visitation room, Mom and I took a seat at the same table I'd sat at the last time. I let her sit so she would be able to see him as he came into the room. When he did, I forced myself to stay silent. Dad was even thinner than the last time. I knew that some men lost weight in prison from all the time they were able to spend lifting weights or running in the yard. Dad just looked like he'd forgotten to eat. His cheeks had become hollow, and there were dark bruise-colored circles under his eyes. He walked slowly, pained. I covered my mouth to hide my shock. He seemed like the most exhausted person on the planet.

And yet, when he saw us, he smiled. It was possibly the most genuine smile I'd ever seen on my father's face—like a man in a desert who'd discovered an oasis. When he reached our table, Dad hugged me first. The fabric of his uniform was scratchy, but he smelled clean, like laundry detergent and bleach. He held me close to him and kissed the top of my head, something he hadn't done in years. When he pulled away, he smiled again.

Dad shifted to my mom and the second he touched her, she lost it. Big, fat tears rolled down her face, and her mascara went with them. Dad rubbed her back in small circles, the way you might comfort a child. He was whispering something in Mom's ear that I couldn't hear and she was nodding. I turned my head, not wanting to invade their moment. The reunion of my parents felt uncomfortably intimate, though I was sure this room had seen many such embraces. Mom kissed Dad's cheek and then his lips, before a guard loudly cleared his throat and they stepped apart.

"It's really good to see you, Celine," Dad said, sitting down. "You look beautiful."

"Thank you, Art." Mom couldn't stop staring at him.

It occurred to me that in all my angry and frustrated moments, I hadn't thought much about what this tragedy was doing to their marriage. I didn't think much about my parents' marriage at all, really. It was nice to see them like this. It was the most affectionate I'd seen them in a long, long time. *Maybe absence does make the heart grow fonder.*

"And you look so grown up, Ashlyn. Even in just the last few weeks. Have you done something different with your hair?" He was looking at me as if he'd never seen me before.

"I cut it."

"I caught that during your first visit," he said with a small smile. *Oh.* "There's something else. Confidence maybe." I blushed. I couldn't help it. I was shocked that he noticed something like that. About me. "Does that mean you've finished out the summer at work on a high note?"

"Yes," I said definitively. I wanted to sound as confident as I apparently looked.

"Ashlyn turned out to be quite the hero," Mom said proudly. She proceeded to tell my father the whole story about Deb and blowing the whistle, while I sat there feeling equal parts busting at the seams and totally embarrassed. There weren't many instances I could remember where my parents bragged about me, so it felt weird and good and wrong and scary. But I knew I didn't want to forget it.

Dad's eyes grew wider as Mom talked. He crossed his arms over his chest and leaned back, settling in, enjoying the story. When Mom finished with Mr. Allen's praise of me that morning, Dad was shaking his head in disbelief. "Ashlyn, that is quite a story."

"It was nothing," I mumbled, shrinking back into old-me mode. I couldn't quite wrap my head around positive attention from him.

"It most certainly is not nothing. You might've saved Mr. Allen's business from ruin." He uncrossed his arms and leaned closer to the edge of the table. Closer to me. "It took a lot of courage to speak up, especially about your superior. I'm not sure I could've done the same."

If I'd been sitting on that wall on the ropes course at Sweetwater, I most definitely would've fallen over backward. It was without a doubt the most personal thing I'd ever heard my father say. He rarely admitted weakness of any kind. And he had never, ever, acknowledged I could do something he couldn't. My head swam a little. I glanced over at Mom, who nodded at me.

I closed my eyes, took a deep breath, and looked my dad square in the eye. "Speaking of speaking up, Dad, there's something I wanted to tell you." My voice shook, but I marched on.

Dad folded his hands in his lap. He looked ready to listen. It was unnerving, but also encouraging.

Another breath in. Exhale. "I'm not going back to Blue Valley. I'm going to spend senior year at home. With my friends. And with mom." I wanted to look away from him, shrink like I always did, but I willed myself to keep talking. I reminded myself that my voice was strong and change had to start with me. "I think I've more than paid the price for my mistake. My grades are spotless. I've gained leadership roles in my activities. I've had a perfect discipline record. And I would imagine Mr. Allen would be happy to write me a letter of recommendation to any college I want."

Dad didn't say anything. Still, I held his gaze. I wasn't going to back down, now that I'd climbed to the top of this mountain. His chest was rising and falling as if he was trying to stay calm. He picked at the cuticle on his index finger and looked down, like he was trying to formulate a response. Was he going to blow up? Was he going to put his foot down and come up with some new ridiculous plan, already in place, for me?

Before he could speak, Mom did. "Art, she deserves this. And I'm going to need support during my continued recovery. It would be nice to have Ashlyn with me." Her voice cracked. "I want my baby at home." She wiped her eyes. "I went to see our financial adviser yesterday." She had? "And he will put the money earmarked for tuition into Ashlyn's college savings account." Wow. Go, Mom.

Part of me wanted to get up and do an end zone dance and say, "Take that, Dad!" But I also didn't want to damage the already cracked relationship. I reminded myself that this was a choice, my choice, and I'd rather repair it than tear it down.

"So that's the plan. Okay?" I said to him. A little piece of me died inside when I said "okay." I knew I didn't need his approval on this. And he knew it too. It was done. Mom had decided for both of them. But it didn't stop me from wanting it.

After a century of silence, and who knows what racing through Dad's head, he opened his mouth. I held my breath.

"Okay."

"Okay?" I repeated, not quite believing that it had been that easy.

"Okay." He nodded and pressed his lips into a line— not quite a smile but not unhappy either. "I've talked to a lot of other fathers in here and if there's one common theme to those conversations, it's that I should be grateful for what I have. When we have group, everyone talks about their kids and the stuff they miss by being in here. It's heartbreaking."

Hold up. My dad goes to group? As in group therapy? And did he say missing kids' stuff breaks his heart? I wanted to clean out my ears to make sure I hadn't misheard him.

"I think," Dad said, and paused. He swallowed hard, struggling to speak. "I think I owe you an apology, Ashlyn."

Was this actually happening? I just stared at him.

"When you got arrested last year, despite your lack of guilt, I behaved irrationally. You may have survived at Blue Valley, even thrived, but now I understand that I should have made a different decision. I missed out on a whole year of your life and now I'm missing another." He hung his head a little. Did he actually feel bad about it?

I wanted to believe him. But I also didn't want to get my hopes up. I had seventeen years of being Arthur Zanotti's daughter to know not to do that. In a perfect world, Dad would keep talking and tell me he wanted to apologize for not only missing last year and the upcoming one, but truly, for missing out on who I was for much longer than that. I wanted him to be sorry for always telling me what to do, for *knowing* his way was better than mine, for not giving me the freedom to make my own choices and follow my passions. I wanted him to apologize for not seeing me, for not hearing me, or maybe he had and purposely ignored it. He didn't say those things. Prison may have given him a new perspective, but you couldn't undo years and years of thinking a certain way in a few months and a couple of chats around a circle. But we had time.

"I'm glad you'll be home with your mother," Dad continued, his voice small, not unlike mine was when he chastised me.

"We're glad too," Mom spoke up. "And Ashlyn and I have made another decision. When we're all back under the same roof, we're going to work on us." Dad looked at her blankly. "We're going to go to family therapy, Art. Families need maintenance, just like cars. We don't want to end up broken down on the freeway again." I stifled a giggle, picturing my dad trying to change a tire on his SUV on the beltway. Mom looked at me, probably having the same mental image, and laughed. "They said stuff like that at Hart Canyon. It made sense to me," she said with a shrug.

Dad nodded slowly. "Okay."

"Also, I'm getting a job and I'll be taking over the running of our household. I won't be a silent partner in this family anymore."

I expected my dad to balk at that. Not that he should be angry my mom wanted to have a bigger role, but that she was horning in on "his" area of expertise. He'd always been in charge of money and bills. Instead, he cracked a smile. Mom smiled back.

"Your mother used to be the bill payer back when we first got married," Dad said. "She was a champion coupon clipper and balanced the checkbook every Saturday morning."

I couldn't imagine that. My mom went to yoga every Saturday while my dad golfed with clients. How had they gotten so far off that path?

Mom swatted Dad playfully, and then grew contemplative. "We need to find us again, I think."

Everything inside me shuddered with emotion. She was so right. I didn't even know who "us" was anymore. I dared to look at my dad and this time, there were actual tears. I'd never seen him so vulnerable. Mom covered my dad's hand with hers and mouthed to me, "Why don't you give us a minute?"

I got up from the table, pushed my chair in, and let the guard open the door for me. I looked over my shoulder at my parents, talking in soft voices, faces close. My mother and I had just jumped down from the wall. Finally.

I went out to the car to wait for my mom. I retrieved my phone from my backpack and dialed Tatum's number for the first time since I left home in June, my hand shaking. She answered on the third ring.

"Ash? Is that really you?"

"It's me," I said, my voice coming out strangled, as hot tears pricked the corners of my eyes.

"Where are you? Is work over?"

I inhaled deeply and smiled into the receiver. "I'm on my way home."

Acknowledgments

I learn something new with every book I write, but the thing that is constant is this job can't be done alone. Thank you to Jillian Manning for cultivating this vision, and to Sara Bierling, Matt Saganski, and Mary Hassinger for picking it up and running with it. I'm so grateful to the whole team at Blink for all your hard work and support. Huge thanks to Kevan Lyon for always steering the ship in the right direction.

Thank you to Amy Burns, Jill Burdick-Zupancic, Penny Slawkowski, and Susan Bruno for sharing your expertise. To the writers and readers who make this process more joyful—you're my favorites: Katherine Locke, Rebekah Campbell, Rebecca Paula, Leigh Smith, Sarah Emery, Katy Upperman, McCall Hoyle, Alison Gervais, Amanda Summers, Olivia Hinebaugh, Lisa Maxwell, and Suzette Henry. To the friends who have stuck by me for literal decades and helped shape the friends I write about—I love you, you're the best.

Every time a teacher, librarian, blogger, or bookseller connects a book with a reader, an angel gets their wings. I am forever in debt to those book superheroes who have read my stories, shared them with someone else, written a review, attended an event, invited me to speak, or otherwise supported me. I could not do this without you.

Thank you always to my family, especially my parents and my in-laws, who bend over backwards to love and support me. And most of all, thank you to my husband and daughter, who are my home—you make it all worth it.

It Started With Goodbye

by Christina June

Not all stories begin with once upon a time ...

Tatum Elsea is facing the worst summer ever: she's stuck under stepmother-imposed house arrest and her BFF's gone ghost. Tatum fills her time with community service by day and her covert graphic design business at night (which includes trading emails with a cute cello-playing client). But when Tatum discovers she's not the only one in the family with secrets, she decides to start fresh and chase her happy ending along the way. A modern Cinderella story, *It Started with Goodbye* shows us that sometimes going after what you want means breaking all the rules.

Available wherever books are sold!

BLINK

Everywhere You Want to Be

Christina June

From author Christina June comes *Everywhere You Want to Be*, a modern retelling of the Red Riding Hood story.

Matilda Castillo has always done what she was told, and as a result she watched her dreams of becoming a contemporary dancer slip away. So when Tilly gets a once-in-a-lifetime opportunity to spend the summer with a New York dance troupe, nothing can stop her from saying yes—not her mother, not her fears of the big city, and not the commitment she made to Georgetown. Tilly's mother allows her to go on two conditions: one, Tilly will regularly visit her abuela in New Jersey, and two, after the summer, she'll give up dancing and go off to college.

Armed with her red vintage sunglasses and her pros and cons lists, Tilly strikes out, determined to turn a summer job into a career. Along the way she meets new friends and new enemies. Tilly isn't the only one desperate to dance, and fellow troupe member Sabrina Wolfrik intends to succeed at any cost. But despite dodging sabotage and blackmail attempts from Sabrina, Tilly can't help but fall in love with the city, especially since Paolo, a handsome musician from her past, is also calling New York home for the summer.

As the weeks wind down and the competition with Sabrina heats up, Tilly's future is on the line. She must decide whether to follow her mother's path to Georgetown or leap into the unknown to pursue her own dreams.

Available wherever books are sold!

BLINK®